WAR MAGE

MAGITECH CHRONICLES BOOK 4

CHRIS FOX

CHRIS FOX WRITES LLC.

Copyright © 2018 Chris Fox
All rights reserved.
ISBN: 1725797615
ISBN-13: 978-1725797611

*For John Kerr 1970 - 2018.
You'll be missed, man.*

PREVIOUSLY ON TECH MAGE

Whenever I start the second or later book in a series, I have a dilemma. Do I go back and re-read the first book(s), or just dive right into the latest release?

I include these previously on sections as a solution for those who want to dive right in. You'll get a quick recap of events from the earlier books, each broken into its own chapter, so they're easily skippable.

If you want to know more about the setting, there's a whole bunch of lore, artwork, and other goodies at magitechchronicles.com (including a mailing list). And yes, I am working on a roleplaying game too.

Okay, let's get to it.

In an announcer's voice: *Last time on* **The Magitech Chronicles...**

The story begins with Major Voria, who is arriving at a floating palace over the world of Shaya.

Shaya refers to a goddess who got kacked (that's totally a

word). Her body is, apparently, a giant hippie tree that crashed on a barren moon. Because Shaya's all magicky, her body created a breathable atmosphere around that part of the moon.

Voria meets with the Tender, a superhumanly beautiful woman. She's the Guardian of Shaya, a demigod mystically empowered by Shaya to watch over her people.

The Tender told Voria she'd deciphered an augury showing Voria's involvement in a war with the draconic Krox, foreshadowing some awesome dragon on starship combat. Then we switch to another PoV.

Aran wakes up in restraints with a number of other prisoners / slaves.

His captors are a pretty girl-next-door type named Nara, and a muhahaha style villain named Yorrak. Yorrak tells the slaves that they're about to make a run on the body of a dead god, called a Catalyst.

This particular Catalyst, a giant floating head full of very angry tech demons, is called the Skull of Xal. The slaves clash with the demons, who tear most of them apart. Aran makes friends with a man named Kazon, and the two fight their way past the demons. They have a choice: Die, or dive into the scary purple god-light where Nara and the slavers disappear. They choose to brave the light, and enter the mind of a god.

Aran sees Xal's memories, and for a brief instant understands the secrets of the universe. He learns Xal was killed by a gathering of gods, convinced by Krox that Xal had betrayed them.

All this god-politics stuff becomes important later, but at this point all we really care about is the fact that Aran comes out of the Catalyst with *void* magic.

We also learn that magic items can catalyze, too, and

Aran's spellblade awakens after touching the mind of Xal. It hasn't yet reached snarky-sidekick-level intelligence, but you guys know that's coming. Although, in this case, the sword is more murderous than snarky.

Kaz survives, too, and also gains *void* magic. When they come out of the Catalyst, Kaz attacks Yorrak, and Aran helps him. Yorrak responds with a morph spell that turns Kazon into a hedgehog. =O

Aran finishes off Yorrak while Nara and her friends join the mutiny. Together, they overcome Yorrak's guards, but Nara immediately takes over and makes Aran a prisoner. We're shocked (we're not shocked).

The joke is on Nara, though, because Voria conveniently arrives with the Confederate Battleship *Wyrm Hunter*. Nara pilots Yorrak's spellship, but Voria easily catches her and disables her vessel.

Nara begs Aran to help fight, and claims that if the Confederates capture them, they'll mind-wipe them and conscript them into the Marines. Aran agrees to help, because plot.

Voria sends a boarding party of tech mages, under the command of Captain Thalas (aka Dick Sock), who kicks the crap out of Aran. Aran does manage to disarm him first, ensuring that Dick Sock has ample reason to hate him for the rest of the book.

Nara also attempts to betray Aran, and claims he was one of the slavers and she was one of the slaves. Captain Dick Sock is not impressed, and takes both her and Aran prisoner.

It turns out Nara was right. Voria mind-wipes her, destroying her mind and replacing her with an innocent woman with no memories. This raises some very troubling moral questions about slavery, in case you ever need a quick excuse to tell your English professor that *Tech Mage* is totally valid for your book report. Make sure you use the word "themes" when you try to sell it.

Voria spares Aran, though she doesn't explain why. The reader already knows it's because Aran was in the augury the Tender showed her. Aran isn't sure how to feel about this, and of course doesn't trust Nara even though her newly wiped self seems sweet.

Anyway, the wonder twins are introduced to their squad of tech mages: Specialist Bord (the comic relief), Corporal Kezia (a short, pretty drifter who talks like the characters in the movie Snatch, Irish Travelers), and my personal favorite...Sergeant Crewes. Crewes is a badass who brooks no nonsense, and has most of the best dialogue in the book. Love that guy.

Anyway, Aran and Nara get a Team-America-style training montage (Montage!), where they learn how to use spellrifles, spellarmor, and other basic magic.

Voria takes Aran to a place called Drifter Rock so they can load up on potions, especially healing potions. Thanks to the convenient augury, she knows he will be instrumental in their battle against the Krox, and she uses this as an opportunity to get to know him.

Voria trades her super-powerful, ancient eldimagus (living magic item) staff for every potion the drifters have. This includes a potion the drifters claim can bring someone back from the dead, which was my attempt at sneakily foreshadowing the fact that someone was going to get resurrected. That particular cheat is rampant in *Dungeons & Dragons*, which inspired much of the setting for the *Magitech Chronicles*.

Enter Nebiat, the antagonist (dun dun dun). Nebiat is an ancient Wyrm who likes to spend her time in human form.

She uses binding magic to mentally enslave the governor of a planet called Marid, and we're all *gasp*, because that's the planet from the augury.

The Krox invade with a full dragonflight and a bunch of troop transports. They wipe out the defenders, who come from a planet called Ternus. Rhymes with burn us, as in "Shit, these dragons are burning the crap out of us."

At this point, the politics in the book aren't very clear. Ternus is a human world with no magic, and they have the largest technological fleet in the sector. But they suck at defending against magic, and for that they need Shaya. Both Shaya and Ternus are part of the Confederacy, though Shaya is clearly in charge while Ternus is the annoying younger sibling.

To complicate things further, there is a third group called the Inuran Consortium. The Inurans buy technology from Ternus, and take magic from Shaya, then use both to make spellrifles, spellarmor, and spellships.

Voria needs those weapons and armor if she's to have any prayer of taking down the Krox. Fortunately, the head of the Consortium is looking for Kazon, the guy who got turned into a hedgehog earlier in the book. Kazon turns out to be the son of the Inuran Matriarch, and controls a shitton of voting stock she'll lose if he dies.

The *Wyrm Hunter* arrives in-system and we finally get some dragon-on-starship combat. The *Hunter* kills the mighty Wyrm Kheftut (Nebiat's brother), then links up with the Ternus defenders who survived the battle with the Krox.

For those who asked: yes, both Kheftut and Nebiat sound Egyptian, and that is a theme for the Krox (woohoo, another one for your book report). And yes, there are subtle links to my Deathless setting, which also links heavily to Egypt.

Voria comes up with a plan, and manages to take back the orbital station the Krox conquered. This plan is a success only because Aran and Nara do an end run and drive the binder off the station, so they're the heroes of the day.

Unfortunately, there's a complication. Captain Dick Sock orders the Confederate Marines to suicide against the Krox position to weaken the binder. Aran, Nara, and Crewes mutiny to stop this. They save the Marines, but Dick Sock wants them dead—especially Aran.

Things come to a head when Voria finally meets with the Inurans. She trades back Kazon (who turns out to be her brother, *gasp*), but Kazon insists they also free Aran, since Aran saved his life at the Skull of Xal.

Dick Sock demands Aran be put to death for assaulting a superior asshole, and has the law on his side. Technically, Voria has to execute Aran. Or course, technically, she's been stripped of command, and Thalas should be in charge.

Shit.

Voria is already in deep. She's been officially stripped of command, but refuses to step down. If she does, she knows her people—and the people on the world below—will die.

So Voria charges Dick Sock with treason, and executes him on the spot. This solves her immediate dilemma, but also creates a whole bunch of problems that she's going to run into in the next book.

Crewes steps up and asks Voria to promote Aran to Lieutenant, because Crewes doesn't feel qualified to lead and thinks Aran can. Voria's hesitant, but agrees because of the augury.

The Confederates head down to the planet, and, because Nebiat has bound the governor, it's a trap. =O

Hundreds of Marines and thousands of citizens are killed in a surprise Krox raid.

Aran manages to kill two different binders, but pays a high price: Bord is killed. It's terribly sad. I mean, you felt bad, right? Bord was kind of an ass, but he was amusing. He at least deserves a moment of silence, you savages.

The Krox retreat back into the swamp, leaving the Confederates to recover. Voria suspects the governor, but doesn't have proof yet. She heads to the local archives and meets with the head archivist (powerful mage / librarian).

She learns what Nebiat is after in the swamp: some sort of potent *water* Catalyst that appeared during the godswar, when a god's body crashed to this world and formed the crater the city was built in. Voria realizes she needs to get out there, but before they can leave there are a few things she needs to take care of.

She talks to Aran about how terrible it is to lose a man under your command, then she's all *Psych!* She uses the potion they got from the drifters to bring Bord back from the dead.

Cheating, maybe, but I don't like killing characters when I can avoid it. As Rick would say, "We can only do this a few more times, Morty." That means I can't keep doing fake-outs. Someone has to get the axe, or you'll think people have plot armor. Will someone die in this book? Now you'll wonder...*muhahahaha*.

Anyway, Voria confronts the governor, proves he is bound, and has him removed from power. She calls for volunteers, then the Confederates and their new colonial militia allies head into the swamp to find Nebiat.

There's lots of *pew pew RAWR I'm a dragon*, and Aran kills the binder who got away on the station. They find

Nebiat's super-secret ritual at the heart of the swamp, and they begin their epic brawl.

It's clear from the start that the Confederates are outmatched. How were Aran and Voria going to beat a much more powerful army of dragons? Many readers began suspiciously waiting for the *deus ex machina*. I mean, I had to have one. There was no other way for them to win.

Things got worse when the Marines finally arrived at the battle with the newly minted militia. They were wiped out to a man, and their bodies were animated and sent to attack Voria and Captain Davidson.

Throughout the book, I kept mentioning the Potion of Shaya's Grace that Aran received as a gift from Kazon (along with his new Proteus Mark XI Spellarmor). Aran pops the potion, which makes him faster and stronger, and gives him the ability to see several seconds into the future.

Aran grabs Nara and the two of them fly up to the summit of the mountain where Nebiat has placed the ritual. On the way up, Aran makes the (not so) casual observation that the mountain looks like it's a real face.

He brawls with a bunch of enforcers while Nara tries to stop the ritual. We've seen her latent true mage abilities manifest several times, so we aren't surprised when she steps into the circle and begins manipulating the spell.

This is the part where I hoped all my little hints paid off. The mountain was actually the ancient Wyrm Drakkon. Drakkon is crazy-powerful, and super-old. If Nebiat enslaves him, the Confederates are screwed, and that's exactly what her ritual is designed to do.

Voria hoped destroying some of the urns holding the magical energy would stop the ritual, but they were only able to blow up the *spirit* urn. *Spirit* magic is used in...*drumroll*...binding. (If you want more details about the magic system, I've got a ton of it at magitechchronicles.com, including a video.)

Nara realizes the spell can be completed if she removes the binding portion. The rest of the spell is designed to wake a creature from mystical slumber.

She completes the spell, and the mountain stands up. Drakkon crushes the Krox forces, and Nebiat goes full GTFO. She flees the planet, and doesn't stop running until she reaches her father's system.

Voria, Davidson, Aran, Nara, Crewes, Kezia, and Bord all Catalyze in a blast of magical energy from the *water* Catalyst.

This provides a glimpse into Marid's mind. Aran experiences the god's death, which happens some time after Xal. Her last act is to create a living spell, one designed to stop Krox even though Marid herself died. That spell is very important in the book you're about to read.

Drakkon (finally) explains the Big Mystery (™) to Aran. Nebiat wanted to enslave Drakkon, because he's the Guardian of Marid. Controlling him would give her an army of drakes with which to assault the Confederacy, and Ternus would fall within months.

Drakkon was vulnerable, because in his grief over his mother's death he went into something dragons call "the endless sleep." Before seeking solace, Drakkon used a potent spell to move the world where Marid died. He put it in a far-away system, where other gods would struggle to find it.

Then Drakkon positioned his body over the wound that had slain Marid. He covered the heart wound, muting the magical signature and preventing primals from all over the sector from being drawn to that world.

Now that he's awake, he's pledged to raise the drakes on

Marid, and when the time is right he will bring them into the war against Krox. So, in the end, Voria accomplished her mission. She stopped Nebiat, but sacrificed almost her entire unit to do it.

Aran and Nara lived, but both are missing their past. Aran desperately wants to reclaim his, while Nara is still hiding from hers.

Crewes, Davidson, Kezia, and Bord survived, but everyone else died. The survivors are tired, and they are out of resources...but they are alive.

Now, Major Voria must atone for her actions.

Nara must learn to be a true mage.

Aran must learn who he really is...

On to Void Wyrm!

PREVIOUSLY ON VOID WYRM

Void Wyrm kicked off with Voria returning home to find herself on trial. We're introduced to the tribunal, which consists of Admiral Nimitz from Ternus, Skare from the Inuran Consortium, and Ducius from Shaya.

Ducius turns out to be Thalas (Dick Sock)'s father, and is more than a little pissed that his son died. He's determined to see Voria executed, and lobbies hard for that. Skare, who looks a bit like Rick from *Rick and Morty*, remains impartial. Nimitz wants Voria prosecuted, because of the catastrophic losses to the Marines on Marid.

Mid-trial the Tender and Voria's famous war mage father, Dirk, show up to offer testimony. Aurelia (the Tender) reveals that it was her augury that caused Voria to act as she did, and begs leniency. There's some posturing, a vote, and Voria is stripped of command and demoted to the rank of captain.

She's understandably discouraged, but Aurelia and her father offer hope. Aurelia has another augury, this one pointing to a world in the Umbral Depths. They can get her a broken down piece of crap ship, if she can find a crew. Voria realizes that a loophole will allow everyone to take four weeks of leave after their campaign on Marid.

While all this has been going on, Aran has been enrolled in a war mage Kamiza (martial arts dojo), under the tutelage of Ree, an insufferable Shayan noble who addresses Aran as Mongrel. She's racist against drifters, and she's mean to Nara. Yeah, we don't like her.

The master of the Kamiza, Erika, is one of the most famous war mages in the sector. She's also working for Nebiat, and has been bound for decades. She dangles Aran's past in front of him, offering to tell him about the Outriders. But first, he needs to prove himself through training.

He gets a montage (montage!), and improves his physical conditioning and combat abilities. Then, we switch over to Nara.

Nara has been enrolled at the Temple of Enlightenment, the Shayan university devoted to magic. She's greeted by a strange flaming girl who introduces herself as Frit. Frit is the emo goth kid from every CW show, except that she's an Ifrit, with void flame. She becomes Nara's only friend and ally at the temple, against her new Master...a dick by the name of Eros.

Eros is the archmage who runs the Temple, and one of the foremost mages in the sector. He refers to Nara as Pirate Girl, and generally treats her like garbage. But he does teach her how to duel, and how to hard cast spells. The very first thing he does is disintegrate her spellpistol so she'll have to rely on her own casting.

After Nara's montage, Aran gets word that one of the stipulations in Voria's trial concerned him. Instead of being awarded a whole bunch of medals, he's being given no special commendation. Instead, all his medals are going to

Thalas posthumously. They're honoring the racist guy who expended Marines like bullets, and Aran is less than thrilled.

He rushes off to Voria, and she, of course, ropes him into this new quest to go into the Umbral Depths. This time they're after a world there that Aurelia discovered, and she believes there is a tool of incalculable power there (spoilers, there is). She asks Aran to convinces Crewes, Bord, and Kezia to join them, while she heads off to convince Nara.

Aran starts with Crewes, and we get our first look at Crewes's home life. He's staying with his mom, who's not at all impressed by him, and likes to drink warm beer (who does that?). He's more than happy to go with Aran just to get out of there, particularly because it turns out the prosecutor in Voria's trial was his own brother.

Aran has less luck with Bord and Kezia. Kez is unwilling to leave her family without more to go on, and it's clear that Bord has it bad for Kezia, so he stays too. Aran and Crewes return alone to Voria's new ship...the *Big Texas*.

The *Big Texas* is a broken down Ternus cruiser that the *Serenity* would look down her nose at, and it comes complete with its own mechanic. Pickus is a technological wiz, but knows absolutely nothing about magic.

They leave Shaya, but on their way to the planet's umbral shadow they're attacked by a massive *air* Wyrm. It turns out to be Khalahk, a Wyrm from Virkonna. He's there because Nebiat told him about Aran, who Khal blames for killing his grandson Rolf (see *The Heart of Nefarius* for details).

Khal far outclasses the *Texas*, but Aran launches a daring plan and they manage to slip away into the darkness while something large, dark, and tentacled wrestles with the Wyrm.

The *Texas* is a huge mess badly in need of repairs, and Pickus proves his ingenuity. He keeps the vessel limping along long enough for them to find the planet from Aurelia's augury. It is shrouded in darkness, but as they approach, magma balls streak up from the surface and slam into the *Texas*.

The already damaged vessel breaks into two pieces, with Nara and Aran being flung one way, while Pickus, Crewes, and Voria are flung another. When they land they are assaulted by arachnidrakes, which are just what they sound like...disgusting spider dragons. Eww.

Nara summons a giant illusion of Drakkon, which scares them off long enough for our heroes to sneak away. They find a little cave and batten down while they try to figure out where they are and what they're supposed to do.

Aurelia's augury is guiding them toward a large mountain, which they can see in the distance. Unfortunately, in order for them to fly the several kilometers to get there they need to brave the arachnidrakes again. That's suicidal without some sort of distraction. Crewes volunteers, but before he can do so they hear a commotion in the distance.

Khalahk has arrived, and is tearing apart arachnidrakes and the remains of the *Texas*, clearly searching for them. They use him as a distraction and make a break for the mountain.

Yay, they make it! They're greeted by a more civilized looking arachnidrake who claims to be a custodian. They are, unsurprisingly, expected by the goddess it works for. He gives them quarters to rest in, so they may prepare for an audience with the Keeper of Secrets, Neith.

Voria is brought first. Before arriving she spends a little time in the library, which purports to hold all knowledge, all the way back to the beginning of time. Voria investigates

Nebiat, and learns that she's loose on Shaya. Not only is Erika bound, but she helps Nebiat bind Voria's father, Dirk. Her plan is to not only murder the Tender, but cause a civil war between the drifters and the Shayans.

Voria is understandably pissed, and also emotionally scarred, since she saw her father naked. She goes to her audience with Neith, who is *drumroll* a really big arachnidrake. Shocking, I know. Neith explains to Voria that she has manipulated events to lead to this moment, that Khalahk attacking was necessary to them being able to reach this place.

She explains about the *First Spellship*, which Voria will need to find if she's ever to beat Krox. To this end, Neith gives her the ability to perceive possibilities like a god. She also gives her a potent Eldimagus with its own personality... which likes poop jokes. Ikadra the staff is the key to the *First Spellship*, and also acts as a spell matrix for the *Talon*, the vessel Neith provides them to get home. But I'm getting ahead of myself.

Aran also has an audience with Neith, and finally learns about his past. Neith shows him formative scenes from Aran's upbringing on Virkonna, and drops the shocking revelation that Aran's entire life has been sabotaged to make him unremarkable. This hid him from Neith's enemies, and allowed him to reach this moment.

Aran was an unremarkable Outrider, but now Neith needs him to be an unstoppable killing machine. Neith grants Aran upgraded *fire* magic, which allows him to be both faster and stronger. She also enhances Aran's armor with the same ability, and catalyzes Aran's as yet unnamed sword with *fire* magic, making it even stronger.

Nara has a similar audience, and is given vastly increased cognitive ability. She's offered her past, but declines, saying she doesn't really want to be that woman any more. The past is best left right where it is.

Pickus and Crewes also get cool *fire* magic powers, and the crew rockets back to Virkonna. Khalahk ambushes them again, of course, but this time they're armed with a state of the art spellship, and thanks largely to Aran's ingenuity they whoop his scaly ass.

They arrive back at Shaya and immediately divide forces. Voria takes Ikadra to see if she can reach Aurelia before Nebiat begins her attack. Everyone else goes with Aran to stop Voria's father from igniting a civil war by crushing one of the largest drifter cities with one of Shaya's own limbs.

Aran, Nara, and Crewes join forces with snotty Ree and her war mages. They battle their own master, Erika, who cuts down most of the war mages and flees to join Dirk. Aran presses the attack, and they catch up to Dirk, Erika, and Eros. They've all been bound, and are working together on a potent ritual.

Erika and Dirk engage Aran and his ragtag band, while Nara tries to stop Eros from finishing his ritual. She realizes that, if completed, it will summon the heart of a star into the tree, causing a massive explosion. The 2nd burl will be blown off the tree, and onto the community below.

Nara quickly modifies the spell to convert heat into light, reducing the power of the explosion. Aran has an epic fight with Dirk. He and Crewes barely take him down, but Aran pulls it out at the last second. Almost as if the author planned it that way, somehow.

The explosion happens and they're sent spinning out into the air miles above the ground. Pickus uses his new *fire* magic to pilot the *Talon* to them, and they use it to blast the second burl into chunks of wood. Those chunks land safely outside the city, and not only does this save the drifters, but they're able to loot the hyper valuable shayawood, and bring a massive amount of wealth into their impoverished community.

Dirk dies, but Erika and Eros are both saved.

Meanwhile Voria and Ikadra show up at the Tender's palace and witness a massive magical battle between Aurelia and Nebiat. The palace is shredded as Voria uses Ikadra to add her own powerful spells.

Aurelia has clearly been poisoned, and badly needs the help. Together they drive Nebiat off, but Aurelia is killed in the process. Nebiat has won. She morphs into a bird and leads the Shayan spellfighters on a chase before escaping back into the city below.

Eros is selected by Aurelia as the new Tender, once the bindings have successfully been removed. Nara and Aran both go back to studying in their respective schools, and Voria's rank and reputation are reinstated.

The final chapter of the book was from Frit's point of view. She seemed like a minor character, but in this scene she longs to be free. While she is pining, a tiny dragon lands outside her window, and introduces herself as Nebiat. She has plans for Frit. Very important plans muhahahahha.

Three months have passed. Aran and his company have been called upon countless times to hunt down binders. They are doing everything in their power to eradicate the Krox influence on their world, but it isn't enough.

... Welcome to Spellship

PREVIOUSLY ON SPELLSHIP

Spellship kicks off with a new character, Kahotep—the son of Nebiat. Kaho is a true mage, and his brother Tobek is a war mage. Right off the bat, fans were like, oh, man—can't wait to see these guys go up against Aran, Nara, and Crewes.

Well, you didn't have to wait long. By Chapter 2, it's all pew, pew, pew, *whoomp*, BOOM. Aran leads his company to assault the manor where Kaho and his companions are holed up. Nebiat slips out the back, and her hatchlings stay behind to delay Aran and the others.

Ree shows up in a spellfighter with her partner and wrecks Aran's ambush. Thankfully, Frit has been attached to Aran's company and turns the tide by raining voidflame down on their opponents.

Aran goes toe-to-toe with Tobek, the war mage, and they end up in a shocking stalemate, almost as if the author was setting up a confrontation at the end of the book. Aran is at a disadvantage, because he lacks spellarmor, while Tobek has a supercool suit of black spellarmor complete with screaming souls all along the surface. Every time Tobek kills someone, their soul is added.

Anyway, Tobek and Kaho escape through a Fissure. Aran and his company find Caretaker Grahl—the target of their raid—dead of self-inflicted wounds. Their mission was a success, but they're all worried about the hatchlings who got away.

We cut to Frit, who is meeting with Nebiat in a small cafe. Frit has never been allowed to eat food, or to have a public holiday. Nebiat uses illusion to cloak them both so Frit can blend in and experience what freedom feels like. Frit realizes she's being manipulated, but thus far, Nebiat hasn't asked anything of her. She's been nothing but friendly and sympathetic.

Meanwhile, Voria visits Eros, who is failing badly to use the Mirror of Shaya that we saw Aurelia use in the previous book. Eros reinstates Voria's former rank of Major, and gives her back the *Wyrm Hunter*, which has been repaired over the three-month gap from *Void Wyrm* to *Spellship*.

Eros asks Voria to travel to Virkonna to beg for an alliance, which they both know the Last Dragonflight will never grant. It's a cover story, because Voria believes the *First Spellship* is located somewhere on that world. She agrees, of course, because plot.

Aran finally has a day off, and is alone on the *Talon*. He's just sitting down to check out a holovid when he's attacked by a masked assassin. Let's call her a dragon ninja because she's from Virkonna and looks like a ninja. They aren't actually called dragon ninjas in the book or the lore or anything, but that doesn't mean I can't get t-shirts made.

Anyway, Aran battles dragon ninja chick to a standstill, but the fight is interrupted when Nara comes back unexpectedly. The assassin flees, and Aran shares what he learns, which isn't much. The woman was from Virkonna, and has come to satisfy her honor. Aran guesses it might have something to do with him having killed a dragon.

Voria returns to the *Hunter* and assumes command, but finds out that there's a hitch. She's in charge of the vessel, but has no authority over Davidson and his battalion. Ternus is no longer willing to trust her with troops, which stings, and means she's basically a glorified taxi service. She accepts the situation, and meets briefly with Pickus. He's given *life* magic by Shaya. We approve, because Pickus is cool.

We flip back to Kaho, who is meeting with the Council of Wyrms on Virkonna. This gives us our first glimpse at their culture, where dragons rule over humans. Kaho attempts to convince the council to ally with the Krox, instead of the Confederacy. He argues that they are dragon slayers, and provides proof of Khalahk's death. He implicates Aran for the murder.

Back on Shaya, Kazon arrives to speak with Aran. He tells him that he's done some digging around Nara's past, and worries that she's still a threat. He knows Aran trusts her, but cautions that she was a different person before, and could still be dangerous. Crazy, right?

Kazon brings a fancy new set of spellarmor for Aran, which allows several new tricks. It can go into storage mode and become a little bracelet, which makes it portable. It allows him to cast spells directly through the fists, so he doesn't need a spellrifle to fire them. The armor also redirects kinetic force as long as Aran has *void* magic to fuel it. All three features become important later, so I had to introduce them here to make them plausible. =p

Savvy readers also noted two facts. Aran felt like he wasn't alone in the armor when he first entered, and Ikadra told Voria that Kazon's ship (made from the same metal) made him uncomfortable because he couldn't pierce it with magical scans. That kind of magitech shouldn't be available in this era. Voria notes his concern, but since she has bigger Wyrms to fry she takes no immediate action.

The *Wyrm Hunter* travels through the Umbral Depths to reach Virkonna, and they are greeted by the largest Wyrm in the sector. Cerberus snaps up the *Hunter* in his jaws, but rather than crush them, brings them down to the planet like a dog returning a toy to its master. Who's a good dragon? Cerberus!

They're escorted to the Council of Wyrms, where Voria pleads their case. The Wyrms refuse to ally with them, and demand that Aran be punished as a Wyrm Slayer. The mysterious (terribly mysterious) assassin turns out to be Aran's sister Astria, from the visions that Neith shared with him. She pleads his case, and gets the Wyrms to agree to allow Aran to perform a March of Honor.

Unfortunately, a March of Honor is just a pretty way to commit suicide. You march across a drake-filled valley, and if you reach the Temple of Virkonna, your enemies get to line up to kick your ass. You fight your way through all of them, and if you reach the top, are judged by Virkonna. No one reaches the top.

But, of course, Aran is wearing a Breastplate of Plot Armor and we know he's going to survive somehow. Aran undergoes the march and fights his way past drakes. He's forced to go alone, but his sister Astria is not so secretly shadowing him.

Meanwhile, Voria is trying to forge some sort of alliance with Olyssa, the only Wyrm Mother who seems at all sympathetic to their cause. Olyssa explains that her rival, Aetherius, is gaining in strength, while her faction is weakening. They've recently lost Khalahk, Rolf, and several other powerful Wyrms.

While there, we're shown that Wyrms like parties, and that they like to party in human form. Their favorite activity is a game that resembles Go, called Kem'Hedj. A few very astute readers correctly pointed out that the name is Egyptian for 'Black, White.'

Voria turns out to be a master, because she can see possibilities. It lets her cheat, and she kicks the crap out of Aetherius. Unfortunately, Kaho is there and sees her do it. Voria is carrying Ikadra at the time, and Voria worries that they may understand the staff's purpose. She retreats back to her ship to see if she can deduce their plans with her new abilities.

Nara spends her time at the local Temple of Virkonna, which includes a massive library. She's been assigned to find the *Spellship*, but has very little to go on. Her only clue is that the Wyrm Father of *Life*, one of the two aspects needed to create the *Spellship*, has removed all mention of himself from history.

At the temple, Nara meets the comic relief. She's introduced to Ismene, a pretty young acolyte, and her pet drake, Pytho. Between the two of them, they piece together that the *Spellship's* magical signature is too massive to hide...unless you hide it beneath another, more powerful signature. Like Virkonna herself.

Nara discovers that there are catacombs under Virkonna, and realizes that she'll need to explore them to find wherever the ship is hidden. Ismene turns out to know an archeologist from Ternus with extensive experience. He's a bumbling scholar, named Wes, who bears no resemblance to the character Wesley from Buffy and Angel.

Wes comes armed with a pair of golden spellpistols that

are even older than Ikadra. Nara is skeptical of his ability to fight, but Ismene is adamant that she saw him gun down five men. Nara relents, and Wes is all too happy to escort Nara into the catacombs, and takes her down the very next morning.

We finally flash back to Aran. He carves a path through the drakes and reaches the temple. There are fifty war mages waiting, and if he can beat them, there are two levels full of hatchlings. The fight looks impossible, but Aran has the advantage of the new armor Kazon gave him.

The next few chapters are probably the best series of fight scenes I have ever written. Aran uses everything his armor offers, and some inventive, new tricks. Aran, unsurprisingly, just barely wins the last fight.

Lightning stabs down from the sky as he is judged by Virkonna, and then he disappears, apparently incinerated. We have to wait like sixty-four trillion chapters to find out what happened to him, since we all know there's no way he really died.

Flash back to Shaya where Frit is slowly realizing that she's going to need to help her sisters escape slavery. She's learned that her people come not from the Blazing Heart, but from the Blazing Heart **of Krox** (dun, dun, dun). She, and all her sisters, are children of Krox. They're fighting for the wrong side of the war.

Nebiat gives Frit all the tools she needs, and Frit leads her sisters to a circle of redwoods where they're going to remove their collars and open a Fissure so they can escape. As they're fleeing, Ree arrives. In an earlier chapter, Ree overlooked Frit being in a restricted area of the library, which Frit really appreciated.

We don't want Frit to kill Ree, or Ree to kill Frit. But we know that one of them is probably going to end up dead.

The Ifrit are badass war mages and true mages, and we get an epic brawl between them and Ree's war mages. There are casualties on both sides, but Ree is forced to fall back. Frit and her sisters escape, though the cost is high.

Back on Virkon, Nara is exploring the catacombs. She goes through a number of cool puzzles, which I absolutely love writing. It hearkens back to my roots as a D&D player. Anyway, she and Pickus eventually reach the place where the first *Spellship* was forged.

They meet Shinura, the Shade of Inura. Shinura is an imprint of the Wyrm Father of *life*, who is *gasp* revealed to be Inura. Shinura explains that while the *First Spellship* was created here, it isn't here any longer. To find it, they'll need to use a temporal matrix to locate the possibility where Inura and Virkonna hid the *Spellship*.

Nara begins the process, but as she does so, Kaho and Tobek arrive. What are the odds of that happening at the absolute worst possible moment? It's almost like the author planned it that way. Wes is shot, but Nara manages to find the right possibility, and they teleport away before Kaho and Tobek can reach them.

We flash back to Voria, who kicks Olyssa's ass at Kem'Hedj. Olyssa realizes Voria must have godsight, and confronts her. Voria admits it, and it makes Olyssa more receptive to an alliance. Then, like two chapters later when Voria is in trouble, she basically does nothing to help.

Voria returns to the *Hunter*, just before the Krox launch a massive assault. They send five carriers. The *Hunter* could take one. Maybe two with the right commander. Five is absolute death, and Voria knows it. She uses her godsight to comb reality for a way to survive.

Voria asks Davidson's Marines to hold the valley where they parked, and to make life hell for any carriers that get close. Thanks to Davidson's enhanced hovertank, they're a threat the Krox cannot ignore. The Krox detach one carrier to brawl with the Marines, and we get a fun combat chapter showing Davidson in action. Love that guy.

Over the next chapter, Voria destroys two more carriers by using foreknowledge of their locations, but it isn't enough. She's going to lose. She sends a missive to Olyssa begging for help, and Olyssa says she'll try. She tells Aetherius, "Stop, or I'll say stop again." Aetherius is not impressed.

After like a hundred-page gap, we finally get back to Aran. He's been brought before Virkonna, and as we've seen with other gods, he gains a Catalization. Virkonna grants him something called *true air* that enhances his existing *air* magic, and she tells him a bit about why she chose to go into endless sleep. She cannot accept her mother's death, because she'd believed her mother infallible, and she knows that without her they cannot win against Krox and Nefarius.

Virkonna returns Aran to the world with the words 'become air', but he has no idea where she dropped him. He's in a dark corridor surrounded by black goop, which we eventually learn is the Blood of Nefarius (dun, dun, dun). Aran is met by a woman covered in the black oil stuff, which may or may not have been inspired by nightmares I had after watching X-Files back in the day.

Rhea claims to be an Outrider, and Aran quickly learns that he's somehow travelled 7,000 years into the future. Nefarius won. But Rhea is excited he is here and claims he has some sort of grand destiny. She also says the name of his sword is Narlifex, and that the blade is legendary. Saves Aran the trouble of thinking up a name.

She leads him through a bunch of oil-soaked corridors,

until he finally reaches a door. We have no idea what lies on the other side, other than Aran's Destiny (TM).

Flash back to Voria. Her ship is boarded by an advanced Krox party, and after she uses her godsight, she realizes she has no choice but to drop Ikadra outside the ship. The Krox will be forced to pursue, and she'll be able to flee. She does so, and buys some breathing room while Kaho recovers Ikadra.

Back to Nara. Using the temporal matrix she finds the *Spellship*. It's in an empty hangar, but it is coated in some sort of black oily goop. Worse, she knows that Kaho won't be far behind them since he can simply use the same matrix she did.

She has Wes go find cover, while she takes up an elevated sniping position. They attack Kaho and Tobek, and Wes is much more impressive than she expected. The hatchlings are still too strong, and Nara is forced to go invisible and hide. She watches powerlessly as Kaho walks to the *First Spellship*'s airlock.

The door opens, and Aran is standing on the other side. He lops off Kaho's hand, and snatches Ikadra. Kaho quite rightly flees like any sane true mage, and waits for Tobek to engage.

Tobek and Aran start to brawl, while Nara heads inside the ship to find a way to send it back to their native possibility. Ikadra shows her how to amplify her magic, and uses void flame to *pew, pew, pew* all the black oil as they make their way to the bridge. They find Rhea, and Nara burns away some of the oil covering her.

Meanwhile, Aran is getting his ass kicked. His spellarmor has gone into storage mode, and there's a band of blue runes covering the entire outside of it. Aran assumes that this is some sort of awesome power-up from Virkonna, and confidently engages Tobek.

Aran is wrong. So very wrong. Virkonna sealed the armor because it is infused with the Blood of Nefarius. So Aran has no spellarmor, and Tobek does.

He's outclassed, but uses some inventive tactics to hold his own for a bit. There's a wisecrack about face protection since Tobek doesn't wear a full helm, and then Aran has a Karate Kid wax on, wax off moment where he realizes what Virkonna said to him at the end is the key to victory.

Become air. So Aran does. He becomes magical lightning and flows up Tobek's nose and into his brain. He cooks it from the inside, and kills his rival. We're all like, "Wow, that author sure is inventive. I never saw that coming. If I did see that coming, I'll refrain from emailing the author and telling him, because I want to let Chris keep living in his bubble."

So back to Voria. She's screwed. The last two carriers have her pinned, and they launch a spread of nukes. It's over. Except that the *Spellship* arrives and intercepts the blast. Voria is teleported to the Bridge, where Nara returns Ikadra.

Ikadra asks if he can deal with the Krox carriers. Plllleeeeaasse. Voria says yeah and he casts the legendary So Fat spell. The carriers have their gravity increased a hundred fold, and plummet to the ground. Boom, dead Krox.

Our heroes won, but at a cost. The Blood of Nefarius coating the *Spellship* was theoretically destroyed during the nuclear blast, but what if some survived? Virkon could be doomed. The ship itself is still covered internally, and Voria will need either Eros or possibly the Inuran Consortium to help her cleanse it.

That's the end, right? Cue the Star Wars ending credits. Not so much.

Aran and Nara hook up. Fade to black hook up, because I don't really write sex scenes. What if my mom reads these?

Nara has a nightmare where she is sneaking aboard the *Spellship* with a sniper rifle. She slowly makes her way to Voria's quarters and finds her combing her hair before bed. Nara executes her. Ruthlessly, without a moment's hesitation.

Nara wakes up with a terrified gasp, and finds Aran in enforced magical slumber. A large figure sits in the corner of the room, enshrouded in dark armor. He introduces himself as Talifax, the Guardian of Nefarius. He explains that Nara *will* kill Voria. He's ensured that possibility.

Man, I love cliffhangers.

...Which brings us to **War Mage.**

PROLOGUE

Skare sketched a *void* sigil to deactivate the wards outside his office, then tapped a seven-digit sequence on the alphanumeric pad next to the door. There was no visible indication, but the buttons also sequenced the DNA of anyone who touched them, adding a third level of security.

He carefully removed his jacket and set the rich, Shayan silk on the hook next to the door. A pitcher of lifewine floated to within easy reach, immediately followed by a simple, glass cup. He gave a nearly imperceptible nod and the pitcher filled the glass.

Today was a day for indulgences. Today he met with the Guardian.

Skare swirled his glass, enjoying the way the rich scarlet caught the light. He sat in the high-backed chair behind the wide, immaculate desk. As he sat, the desk rippled and data began streaming across its shiny surface. Reports from all over the Consortium, as well as troop movements for both the Confederacy and the Krox—his two chief enemies.

A red envelope flashed on the corner of the screen, and

Skare tapped the missive to accept it. The data shimmered out of existence, and a holographic representation of Kazon's bearded face emerged from the desk. The man wore an uncharacteristic calm.

"I'd assumed you'd start screaming at me the moment I accepted your missive." Skare cocked his head and stared down at the young man's illusion, made even younger by the mind-wipe that had robbed Kazon of much of the political savvy that had previously made him such a threat. "You must want something badly if you're willing to forgo your hatred."

"Thank you for accepting my missive, Skare." Kazon inclined his head respectfully. "I apologize if my last was… rather explosive. After speaking to Mother, I've decided on a more moderate course of action."

"I didn't realize you were capable of moderation, in anything." Skare raised a slender hand to mask his smile. He loved baiting the boy, though of late that had grown increasingly difficult.

Kazon inhaled slowly, and while his eyes blazed with promised retribution his words were almost…gentle. "You are doing amazing things for our profit margins. For that you have my gratitude. But I am very concerned about this new metal. You won't even tell my mother, or the board, what it's called. Much less where it comes from."

Skare sipped his lifewine. He savored it before swallowing, and only then did he answer. "Despite your faults, you're a smart man, Kazon. But like many smart men, your very intelligence will be your downfall." Kazon's face darkened, but Skare raised a hand to forestall him. "I realize the mindwipe wasn't your fault. But it happened, like it or not. And it robbed you of the cunning you were so famous for, my friend. I won't tell you—or anyone else—the source of the metal, because doing so risks the secret of its creation. If that gets out, then our competitors will catch up in months. Certainly no longer than a year." Skare delivered the lie with complete conviction, utterly positive that Kazon would detect no deception. "Much better that I keep that secret close—for decades, if possible. By then, we will be the undisputed supplier for the entire sector in, well, virtually every industry."

Kazon steepled his fingers, and eyed Skare with apparent calm. Skare didn't like this new demeanor, nor did he understand where it had come from. Kazon was a hothead, and always had been, even before the wipe. Unless he wasn't. Unless it had all been an act. Had he underestimated this boy?

"I understand." Kazon lowered his hands and sat back in his chair. "Keep the source to yourself, then. But this metal concerns me. A...friend returned the spellarmor I gave him, claiming that the goddess Virkonna told him it was corrupted. Can you explain why a goddess might say that?"

Skare made no attempt to hide his amusement. He took another sip.

"You're just going to sit there and ignore my question?" There was the anger. Kazon's eyes positively blazed now. It had taken more to achieve than it had in the past, but at least it was still possible to goad the boy.

"Of course not." Skare set his empty glass on the corner of the desk. "Kazon, you are a man of principles. I've always admired that about you. But it's also the primary reason you decided to turn the voting rights to your stock over to your mother. You don't have the stomach for business. Some of the most dangerous weapons in the world are considered to be 'corrupted' in some way. That extends all the way back to ancient Terra and their initial use of nuclear weaponry.

They irradiated entire continents for centuries. Is *that* not corruption? A weapon isn't corrupt. A weapon is simply a weapon."

"And Virkonna herself warning us?" Kazon demanded. His hologram held up an oily, black bracelet and the scryscreen perfectly captured the metal, banded in white-blue runes. "Do you lend no credence to the words of a goddess?"

Skare almost reached for the image rippling across his desk, so great was his hunger. He longed to inspect a binding that had been placed by a literal goddess, to unravel its workings. But he couldn't risk showing any interest at all.

Skare fixed Kazon with his most imperious stare, then shook his head. "The gods are no more. They call it sleep, but we know the truth. Virkonna is dead. And if she is dead then she could hardly have cast that spell, could she?"

"Then how do you explain the intricacy?" Kazon removed the bracelet from Skare's field of view. "My mages have no idea how it was cast, but every last one claims it's beyond any complexity they've ever seen. It could be a ninth level spell. Our best archmages, working in tandem, have only managed a seventh."

"So someone powerful bound one of our new suits. Noteworthy, but hardly more so than a hundred other concerns." Skare gave a noncommittal shrug. "My time is valuable, Kazon. I have a meeting that started five minutes ago. Good day." Skare motioned and Kazon's head dissolved into particles. He knew the missive's end was abrupt, but he could not allow Kazon to witness what was about to happen.

A wave of cold emanated from the corner of his office, the only sign that the Guardian had arrived. It wasn't the first time Skare had met Talifax, but it was the first time he'd been able to do so as a near equal.

"Welcome." Skare didn't rise, but he did swivel the chair to face Talifax.

The dark armor made identifying Talifax's species impossible, but whatever it was, the limbs were too thick. The body too wide. An Eleph, perhaps? Skare wondered every time he met with Talifax, but still had no way to confirm his guess, and doubted he ever would.

"You have asked and I have come, a privilege I do not award lightly." Talifax's voice was disturbingly normal, completely misaligned with his body. "What is it you seek?"

"I need more." Skare clutched his empty glass, but resisted the urge to refill it. He knew holding it was a sign of his weakness, and he sought to master it. Unsuccessfully. "What you've provided isn't enough, not to accomplish the task I have been given."

Talifax considered the request for a long time, then finally gave a short nod. "Very well. I will provide you with another shipment. But be careful, lest your hubris cause you to mistake your place. The task is important. You are not."

Then Talifax was simply gone.

Skare would give up nearly all his wealth to know how the Guardian did that. Talifax ignored wards, and came and went as he wished. It suggested access to some new form of magical travel, or an ancient secret that had been long forgotten.

He gently chided himself. Right now the source of that magic, or even the magic itself, wasn't important. He'd secured another shipment, and that would finally give him what he needed to convert Jolene to his cause. In a few more days, the Inuran Consortium would belong fully to him, and through him to Nefarius.

A silent, bloodless coup would rock the very foundations of power in the sector.

1

KHEROSS

Aran wasn't certain what sort of reception he'd get when he stepped off the *Talon* into the *First Spellship*'s cavernous hangar. He'd been prepared for a snobby Caretaker here to cleanse the legendary vessel. He wasn't at all expecting Ree to be the person they sent. War mages weren't generally relegated to cleaning starships.

Ree stood at the base of the shimmering ramp, glaring imperiously up at him from her golden spellarmor. Her spellblade was buckled around the waist, and her helmet was clutched under one arm. A river of scarlet cascaded down her shoulders, framing the kind of ethereal beauty Shayans were famous for. Behind her stood a dozen war mages in similar garb, and those few with their helmets removed shared her bland expression.

"Is Pirate Girl with you?" Ree called in a clear voice that echoed through the *Spellship*'s bay. It was one of many such bays, and the *Talon* took up only a small part of this one.

Aran stepped onto the ramp to give Nara room to follow. She joined him silently and they walked down to the base of the ramp, where Ree stood glaring.

"I have a name," Nara growled when she got close, her expression murderous. She not so casually leaned on her staff, which had been empowered by Neith. Four fire rubies orbited the onyx tip, and they bathed the silver staff in potent energies. "What do you want, Ree? I'm not in the mood for your antics. Voria said you were here to clean the ship, not hassle true mages."

Aran blinked at Nara. It wasn't that she didn't have cause to treat Ree that way, but normally Nara would be much less aggressive. What was going on with her? She'd been in a foul mood ever since they'd left Virkonna, and Aran had no idea why. One minute they'd been enjoying some very physical R&R, and the next she'd become colder than the void. Maybe he was just bad at it.

"You were in on it, weren't you?" Ree demanded. Her eyes narrowed, and she took a threatening step closer to Nara. Nara didn't back down a millimeter.

"If she was," a sun-haired war mage called from behind Ree, "she won't be leaving this bay alive." The man's aggressive stance was mirrored by the others, and he could tell they were working up their courage.

Aran needed to diffuse this, and quickly. Trouble was, backing down would only encourage Ree's people to press the assault.

He took a deep breath and rested his hand very pointedly on Narlifex's hilt. Was the weapon a little bigger than it had been the day before? Ree's attention shifted to him, and the others quickly followed her gaze. "Ree, we've only just gotten back. It's been a tough trip, and we're exhausted. I get it. I'm a mongrel. She's a pirate girl." He paused and nodded at the closest war mage, whose hand was trying to throttle the hilt of his spellblade. "But if that kid steps any closer to Nara, you're going to need every bit of your *life* magic to stitch him back together." He stared her down hard, ready to follow up on his threat if needed. "I'm not the same wipe you trained, Ree. I've got my memories back, and have spoken with a goddess. Don't push us. I'm asking nicely."

Ree eyed him appraisingly for long moments. Her people began to shuffle nervously behind her, but still she said nothing. Finally, she licked her lips and spoke. "You've grown. So has the blade. Take a breath, Jayke. Let's hear what Pirate Girl has to say in her defense."

"It would help if I had any idea at all what the void you were talking about," Nara snapped. Aran could feel the magic coiling within her, and prayed she wouldn't do anything rash. "What is it you think I'm in on?" She had the same freckles and the same dark hair, but it just didn't feel like Nara.

"Don't pretend you don't know." Ree gave an exasperated sigh. "Your friend, Frit. She's working with the binders. She freed a bunch of Ifrit, and we tried to stop them from escaping. A lot of my brothers died in that fight." Ree folded her arms. "So, were you in on it? Where did she go? I've got a score to settle with that traitor."

Nara's entire demeanor shifted. Gone was the confidence and the derision. Instead Aran caught a glimpse of the compassion he'd come to expect. "Frit's gone rogue?"

At the sight of Nara's clear confusion, even Ree deflated, and her people began to relax. "You really don't know where she is."

"When did this happen?" Nara whispered. Her shock appeared total.

"Four days ago. They escaped into a Fissure and we haven't seen them since."

Aran removed his hand from Narlifex's hilt. The blade

pulsed disappointment. "You said she was working with binders. How did you know?"

"We never found direct evidence, just a warning augury about binder activity involving her. The flamereaders couldn't give me more," Ree admitted, "but Frit's actions when we confronted her prove that she was the ringleader. She freed almost forty Ifrit, every last one a war mage or true mage. We interrogated the souls of those who died during the assault, and two mentioned going to meet Nebiat at the Heart."

"That's troubling." Cold Nara was back. "And it doesn't sound at all like Frit. If she did this, there had to be a reason."

Ree's eyes flashed with a spark of *life*, though only for an instant. "I'm not surprised you're defending a traitor."

Nara waved at the hangar around them, which still bore many dark stains. "Aren't you supposed to be cleaning the walls, premaster? Not interrogating us about the botched op that you failed to complete. Seems about all you're capable of, since you obviously weren't able to stop 'the traitor'."

"Nara," Aran snapped, which drew the attention of both women. "You aren't helping." He turned his attention to Ree. "She's not wrong. Voria said you'd agreed to help us clean the *Spellship*. If that's true, we're grateful. Frit might have gone rogue, but we haven't. We've just spent the last month up to our asses in Krox, and we're lucky to be alive. Now we're back, and finally getting ready to take the fight out to them. We're going to need you, Ree. Same side, remember? You don't have to like us, but you do need to work with us."

Ree's expression softened to thoughtful, as did a few of the others. Not the man who'd called for Nara's head though. Jayke still glared at Nara, and Aran didn't like the way his hand still choked the hilt of his spellblade.

"Let's get to work." Ree raised a hand into a clenched fist and the war mages began to spread out through the hangar. Each moved to a section covered in the sticky black blood, and they began using light bolts from their spellrifles to clear patches.

The work looked exhausting, even firing level one bolts. It was going to take weeks, or even months, unless Eros had a lot more *life* mages to lend them. This Blood of Nefarius was insidious. Slow, but always growing.

Narlifex thrummed in his scabbard, drawing Aran's attention. He glanced around to see what the blade had noticed, and saw a figure step into the far side of the cargo bay. It was shrouded in darkness, and not the normal sort. It was the same ability he'd seen Rhea demonstrate when he first met her, and it cloaked the figure, preventing Aran from identifying it.

Most of that encounter had been a blur, but he remembered a roar from somewhere in the ship when he'd first arrived. Had this thing been hiding here the whole time? The ship was certainly big enough, and it might not be the only thing living in the shadows.

"Didn't Rhea say there was something else living on this ship?" Nara asked, pointing.

"Yup," Aran shot back. "Grab Crewes and the others. I have a feeling we're going to want all the backup we can get."

Nara nodded, sketched a few sigils, and then vanished.

Aran rested his hand on Narlifex's hilt and walked calmly across the hangar toward the patch of darkness. It was simply standing there, watching. It hadn't made any hostile move as of yet, so he figured the best opening play was talking. Rhea had been willing to talk. Hopefully this thing was too.

"Premaster!" Jayke roared, pointing suddenly at the patch of darkness. He sprinted toward the figure, and as he ran both his armor and spellblade exploded into a clean brilliance, the very essence of *life*.

Some *void*-touched creatures were vulnerable to that type of magic, but if this thing was, it didn't appear concerned. It stood there watching as Jayke charged. The man raised his spellblade in both hands, and leapt into the air above the shrouded figure.

A wickedly barbed axe appeared in the figure's hand, and the shadow blurred forward, faster than Aran could track. Its weapon flicked out, knocking the spellblade from the war mage's grasp. For one brief instant, Aran thought the shadow might let Jayke live, but then its hand shot out and wrapped around the war mage's throat.

The shadow squeezed, and an awful crack echoed through the hangar. Jayke's body crumpled to the deck, drawing the horrified attention of every surviving war mage. They all saw their friend fall, and rushed the shadow en masse.

"Ree, wait!" Aran began. It was too late. She led the charge, and that left Aran little choice but to support her. Otherwise, there was a good chance this thing would kill every one of her people.

He sprinted after her, and channeled a bit of *fire* to increase his strength. He bounded toward the shadow, studying its forms as it flowed from war mage to war mage. A second spellaxe appeared in its free hand, and it began carving a path through its enemies.

Four died in its first pass, each crumpling into a grisly mess after the axes carved through spellarmor like tissue paper. The second wave was further behind, and Aran leaned into his run to narrow the gap. It wasn't going to be enough. He needed to get this thing to come to him, before it cut down more mages.

Rhea had claimed they were Outriders once, and that they'd fallen to this darkness trying to protect their own. Maybe he could reach that part of this creature.

"Outrider!" he bellowed. The shadow turned instantly in his direction. "Face me."

The shadow hesitated for only a moment, then blurred toward him, its axes cradled loosely in its hands. Aran wished he had his spellarmor, in this case specifically for the spellshield. Narlifex was too slender to parry those axes, so he'd have to rely on dodging.

I. Grow. Narlifex's voice echoed through his mind. The sword, which had begun as a simple officer's saber, had grown and changed before. It had gotten longer, and the blade had darkened. That change had happened at a Catalyst, though, and he hadn't realized it could occur elsewhere.

Narlifex's blade lengthened another few millimeters and curved slightly, fattening at the end to more closely resemble a falchion than a saber. Aran had a brief moment to adjust his stance to compensate for the larger weapon, and then the shadow was on him.

An axe hummed toward his neck, and Aran gripped Narlifex in both hands to parry. His blade rang like a gong, and he was flung backward. He tumbled across the deck, just barely rolling to his feet before the shadow was on him again. Aran dodged a wicked slash, then dropped under another.

There was no way he was going on the defensive.

Aran rushed forward, and aimed a wide slash at the shadow's gut. It hopped backward, and Aran did the same to open a small gap between them. He hurled his spellblade with one hand, and used the other to fling a river of ice at the ground near the creature's feet.

The shadow wobbled, not falling, but also not steady enough to launch a counterattack. Aran was about to follow up when Ree and a trio of her mages swept in on the right. The layer of shadow around the figure diminished under the intensity of their collective brilliance, enough that Aran had his first look at the man.

Sharp eyes glittered in a handsome face framed by long, dark hair. It wasn't unlike many of the men Aran had seen back on Virkonna. The view lasted only an instant, and then a wave of darkness exploded outward, obscuring his features once more.

When it dissipated, the man was gone. In his place stood a massive Wyrm, which towered not only over Aran, but over the *Talon*. Its hellish purple eyes swept over them, saliva hissing to the deck as it sought its next target.

2
SAND ON A BEACH

Nara sketched a trio of *void* sigils as she mentally envisioned her destination. She popped out of existence, and appeared in the *Talon*'s mess.

Crewes lounged on a hovercouch, and still wore his spellarmor. He rarely took it off, thankfully. Bord and Kezia sat playing a game of Kem'Hedj, which they'd been playing a lot of since Virkonna. They'd also spent pretty much every moment together.

"We've got a threat in the hangar. Aran needs all of you. Now." Even she knew the edge to her voice was uncharacteristic, and that terrified her. What was happening to her? She longed for a moment to decompress and confront this, but there simply wasn't time.

"You heard the lady." Crewes rose from the couch and retrieved his spellcannon from the floor next to it. "Bord, Kez, get down to the hangar and get suited up. We deploy in thirty. Nara, see if you can keep the LT out of trouble til we get topside."

Something hot flared in her gut and she almost chewed Crewes out for ordering a true mage about before she caught herself. After a moment she nodded. "Yeah, good plan. See you out there."

She turned from Crewes and hoped he didn't see the tears. The weight of this was just too much. Dealing with gods and wars she could handle, but her mind being eroded like sand on a beach...it brought her back to those first terrifying moments when she'd awakened from the mind-wipe.

They'd taken everything once, and she couldn't bear to lose it again.

Thankfully, she had a wonderful distraction. Combat. She blinked back outside, and focused on the battle. It wasn't shaping up in their favor, from what she could see. Ree's war mages had apparently assaulted the...was that a Wyrm? Bits of golden armor lay strewn about the hangar bay, sometimes accompanied by the grisly remains of the war mages that the dragon was absolutely savaging.

Aran had its attention currently, and stood his ground before it. The dragon's tail lashed about, quick as a serpent, but he flipped over it and delivered a wicked slash with his spellblade. The curved blade sliced deep into the scaly flesh, and sent up a spray of black blood.

The resulting roar shook the entire hangar, and Nara gritted her teeth as she waited for the pain to pass. The Wyrm's wings flared out to either side, and it brought them down in a sudden sweep. An intense gust of wind knocked everyone back, including Aran. The defenders went tumbling across the hangar floor, desperately trying to cling to their weapons.

Aran was the first to his feet, and leapt into the air to hover near her. Blood dripped from his nose, and it looked like a blood vessel had popped in one of his eyes. "I don't recommend hanging out at ground zero for that roar. Crewes on his way?"

"Bord and Kez are getting suited up." She kept her attention on the dragon, which snapped up a war mage in its jaws. It shook the mage violently, then flung him into the *Talon*'s hull with a horrific crack. She winced. "How do you want to deal with this thing?"

"Do you have a spell strong enough to immobilize it? Like a paralyze?" he asked. His attention had also shifted back to the dragon. She studied him sidelong, wishing she had the courage to tell him what was going on in her head. *Focus.*

"Possibly. If you can distract it, I'll see what I can do." She didn't know if her magic were strong enough to stop it, but it wasn't as if they had a lot of other options. They couldn't wait for Voria.

Aran nodded and zipped back into the combat. His magic captured a lot of the same advantages wearing a suit of spellarmor would have afforded, but while he could fly, he was far, far more fragile than someone in spellarmor. That terrified her every time he fought without it.

Nara closed her eyes for a moment, and tapped into the increased cognitive ability Neith had imparted. New memories were returning, but she wasn't able to access them consciously yet. They were fragments, and therefore not useful.

In reaching, she saw something. A complex weave of sigils, embedded in her mind somehow. That must be the spell that was returning the memories. As she studied it, a pulse radiated outward from the knot of sigils, and something tingled in her brain like a long-dead limb suddenly reawakening.

For a moment she was elsewhere.

Nara stared through the scope of a spellrifle, settling the crosshairs over a man stepping out of a hovercar. She exhaled, then cast her spell. A muted-purple ball lanced down to his position, and disappeared instantly inside the back of his head. The target jerked and clutched at the back of his head, but only for a moment. Then he relaxed. None of his guards noticed the curse, and the man continued on his way.

Nara opened her eyes, and the vertigo began to recede. The spell seemed to be showing her memories that were pertinent to the current situation, so perhaps the rifle could be useful somehow.

When she'd first been taken by Voria, she'd relied almost exclusively on her spellpistol, which Aran had said she'd been really good with. She'd been terrible at the spellrifle when they'd practiced.

Nara snatched the rarely used spellrifle from her void pocket and raised the stock to her shoulder. The weapon was too short and too bulky. It didn't feel right. She wanted a violin, but felt like someone had handed her a stick.

She sighted down the barrel, and considered the spell she might cast for a split second. Her target was a Void Wyrm, which meant it should be vulnerable to *life*. But the *life* mages weren't exactly kicking its ass. That suggested it had a certain amount of innate magic resistance, as most Wyrms did.

She couldn't take down the Wyrm, but what if she focused on those defenses instead? Maybe she could weaken them, and make it more vulnerable to *life*.

Nara grinned suddenly. She had just the thing. For an instant, she felt better than she had in days. The rifle kicked as it tore loose a large chunk of *spirit*, and an even larger chunk of *water*. The grey-blue bolt streaked into the Wyrm's open mouth, where it promptly expanded into a massive amount of discolored sludge. The Wyrm coughed, trying desperately to expel the liquid.

"What did you do?" Aran yelled as he darted in and delivered a gash on the Wyrm's flank.

Nara zipped a little closer to him. "That should lower its magical defenses for a bit. Now is the time to hit it with everything you've got."

"I thought you was never gonna ask," Crewes boomed as he rose into the air on a plume of fire from his armor's thruster. Bord and Kezia sprinted underneath as they charged into combat. "Hang in there, LT. Help is on the frigging way." Crewes aimed his spellcannon at the Wyrm, and adopted a look of concentration. The barrel of his cannon began to glow—the standard orange-white heat of magma, but underlying it was something blue.

Not the shimmer of deeper heat, but...was that *water* magic? There was a ripple, and then the spell exploded outward in a spectacular misfire. Ice crystals and steam shot out in all directions, while a small ball of magma impacted anemically a few meters from Crewes.

"Shut your face, Bord. I don't want to hear it," Crewes roared before the shorter tech mage had even said anything. The sergeant's voice was tinged with embarrassment. "I was trying to combine water and fire, but uh...mostly got steam. Guess I'll have to stick with tried and true." Crewes lobbed a much more familiar pulsing ball of magma that detonated directly above the Wyrm's wings. "Why don't we start by limiting your mobility, scaly?"

Bord clung to Kezia's back in what appeared to be a planned version of the maneuver they'd done back on Marid. Kez sprinted forward, and Bord raised both hands. A white latticework of sigils burst outward into a protective ward, just in time to shield several wounded war mages from the Wyrm's frantic tantrum.

Ree sprinted forward, and the Wyrm's massive head

swung as it tracked her. It sucked in a quick breath and breathed a cone of dark, purple death. Nara recognized the *void* energy, but had never seen a Wyrm breathe anything like that.

The energies devoured Ree's golden aura, then continued on to her spellarmor. Thankfully, she'd donned her helmet, as Nara had no wish to see what that stuff would do to flesh. When the energy passed, Ree lay in a smoking heap, her golden armor now battered and wrecked. But at least she was moving.

Aran hadn't been idle. Nara watched as he glided silently behind the Wyrm. He raised his spellblade high, and the weapon looked considerably different than it had moments before. The blade was fatter toward the end, and curved now. It had become more of a chopping weapon, and less of a piercing.

Narlifex burst into purplish flames, and sliced into the dragon's spine where the neck met the main body. The weapon sank deep, and the Wyrm bellowed its agony. The roar knocked Nara back a step, and a high pitched ringing drowned out everything else.

The Wyrm began to ripple, then its body rapidly shrank. When the transformation was complete, an unconscious man lay on the deck, with a pair of axes lying next to him. Aran landed a few meters from the body with his blade held defensively before him.

"Nara," he called in a strong voice. "Can you bind this thing into human form? He looks a lot more manageable like this."

Nara deposited her rifle back in the void pocket, then withdrew her staff. "I can keep him slumbering, at least until Voria arrives."

She raised her index finger and sketched a binding, then

flung it at the unconscious Wyrm. It settled over him, an invisible net that subtly reinforced his natural slumber, keeping him confined to a deep sleep. She hoped anyway. Who knew if it would hold him?

The crisis was over. Her problems came flooding back.

Twice in that fight she'd done something uncharacteristic, and both times she could trace it back to one of her new memories. She was changing. Rapidly. She knew about the spell in her head now, too, and could apparently squeeze memories from it like a sponge. What kind of price did that carry though? Who was she becoming?

Aran strode up to her with a friendly grin. "Nice work. I didn't recognize the spell you used to weaken it. Was that new? Definitely a good time to unveil it."

"No, it wasn't new," she snapped. The fury in her own tone shocked her, but it shocked Aran even more. His eyes widened, then his expression shifted to carefully neutral.

He walked past her without another word.

3

WARNINGS UNHEEDED

Voria held her breath as Ikadra carried her through the Shayan sky, toward the pristine battleship. The vessel had been constructed entirely of hardened redwood drawn from the base of the tree itself, and more closely resembled a naval vessel from ancient Terra than it did a Ternus ship of the line.

Her hair floated up around her face as they passed through the membrane, and she tingled slightly as she entered the breathable atmosphere. That hair had gotten longer—past her shoulders now. Not because she liked it long, but because the idea of sparing time for a haircut seemed ludicrous in the face of what they were dealing with.

She focused on the battleship, which she hadn't seen since the fall of Starn. The *Arcanaca* had been the linchpin of their defense, and had suffered heavy damage. All that was gone now, and she looked as ready for combat as ever. Not that you could tell by looking at her. The early Shayan enchanters had opted to hide her weaponry. The spell-cannon was built along the keel of the ship, and would discharge spells from the carved maidenhead meant to represent Shaya.

"Listen, I don't want to sound judge-y," Ikadra pulsed, "but I think that statue is kind of phallic. Like maybe a little."

Voria suppressed a smile. Nara had removed Ikadra's limitations around speaking, and she'd yet to replace them. She hadn't decided if she wanted to just now. Much to her surprise, Ikadra was becoming a real friend, and his unfailing enthusiasm had helped her through some dark days.

"Take us past the phallic statue, to the third deck. Land in plain sight of the war mages, so we aren't mistaken for attackers," she instructed.

"Aren't we expected?" Ikadra asked, though he did fly them closer, in plain view of the defenders lining the third level. The armored war mages saw her, and began to deploy into a defensive pattern.

"We are, but Eros has become increasingly paranoid of late. He sees binders everywhere, and fears every visitor, or so I've been told." Voria pursed her lips as they made the final approach. The war mages were alert, but while their spellblades were within easy reach, none of them drew.

She thought she recognized their leader, though it was difficult to tell with them all encased in their golden Mark IX spellarmor. The leader was indistinguishable from the rest, save for a scarlet patch on the shoulder and a slightly more regal bearing.

The figure inclined its head as Voria landed. "I'm glad to see you survived Virkon, Major. I've heard tales of your... exploits." Voria recognized the clipped tone immediately, a feminine voice not at all unlike her own.

It was so odd, but Voria considered this woman a friend

despite not even knowing her name. They'd only ever spoken when she'd been visiting a Tender.

"How is he today?" She inclined her head respectfully as she approached.

"How is he ever?" The resignation weighed down the words. The figure shook her head. "His paranoia grows worse. He just chased off two Caretakers, and this time he used a spell to do it. I worry."

Voria gave a quick nod. "Thank you." It wasn't really any new information, but it made her feel like she had an ally here.

The figure nodded again as she passed, and Voria continued through an impractically vaulted arch inside the vessel. Here it began to resemble a more traditional warship, with narrow corridors and artful bulkheads that could be sealed in the event of decompression.

The ancient Shayans had done everything possible to disguise this ship's true purpose, and it underscored everything wrong with their society. They found war distasteful, and if it needed to be waged, they felt it needed to be done artfully. Screw art. War wasn't pretty, whatever they thought.

She made her way deeper into the vessel, but instead of guards, she passed golden mirrors along the wall every ten meters. She could feel their immense strength, and tensed as she passed the first one. It showed her reflection, staring a challenge back at her.

The woman in the mirror frowned, and raised a copy of Ikadra as if ready to cast. Each woman in each mirror watched her progress, and she realized they could likely be animated to attack if she didn't pass whatever test Eros had baked into them. She wasn't familiar with the spell, but the level of power dwarfed what she could harness.

Apparently Eros's paranoia wasn't the only change. The

man had grown in strength as well, which was good. He'd likely need every bit of it in the near future. It offered his one advantage, really. Aurelia had been a war mage before she was elevated. Eros was a true mage, and if he bent his considerable intellect toward mastering magic he'd be capable of incredible feats in just a few short years.

She reached another vaulted archway and entered the *Arcanaca's* bridge. The ceiling was a layered illusion, and currently displayed the sky above as if the ship were open to space. The night sky was breathtaking, and also a little terrifying. Not because of the vacuum, but because Voria felt that a Wyrm could streak down at any moment, and that they'd have no protection from its breath weapon.

"I've given you everything you asked for," Eros snapped. Voria's gaze fell to the corner of the room, in the shadows near one of the slowly spinning spell matrices. "You're here to ask for more, aren't you? What do you want, Voria?"

"To ask your advice," Voria countered. She tightened her grip around Ikadra, who'd remained respectfully silent since they'd arrived. He seemed more cognizant of social situations since she'd gotten him back from Nara. Perhaps the girl had had a talk with him. "I'm grateful for the *life* mages you've loaned us. The first several teams have already arrived, and I'm hopeful they'll complete their work before we need to deploy."

"Deploy?" Eros's eyes narrowed and he stepped from the shadows. "I take it that you haven't considered my words at all then. You still plan to take the vessel from Shaya, where it belongs. She is meant to protect our goddess, not to prosecute your war. You've come back to utilize our resources, only to deny us aid when we most need it."

He blazed with an inner strength, a potent force that hovered just outside her vision. She couldn't see the power, but she sensed his divinity. He was much, much stronger than when they'd last spoken.

"It's interesting that you accuse *me* of not listening when you so clearly haven't heeded my words." Anger bubbled up and she made no move to hide it. Voria's free hand shot up and she stabbed an accusing finger at Eros. "You are not a god, Eros. You do not know all, or see all. The godsight you fumble with right now? I've been blessed with the same ability, but unlike you, I've had time to practice it. Krox is coming. Not the Wyrms we've faced so far, but their resurrected father, in all his terrible glory. The hammer will fall soon, and when it does, I intend to be there to deflect the blow. I don't know Nebiat's endgame, but we're approaching it. Why else do you think Virkonna built this vessel? It has a purpose, Eros, and while I admit I don't know what it is, I'll hazard a guess that it is not to sit in dry dock on Shaya while the Krox dismember the entire sector."

Eros gave an irritated wave and a goblet of lifewine floated into his hand. He did not offer her one, though she wouldn't have accepted in any case.

"I've warned you time and again." His voice had fallen to a near whisper. "Something is coming for Shaya. I can feel her fear. Her dread seeps into my mind when I sleep." His haunted eyes snapped up to her. "If that ship isn't here to defend her when it comes, then our whole world will be extinguished. What price for the entire sector to preserve our mother, Voria? Our goddess could live again, and that ship could help. I can feel its strength. Give me time to master it. Give me that staff, and I might be able to resurrect Her. I'm certain of it. We won't need to fight alone. Shaya could crush Nebiat, or do you think her, or her father, could stand against the full might of a true goddess?"

The feverish sheen to his eyes terrified her. She recognized it, that ability to perceive multiple possibilities at once. Yet where she'd been given the ability in a controlled setting by a living goddess, poor Eros had had the ability thrust on him with no preparation. And his mind did not appear to be handling it well.

Could she reach him? She had to try. "It's possible the ship could somehow aid in Shaya's resurrection, but even you must admit that you can't be certain without a great deal of study. And while you are studying, the war is worsening. The Krox are coming, slowly crushing all resistance." She gave a sympathetic sigh. "I'll remind you that I am the vessel's captain, Eros. Not you. I will go where the battle is. If the Krox come for Shaya, I will be here to oppose them, but if they strike elsewhere, then I will move to counter them."

"Uhhh, Voria?" Ikadra's sapphire pulsed. "I'm really sorry to interrupt, but you aren't going to like this. I'm detecting magical combat on the *Spellship*. A powerful Void Wyrm is loose in the hold."

Eros raised an eyebrow and gave a triumphant smile. "Yes, I can see you have things...well in hand, *Captain*." The last word bled sarcasm like a hull breach leaking oxygen.

Voria flushed. "Please excuse me, Tender." She gave a stiff bow, and then strode from the room.

4

INTERROGATION

By the time Voria arrived on the *Spellship*, the intruder had been moved into the *Wyrm Hunter's* brig. Striding into the claustrophobic row of cells reminded her of her first meeting with Aran, just after she'd retrieved him and Nara from the Skull of Xal. She hadn't been down here since.

Aran stood outside the only occupied cell. His hand rested on the hilt of his spellblade, which was considerably larger than the last time Voria had seen it. It wasn't the only change, however. Aran's entire demeanor was different. He stood with quiet confidence, exuding the deadly certainty of a master swordsman.

"What happened?" She moved to stand next to the cell, and inspected the man sitting on the cell's only bench. He looked human enough, with thick, dark hair spilling down the middle of his back. He wore scarlet armor so dark it could be mistaken for black. He was ruggedly handsome, though the cold, hellish light in his eyes ruined that image. "And why is he still wearing the armor?"

"Because it's bound to him." Aran inclined his head

respectfully, but didn't salute. He hadn't since they'd left Virkon, and she didn't have the heart to oppose such a minor insubordination. "He's a Void Wyrm, at least several centuries old. I think he was sneaking onto the *Talon* to get access to Rhea, possibly to free her. I haven't asked him any questions, as I assumed you'd want to be present for the interrogation."

She nodded briskly. "You assumed correctly." She faced the man—or Wyrm, she supposed—and noted the immediate differences from the Wyrms she'd seen on Virkon. They failed utterly to mimic a human, especially hair. The only exception she'd seen was Nebiat. Yet this man was utterly indistinguishable from a normal human, just as Nebiat managed. Even the eyes were perfect, save for the glow.

"What is your name?" she demanded.

The man slowly raised his gaze until it met hers. The area where the pupil should be wasn't black. Each eye glowed with brilliant intensity, and the color was unmistakable. The deep purple of *void* magic, the antithesis of *life*.

"I am Kheross." He cocked his head, then rose smoothly to his feet. He towered over her, and even over Aran. He leaned in to inspect her with those hellish eyes. "You are godmarked. Many times over."

"We are not here to speak about me." Voria leaned closer to the bars, and Kheross did the same. Only a few millimeters separated them. She could feel the cold radiating from his eyes. "Why were you on this ship? How did you get here? And what were you trying to do to Rhea?"

Kheross turned from the bars and moved to sit on the bench. He rested his hands in his lap, and stared listlessly at the cell floor. "This ship was once my charge. I, and the other Outriders, were tasked with keeping it safe. We were told that the day would arrive when the vessel came, sent by Virkonna herself." Kheross looked up then, and his gaze locked on Aran. "When Nefarius attacked our world, we realized she was draining all magic, siphoning all power to grow stronger. Every Wyrm was a target. I realized that the only way any of us would survive was by hiding, but I knew she would see through any disguise. I enacted a ritual to bind six of my strongest children. Each was mind shaped into believing themselves to be human. Each thought themselves an Outrider, and believed me to be the same. When Nefarius came, we were left behind, while every other Wyrm was devoured."

Kheross shuddered, then closed those awful eyes. He kept them closed as he spoke again, his voice thick with memory. "At first, I believed it was because we had succeeded. Very quickly it became apparent that we hadn't been missed. Nefarius simply had a different plan for us. She left a bit of her blood on our world, and over time that blood slowly absorbed all life."

He licked his lips and opened his eyes. His gaze was haunted now. "It began as a corruption. Your temper would flare for no reason. Then, dark thoughts crept into your mind. All of us were affected, but we had a *life* mage and were able to cleanse ourselves. For a time. But the blood is insidious, and it can never really be eradicated. It always returned. Years became decades, and nearly a century after we began our vigil, the first of my children fell to the shadow. He dragged another away, and the pair returned for a third. One by one, they were corrupted, until I was forced to kill them all. All save Rhea."

"Even now, I can hear the whispers." He leaned forward on the bench and rested his face in his hands. His voice dropped to a near whisper. "I just want it to stop. I've been fighting so long, and I just want to rest."

Voria sketched a single *void* sigil and the energy field sprang up around the cell, isolating it. The creature couldn't hear them now, but it could still read lips. She turned away from the bars to hide her face.

"What do you think?" She didn't call him Lieutenant. Somehow that no longer felt appropriate. He might still wear the uniform, but she doubted he would for much longer.

Aran looked up at her with a start, his eyes mirroring her own horror. "He seems to be on the level, but this story could be designed to win sympathy. I don't trust him, not after seeing what he could do. He's dangerous. Maybe the most dangerous thing I've ever fought. I've been fixed on Krox, and I know he's a threat, but I'm realizing now that I can't afford to ignore everything else. We need to know more about this Nefarius, and we need to know about Kheross and Rhea."

"I agree." She turned her attention back to their captive. He stared up at her from the bench, watching calmly. "Before we investigate, I want to see what we can do to remove this corruption. It's had centuries to seep in, but we're at the site of the oldest healing college in the sector. We have access to dozens of talented archmages, and a *life* Catalyst. I will petition Eros, and see if he is willing to perform a full ritual."

"He's not going to like that," Aran ventured. "Kheross killed a lot of Ree's people, and she's already petitioning to have him executed."

"He'll see reason." Voria sincerely hoped that he would. "I'll appeal to his ego. If I tell him I don't think it can be done, he'll have it taken care of the very same day."

Despite her words, Voria worried. This was exactly the kind of distraction they could not afford. They needed to deal with Krox, not be looking over their shoulder for some new threat. Yet she couldn't afford to ignore it. She didn't know what concessions Eros would demand, but she was positive she wouldn't much like them.

5

PAWNS

Nebiat waited patiently as the Fissure completed, then clasped her hands behind her back as the vessel passed through. Kaho piloted silently from the command matrix, his scaly visage fixed on the scryscreen. He'd been much quieter since his return from the possibility where his brother had been slain by the Outrider. He'd not questioned her once, about anything.

She eyed him sidelong as they passed back into normal space, in the shadow of a world that, in theory, was a holy shrine built in her honor. In practice it was a training world, where her children vied against each other to secure her notice.

"Shall I take us home, Mother?" Kaho rumbled. He glanced disinterestedly in her direction, then down at his wrist.

"You must cease this petulance," she snapped, then immediately regretted the loss of control. Nebiat smoothed her dress, and focused on her breathing. Kaho wasn't the cause of her unease. "The Outrider bested you. The fight is over, and your limbs have regenerated."

Kaho met her gaze then, and his eyes narrowed to slits. It was the most emotion he'd demonstrated in weeks. "My brother died at the hands of a mortal. *I* very nearly died, and if I face him again, I am positive I will."

"Have you so little faith in your abilities?" She eyed her offspring contemptuously. "I thought you were made from sterner stuff. Tobek would be disappointed, and if your grandfather knew of your cowardice he would devour you on the spot."

"Cowardice?" Kaho barked a bitter laugh. He rested both scaly hands on the stabilizing ring and glared hard at her. "No, Mother. This is pragmatism. I finally understand my role in all this. No, not my role." He gestured expansively at the bridge around him. "Our role. All of this."

Nebiat waited for him to continue, but he did not. Instead he turned back to piloting.

"No, I do not wish to go home," she corrected, answering his earlier question. "Take us to Teodros." She didn't want to dignify his outburst with a response, but she had to know. "What is this grand revelation of yours, Kaho?"

Kaho didn't answer immediately. He tapped a series of sigils on all rings, and the vessel began curving around her world. It revealed the system's bloody star, which bathed the lava world her father had claimed. There was no sign of him, at the moment at least. He was probably buried under one of the world's magma seas, quietly plotting the return of their progenitor.

Finally, Kaho turned to look at her. The animosity had been replaced with resignation. "We are pawns of gods, all of us. Grandfather doesn't care about any of us. He doesn't care about Ternus. All of this is a means to an end."

Nebiat gave an amused chuckle. "And what is it you think he gains from all of this then, hmm? My father's motives are clear. He wishes to bring back Krox, and thus our control over the sector."

"Oh, I don't doubt that." His words were thick with sarcasm, and Nebiat instinctively curled her hands into fists at the tone. "What I doubt is his need or desire for any of us to survive to see this resurrection. We are resources, Mother. Even you. And we will be expended to achieve grandfather's goals, whatever you think."

Nebiat barked a harsh laugh. "Oh, Kaho. You may not believe it, but you have always been my favorite for a reason. You always see to the heart of the matter. Don't you think I know that? My father will expend me, or you, or anyone else without a second thought."

"Then why aren't you worried?" His grip tightened on the matrix's stabilizing ring. "What's to stop him from putting us in a situation where we are killed, just as you did to me when I faced the Outrider?"

She shook her head sadly. "Do you know why I am still alive while nearly all of my older siblings are dead, little one?"

"No, Mother." He turned his attention back to piloting. The unnamed lava world where her father resided grew larger on the scry-screen.

She moved to stand before the scry-screen, shuddering as they approached her father's lair. It grew larger, an angry molten ball concealing the deadliest predator in the sector. "Because when I realized that I was expendable, I found other expendable servants to be expended in my place. And when that wasn't an option, I quietly deferred to my louder, and more bold, brethren. Note that they are dead, and I am not."

Nebiat folded her arms and turned to the scry-screen. She studied her father's world, and waited patiently until a dark spot grew on one of the seas. Teodros emerged in a geyser of lava, rocketing into the sky and approaching her vessel.

He hovered in the space before her vessel, and his words echoed through her mind. *I have a task for you, Daughter. I need you to deliver me Ternus. Burn their worlds. Scourge their fleets. Our father's rebirth approaches.*

Nebiat shivered, and wondered if Kaho were right. "Of course, Father." She knew he could hear the words, though she hadn't bothered with a missive. "My plans are already in motion. Ternus will fall, very soon."

6

ALWAYS A PRICE

Aran tugged at the collar of the Confederate uniform, and wished he were wearing anything else. Almost everyone scattered throughout the holy chamber wore white or gold, depending on whether they were a true mage or a war mage.

He'd never been allowed into the Chamber of the First before, and gazed up at the ceiling in wonder. It vaulted several hundred meters above, and every bit of it glowed with potent *life* magic. They were close to the goddess herself. Very close.

A pool of golden energy lay near the center of the room, and Aran recognized it instantly. This must be where the potion of Shaya's Grace that had saved him back on Marid had originally come from.

A number of stiff-necked Shayans clustered around Ducius near the edge of the pool, all wearing versions of the same arrogance. All possessed the same ethereal beauty. All wore the same calm expressions, though hostility crept into a few as they glanced in Aran's direction. Others were thoughtful.

Voria was the only other person in the room wearing the blue and gold, and drew the lion's share of these people's animosity. Aran was just an outsider, but the way they eyed her spoke volumes. They considered her one of their own, and that meant her loyalty to the Confederacy represented a betrayal of Shaya. In their minds anyway.

A hush descended as a tall man in white robes strode into the chamber. His dark beard had been combed to a neat point, and his hair artfully styled. Power pulsed from him, a song that the pool echoed. They were one and the same, the song said, the same divine power.

Aran reached instinctively for Narlifex's hilt, a raw fight or flight response in the presence of something that dwarfed his own power. Eros had become something far greater than any mere mortal, and unlike his predecessor he didn't seem interested in hiding that fact. He wore his power openly. Flaunted it, even.

"Let's get this over with," Eros groused as he approached the pool. He was flanked by several war mages, Ree among them. Her armor had been lovingly repaired, with no hint of the damage she'd suffered from Kheross.

Ree glared at Aran as she strode by, snarling the word mongrel under her breath, infusing that word with all the fury no doubt inspired by the death of her brothers in arms. Because somehow that was his fault.

The Aran that had left for Virkon would probably have taunted her back. He'd seen too much since then to care about petty bullshit, though. He offered Ree a respectful nod, just as he'd do for Voria, or for Eros. Nothing more and nothing less.

Ree eyed him suspiciously for a moment, but then followed Eros toward the ritual circle. Two other war mages flanked her, and both glared at him as they passed. The trio knelt outside a wide circle that covered the entire center of the cavernous chamber.

Eros moved to stand before that pool, and knelt next to it. He cupped his hands, scooped a handful of golden blood, and drank it reverently. A line of white-clad mages formed behind him, and one by one, each stepped forward and drank as he did. Their eyes began to glow a soft gold, and Aran could feel the power pulsing from them.

"This is where it gets interesting," Voria whispered as she paused next to him. "Can you imagine what could be accomplished in this room?"

"I hope we're about to find out." He nodded at the entryway.

A pair of hovercouches floated into the room, each bearing an unconscious figure. The first carried Kheross, and the second bore Rhea. He studied the Outrider, though he guessed the term wasn't accurate. She was a Wyrm, even if she herself didn't know it. Talk about a mindfrag.

Her golden hair had been washed and combed, and she now wore a simple white gown that was gauzy enough to leave very little to the imagination. Aran looked pointedly away. He had a responsibility to take care of her, like a sister, not a concubine.

The pair of hovercouches floated into the ritual circle, and halted not far from the golden pool. A faint odor filled the room, and Aran realized he was smelling cooked flesh. Wisps of smoke rose from Kheross's eyes. The flesh around them blackened, and the purple light flared more brightly as if trying to push back the golden glow from the pool.

Rhea began to writhe as her eyes also smoked, and gave a pained grunt as she tried to wriggle away from the golden light.

"Why aren't you a part of this?" Aran whispered to the

major. "Shouldn't you be one of the mages up there? You've got *life*, right?"

"Yes, and by right I should be up there." Voria delivered a muted sigh, but the intensity never left her gaze as she studied the ritual. "Eros is making a point. I am no longer Shayan. I am a foreigner who has come asking for Shayan aid. If he included me in the casting he wouldn't be able to exact nearly as large a price from me."

"He wants the *Spellship*." Aran's grip tightened around Narlifex, and the hilt thrummed in his hand as the blade picked up on his mood. "Even after everything we saw on Virkon, he still believes this about protecting Shaya."

Voria nodded sadly. "He'll let the sector burn if it means protecting this world. In a way, I understand the fervor. He shares his mind with a goddess, so of course that goddess and the world that serves as her tomb are of paramount importance. Her blood runs in our veins. We are her children."

The golden glow around each mage intensified, and one after another they began sketching sigils. Aran had often watched Nara put together jigsaw puzzles, and this was similar except that each mage was creating its own pieces. *Life* and *water* sigils flowed up to join the growing latticework. They swam around each other and slowly formed a dome over both couches.

That dome was nearly complete when a slow flow of golden motes rose from the pool to join the sigils. The magic infused the spell, greatly intensifying the native energy. Aran wished Nara were here to explain exactly what he was seeing. Voria could likely do it too, but she had more important concerns so Aran studied the strange ritual in silence.

It went on for long minutes, and became harder to watch as both Rhea and Kheross writhed in agony. More streamers of smoke rose, not just from their eyes. It poured forth from many different points on their body, a dense black smoke that was pulled into the dome of light.

The dark energy pooled above it in an oily sphere, both defined and imprisoned by the sigils of light. That sphere grew and grew, and as it did Kheross and Rhea began to scream. Their hoarse cries split the chamber, and Aran found himself wincing with each one. The agony must be indescribable.

The crescendo of sigils joining the dome finally slowed, and one of the mages stopped casting entirely. The woman collapsed, and was quickly helped away by one of Ree's war mages. A second mage fell to his knees, then a third. Kheross and Rhea had stopped yelling, though both still thrashed weakly.

Finally, the dome began to crumble. The sigils along the edges hissed out of existence, and the spell began to fail. As it did, Eros disengaged from the circle and began sketching a containment spell. A swirling ball of golden energy rose from the pool, and moved to encircle the dark energy that had been siphoned from Kheross and Rhea.

The golden energy swirled around it, wrestling and thrashing as the rival energies battled for control. The golden energy slowly overpowered the dark, until the outer surface was a muted, discolored gold. The entire mass shrank down to a ball the size of his fist, then dropped into Eros's trembling hand.

"We have done all we can do," he muttered wearily as he turned to face Kheross and Rhea. Both were unconscious, either from pain or from the spell. Eros turned to Voria. "I do not think either is fully whole after this. There are still traces of darkness, particularly in the one you call Kheross. I would trust neither. In fact, it might be safer to eliminate that one right now."

The major shook her head. "I am reluctant to discard a being we recovered at the behest of a goddess." Voria turned to face him. "Aran, you've battled this creature and bested him. Do you think he poses a significant risk? Enough to offset any intelligence you might obtain?"

The question caught him off guard. Many of the mages, those still conscious at least, were watching him. Including Ree.

So he answered honestly. "He's a threat, certainly. I wouldn't trust him, and I'd want to keep him bound and under constant surveillance, assuming we let him live." Aran stroked his beard thoughtfully as he studied their sleeping forms. "Learning about the universe they came from could be important. In that timeline, as I understand it, Nefarius took over everything. We might be able to learn more about her, and about how Krox was ultimately defeated. Maybe we can use the same tactics they did."

Voria nodded. "Thank you, Lieutenant." She turned back to Eros. "We will keep the prisoners alive for the time being. They'll be moved to the *Wyrm Hunter*'s brig for interrogation. I will ensure neither is allowed anywhere near the *Spellship*, but there is simply too great a chance they know its inner workings. They spent centuries aboard her. We need that knowledge."

"You haven't yet asked the price of the ritual," Eros pointed out. He approached Voria and stared down at her with a smug smile. "And there is a price, of course."

"Out with it." The corners of Voria's mouth turned down into the beginnings of a scowl.

"The girl stays here." He nodded at Rhea. "I believe she can be rehabilitated, but only if separated from the other one. Given time, she could become a powerful force to help defend this world. She is a Wyrm, after all."

Aran cursed under his breath, which drew an annoyed glance from Eros. "What? I'm going to be the one who has to explain it when Kheross wakes up."

7

DOUBTS

Aran was mildly surprised to realize Nara was already there when he strode into the *Hunter*'s brig. He hadn't spoken to her since they'd subdued Kheross, though he supposed he shouldn't be surprised she also had questions. She probably had the best questions, in fact.

He made no move to disguise his presence as he approached. Nara and Kheross were speaking in low tones, and Nara wore a look of genuine distress. She looked up at Aran and instantly stopped speaking.

"Did I miss anything interesting?" Aran asked as he stopped outside Kheross's cell. The man looked more or less the same, though the darkness that had clung to him was more muted now. His eyes burned with familiar intensity, and Aran recognized the *void* energy. He shared that connection, through Xal.

"No," Nara said. Not hurriedly, but her tone was carefully neutral. "You came to question him too? I was just getting started."

He overlooked that. She's clearly been here long enough

to establish a rapport, but for whatever reason didn't want to share what she'd learned.

"Why don't we start with introductions." Aran inclined his head to Kheross, who sat on the cell's bench with a bored expression. "I'm Aran—"

"Aranthar of the last dragonflight, Outrider of the First Order." Kheross waved dismissively. "Yes, yes, I'm quite familiar with all your various titles. It didn't save us in the end, any more than it will save us this time."

"Cheerful guy, huh?" Nara asked. She gave him a weak smile.

"Seems that way." He turned to Kheross. "We're keeping you alive because it's possible you might know something that can help us survive, both against Krox, and against Nefarius." Aran wrapped a hand around one of the bars. "I can see about getting you out of here, if you can help us. We need intel. We need to know what the timeline you lived in was like. Right now we're facing Krox. Nefarius hasn't resurfaced yet."

"Hasn't she?" Kheross taunted. He nodded at Nara. "She's been touched, just as I have. She's a vessel, Outrider, but not for any god you serve. You've had a spy in your midst the entire time."

Aran expected Nara to laugh that off, but she went pale as a sheet, her freckles standing out on a somber face. He briefly considered asking her what Kheross meant, but he'd be damned if he was going to let this prick steer the conversation. He could speak to Nara later, in private.

"Well that answers my next question." Aran folded his arms. "You're clearly still loyal to Nefarius."

"How can I not be?" Kheross snapped. The *void* magic in his eyes flared. "She is a part of me. She orchestrated my rebirth. The Wyrm I once was ceased to exist decades ago."

"And what about Rhea? Your last living daughter?" Aran demanded. He leaned in close. "Let me be very clear. If you are both irredeemably contaminated, if your loyalties are in question, then you're of no use to us. You might not care what happens to you, but what about your daughter? Do you really want to see her executed because you couldn't be bothered to answer a few questions?"

Kheross's jaw clicked shut and his expression became unreadable.

"Looks like you struck a nerve." Nara sounded very satisfied, and Aran couldn't blame her.

Aran studied the Wyrm carefully, but couldn't discern any emotion. Kheross had buried his feelings. "You've got a choice, Kheross. We had more success cleansing Rhea than we did you. It's possible she could have a normal life, and in time gain some measure of our trust. Or, you can both be disintegrated, and your souls bound and interrogated before being dispersed."

"You practice binding?" Kheross sneered. "And yet you still have the gall to pretend at some sort of moral high ground. You shackle souls. There is no lower deed."

"Magic is magic," Nara countered, "and if we need to use binding to learn what we need, then we'll use whatever it takes."

Aran wasn't as sure. Binding terrified him, particularly the kind used to enslave Dirk and Erika. Shackling another's will, or worse their very soul, just wasn't something he could get on board with. But there was no reason Kheross needed to know that.

"As I was saying," Aran growled. "You have a choice. Cooperate, or both you and Rhea are ashes. And yes, your souls are fair game to these people. The question is, do you want to save your last surviving daughter and give her a chance at a real future?"

"What exactly are you offering?" Kheross pulled his long hair into a topknot, then rose slowly to his feet and shuffled closer to the bars.

Aran resisted the urge to withdraw his hand. "I might be able to arrange for Rhea to be freed. She could go where she wanted and do what she wanted. She could have a real future."

"But for me there is none." He gave a sharp, bitter laugh. "That's what you're saying, isn't it?"

Aran nodded. There was no need to sugar it up. "There's a chance we'll one day trust you enough to let you out of that cell, but I assure you we'd need to be pretty desperate."

Kheross gave a quick, nonchalant nod. "Of course. I'd stab you in the back, and you know it. Though for the time being at least, our aims align. You want to stop Krox, you said. This bargain will I strike. I will tell you everything I know about Krox, and about how you defeated him. In turn, you will release my daughter. She may go where she will."

"Done. I'll speak to the major about it." Aran had no idea how he was going to get Rhea back from Eros, but that was a problem to be solved later.

Aran turned on his heel and strode from the brig. He was mildly surprised when Nara followed. He waited until they were out of earshot before speaking. "What did he mean by you being a spy in our midst? That's crazy, right?"

Nara's expression became a carefully rehearsed version of itself. It was masterfully done, and Aran might not have caught it if he hadn't been exposed to it once in the past. It was exactly the kind of expression she'd worn back when he'd first met her. Before she'd been mindwiped. Seeing it now terrified him, and it lent weight to Kheross's assertions, however crazy they sounded.

"Of course it is." Nara gave a stilted laugh. "He just makes me uneasy. Hey, listen, I need to go meet with Eros. Catch up with you later?"

"Yeah, of course." He gave her a smile that he doubted reached his eyes. "We'll catch up later. I need to go talk to Voria anyway."

Aran's mind was troubled as he watched her walk away. Could he still trust Nara? She was an ally, wasn't she?

8

RUN

Nara had no intention of going to meet Eros. She hated lying to Aran, but as more and more memories came flooding back she'd come to a very powerful realization. She was dangerous. Old Nara had hurt Aran. She'd never forget the way he looked at her in the beginning, the absolute terror in his eyes.

If she were becoming that woman again, then the smartest thing she could do was get away from her friends. Unfortunately, getting away required a ship, and she only had access to one. Aran would never forgive her. Neither would any of the others. There had to be another way. Maybe she could hitch a ride on a transport, or find some other way off world.

She hurried to her quarters and packed her few belongings into a pack. As she stuffed in a second uniform a spike of pain shot through her temple. As before, part of her head began to tingle, heralding the awakening of another memory. This one, however, was far more powerful. The room around her disappeared, and she was in the memory.

Nara was strapped into a harness in what appeared to be

a shuttle. It flew unerringly straight in a way that suggested they were post-atmosphere, though she couldn't see outside and thus had no idea of the destination. She wasn't able to move her body, but caught sight of people sitting to her right and left. Both wore black, form-fitting uniforms. Not quite body armor, or if it was armor, it was the lightest set she'd ever seen.

Each cradled a long-barreled rifle, as she herself did, she realized. She studied that rifle and found it matched the one from her previous memory, though she sensed that this memory came before the other.

"Thirty seconds to the cradle," an emotionless voice crackled over the comm. "Deposit your rifle and armor, and report for debriefing."

The shuttle made an audible thunk as it docked with something, and then the rear wall slid up into the ceiling to reveal a corridor leading into a station. One by one, Nara's companions rose, and she fell into step behind them. They did not speak. There was none of the chatter she'd expect between soldiers. Each Zephyr—the word came unbidden—wore a visor with a cord attached to their spine.

Nara realized that she was also wearing a visor, which framed her vision. The screen was currently blank, except for an X-3 label that she sensed was her name. Memories of various readouts in a number of combats flared into existence in the back of her mind. She'd been trained to use this visor, this armor, and this rifle, with these people. She had no idea how many times they'd been deployed, but she got the sense that it was over a period of at least several years.

"Closer to a decade," a voice rumbled from the space next to her. She recognized Talifax immediately, and every part of her longed to run in the opposite direction. "We have arrived at the Cradle, a level one facility in Ternus space.

We're in an asteroid field, the remains of a shattered moon. There is no reason to come to this system, which made it perfect for Ternus to conduct their experiments."

"Experiments?" She wasn't sure how she spoke, since memory-Nara's mouth didn't move. The memory continued to play out, and Nara was now making her way up a slate grey corridor. They were approaching a sterile mess hall, with chrome walls and uncomfortable chairs. It was currently empty.

"Ternus has long lagged behind in magical theory," Talifax explained, without a hint of condescension. "They know this, and they are not fools. So they sought to expand their understanding by commissioning the Zephyr program."

A thrill tingled through part of her mind at the second use of that word, unlocking many associated experiences. She remembered training. She remembered being forced to approach Sanctuary, an *air* Catalyst. There was a flash of storms. Water on her face. They were boarded by another vessel, and attacked by strange, green-skinned monstrosities.

Then she was back in the memory. Nara walked to the counter in the mess and picked up a tray. It contained several sealed sections, each with a different color of paste. She brought the tray to a table, and began to eat mechanically, her back to the wall so she could see the other Zephyrs, each with their back to a wall, eating mechanically.

"Why are they so...similar?" She asked, again unsure how she was speaking. Nara's mouth didn't move when the words issued.

"Neuro-associative conditioning," Talifax explained. "You were exposed to highly experimental drug therapy, and fitted with a harness in the suit that administered drugs as the handler deemed fit. Any individuality was ruthlessly culled, and each of you was monitored at all times. This process began when you were eight years old, and has continued for a decade and a half before your liberation."

Past Nara finished the paste and rose from the table. She deposited the tray in a receptacle, and then walked slowly out the opposite side of the mess. She threaded down another corridor, then stopped in front of an unremarkable door. It slid open at her approach, and she entered the room.

It contained a narrow bed, a nightstand, and a harsh light set into the ceiling. Nara flopped onto the bed and withdrew a comm unit from her pocket. She began playing some sort of game of the variety she'd seen Pickus play, and was apparently quite skilled at it.

"Why are you showing me this?" Nara demanded. She hated being so powerless.

"This is a formative moment in your development." A ghostly vision of Talifax's form appeared in the corner of her vision, his dark armor revealing nothing other than that he had bulky limbs. "This is your earliest past, but on this particular day your entire life changed. For you see, Ternus had no true understanding of the forces they were trifling with. One after another, they sent their Zephyrs to the Catalysts in the sector, but when they reached the Fist of Trakalon they were noticed."

An explosion punctuated the word *noticed*—deep, and not distant enough for her comfort. Memory-Nara rose from her bed and placed the sniper rifle in the corner. She withdrew a very familiar spellpistol from a holster on her hip, and waited silently next to the door.

"What's happening outside?" Nara wished she could control her own body, just for a few minutes.

"The Zephyrs were noticed," Talifax continued as if she hadn't spoken, "by me. I saw your potential, and nudged Yorrak into attacking this place. He believed he would find wealth here, and was bitterly disappointed when you were the only thing of interest."

Nara slipped through the door, then tapped a button on the keypad on her wrist. The suit shimmered and disappeared from view.

"His thinking was quite limited." Talifax drifted in the corner of her field of view as memory-Nara advanced up the corridor looking for threats. "He did not value the Ternus research, which was, of course, a mistake that ultimately proved fatal. He did not understand what Ternus had created, or how you might use it to escape his rule."

Nara crept around the corner, and peered at the intruders. There were four of them, each eight-legged creature made of something that resembled stone. One of the spiders leapt on X-4, a woman she'd fought beside many times. X-4 removed a vibro-knife from her boot and began stabbing the creature in its many eyes even as its razored legs bathed her in her own blood.

Behind the monsters, a scarlet ruby glittered in the darkness. A figure stepped from the shadows, and Nara gasped in spite of herself. Terror pulsed through her—inexplicable and complete. Memory-Nara had no such compulsion, and calmly drew a bead on the man in dark spellarmor.

"Yorrak," she whispered, as memories slithered into her mind.

"Yes. He was quite cruel to you, during your years of servitude." Talifax seemed neither pleased nor displeased by the situation. "It shaped you. Molded you. Voria's mindwipe removed your memories, but not the programming underneath. Your neurons have been shaped. Honed. And further enhanced, because Neith assumes you are her pawn, not mine."

Nara's terror mounted as he used a name that no one else seemed able to say. She beat frantically at the confines of her mind, longing desperately to be back in her body.

"You will return to your body in time." The voice was smug now. "But I am not quite done with it. While you have been unlocking your memories, you have not been...idle."

The implications slashed at her like shards of glass. When she'd dreamed of killing Voria, it had seemed utterly ludicrous. If Talifax could really control her body at will, though, then she could be doing it right now. Her friends were in danger, and it was her fault.

9
THE DEMON'S CHOICE

Frit wasn't really sure what to expect when they arrived at the system containing the Blazing Heart of Krox, but whatever it was, this exceeded it. She and her sisters hovered in the umbral shadow of a molten ball of rock, but it wasn't the planet that interested her. It was the star the planet orbited.

An untrained eye would call it a red dwarf, but she could feel the magic pulsing from it, and knew this was no star. Rather, it was the Heart of Krox, the repository for the god's vast reserves of *fire* magic. This wasn't just a god. It was *her* god. The god that had given her form, even after that god's death.

"Sister?" Fritara asked timidly. She drifted closer to Frit. "What do we do now?"

That was the real question. Frit had done what she'd set out to do. They were free, but now she had no idea what to do. What did freedom mean? It was terrifying. Where would they go?

"I don't know," she admitted. Frit took in all of her sisters. "I'm scared. I don't mind admitting it." She pointed closer to the Heart of Krox—the corona, had this been a sun. "I can see our people there, flitting about. Do you see them?"

One by one, her sisters turned to look at the star. Their connection to the Heart had already dramatically enhanced their senses, and it allowed them to perceive things humans or Shayans would have called impossible. She could see across the million-kilometer gap as if gazing across a park.

"That's what we were...before?" Rita asked.

"I think so." Frit drifted a little closer to the Heart. Bathing in its light felt wonderful, and her entire body tingled. She longed to get closer. To bask in that light. All around her the others slowly donned beatific smiles. "We've finally come home."

Magic surged behind her, and Frit spun to face a rapidly expanding Fissure. Someone else was coming through, though that had been expected. A large, grey cruiser emerged, and moved unthreateningly in their direction. It stopped a half-kilometer away, and two figures emerged from a cargo bay.

The first was a Krox hatchling Frit thought vaguely familiar. The second captured her full attention, though. Nebiat wore her human form, her dark skin highlighted by a scarlet dress that flattered her figure. A cascade of ghostly, white hair framed her elegantly, contrasting perfectly with the dress. She and the hatchling drifted closer, and it took Frit until the pair reached them for her to recognize him as the true mage they'd battled back on Shaya what felt like a lifetime ago.

"Sisters, I am so pleased to see you." Nebiat glided to Frit and kissed her on both cheeks. She leaned back, and gave them all a warm smile. "You survived the crossing. Nearly all of you, it seems."

"We fought with Ree and her war mages when we escaped." Frit's hands curled into fists. "We lost four sisters. The cost was high, but we're...home, I guess."

"You don't sound particularly thrilled." Nebiat raised a delicate, white eyebrow.

"Who is your friend?" Frit asked, deflecting the question.

"My son." Nebiat rested a motherly hand on his shoulder. The hatchling flinched, but did not pull away. "I believe you met Kahotep briefly on Shaya, before you defected."

"It is an honor." Kaho gave a graceful bow with his wings flared out and his tail curled artfully behind him. "We are cousins, in a way. Both children of Krox, ultimately."

Frit couldn't set aside her dislike for the Krox, not after Nara's stories. But so far as she knew, this one hadn't done anything to them, and he wasn't wrong about their kinship.

"It's a pleasure to meet you." She bobbed a small curtsey, and all around her the other girls did the same. Only Fritara didn't repeat it. She watched everyone, and Frit noted a calculating look to her gaze that she didn't much like. "So, I don't suppose, maybe, you could introduce us to our people? Do they know you?" She glanced over her shoulder at the Heart, then back at Nebiat.

"I can." Nebiat nodded, and her smile never slipped. "But you must understand that such introductions are unnecessary. I have brought with me a pattern inducer, the very device used to mold you into your current forms. If you wish, I can return you to your natural state. You will be as they are, free to bask in the glow of your god."

Frit watched her sisters to see how they'd react to the offer. Most avoided eye contact, and all looked uncomfortable. Even Fritara.

Frit turned back to Nebiat. "I can't speak for everyone, but I don't want to give up what I've become. It's all I've ever known, and while it's true that I'd be like them if I'd never been caught...well, I *was* caught. I did live as a Shayan, basically. I'm grateful for all you've done to get us home, but I don't think I want to stay here."

She realized that she didn't want to meet them. Not one little bit. They were floating balls of light orbiting a god known for controlling the minds of his vassals. Turning them into willing slaves. She'd already seen what slavery was like, and the theft of will only made it worse.

"I do not wish to give up my body." Rita bit her lip, her short hair floating in the void around her. "If we go there, and we don't want to change, do you think they'll let us stay?"

"Mother?" Kaho asked, bowing deferentially. She gave him a nod, and he turned back to them. "I do not believe you understand what your natural state entails. Your people won't care if you are there or not. They do not possess language, only vague emotions. They are empathic, to a limited extent, but they do not communicate or bond as we do."

Frit turned back to her people, horrified beyond reason. "That sounds so lonely." She badly wanted to leave this place, and wanting that crushed her. She'd given up everything to be here. Now what? Where could they go? They had no allies, except for Nebiat.

"I understand and sympathize," Nebiat said, her tone oozing support. "You cannot be as you were, not after everything you've been through. So what will you do now?"

The fact that she didn't offer her opinion raised Frit's guard. Nebiat was far too canny not to have a plan for them. Perhaps she wanted them to arrive at the solution on their own, so they thought it was their idea. Frit decided to take a shortcut.

"Oh, out with it already." Frit squared her shoulders in a very Eros-like way, and drifted a bit closer to Nebiat and her hatchling. "You knew what we'd find when we arrived here. You knew it the first day you met us in that clearing. You knew damned well we wouldn't want to stay here once we realized what it meant. You've had a plan this entire time. So let's skip the part where we pretend you're doing this to help us. What do you want from us?"

Most of her sisters glanced awkwardly away at her outburst, but Fritara simply stared, aghast.

Nebiat gave Frit a compassionate glance, then turned to the others. "Your sister's words are blunt, but her concern is warranted. You all know I'm embroiled in a war with your former home. Shaya seeks to eradicate the Krox—make no mistake of it. If we were to retreat back into the Erkadi Rift today, how do you think they would respond?"

No one answered. Nebiat pointed at Fritara. "You, there. You look like you want to say something, little sister. What is it?"

Fritara wilted a bit at the attention, and hid part of her face behind her flaming hair. "If you retreat, then the Confederacy will muster all their forces. They will build an army, and when they're ready they'll come into the rift to wipe you out."

"This one understands." Nebiat smiled proudly at Fritara. "We are battling for our survival, and you each have a choice." Nebiat's expression shifted to a more somber mask. "Either you can help us win the war, and secure a place for your people, or you can pick a corner of the sector to hide in. Either route is viable. There is nothing wrong with hiding, and if that's the route you chose, I will wish you well."

Her answer infuriated Frit, because she saw the manipulation, while many of her sisters seemed to miss it. It was the demon's choice, which was no choice at all. Either they forged an unknown destiny when they had no knowledge, no resources, and not even the social skills necessary to seek the help they'd need to find a new home. Or they joined Nebiat's war effort, where they had a clear purpose, one that utilized the skills each had spent a decade or more mastering. One that gave them purpose.

"I'll go with you," Fritara piped up.

Others followed, and before long everyone had agreed. Nebiat looked to Frit. "Will you come too, sister?"

"Of course." She smiled prettily at Nebiat. Someone had to make sure that her sisters weren't taken advantage of, and while everyone else was buying her bullshit, Frit was one hundred percent certain Nebiat wanted them only as weapons. "Where do we start?"

"Excellent." Nebiat beamed a radiant smile at them. "I will escort you to a Ternus facility, one where they experimented with magic. It is my hope that we can find a particular piece of technology that will allow us to slip past their early warning systems, and put an end to them once and for all."

Nebiat began flying back to her ship, and a flood of Ifrit followed. Only Kahotep lingered, and he shot Frit a pitying look. "You see it too, don't you? Most don't."

She nodded sadly.

Kaho drifted over to give her shoulder a sympathetic squeeze, then followed the others. Only when he'd nearly reached the ship did Frit force herself to follow as well. She was positive she was going to regret this, but as with every part of her life, what better choice did she have?

10

WAR

"LT, we have to move." The sergeant's voice yanked Aran up from dark dreams, and he rolled out of his bunk to find himself soaked in sweat. Every part of him ached from the previous evening's session with the squat rack, Crewes's favorite therapy. Not as much as the internal ache, though. The confusion surrounding Nara's behavior had permeated his nightmares.

Crewes loomed over his bed, already wearing his armor.

"What's up, Sergeant?" Aran blinked himself awake as he slid from the bed and buckled Narlifex around his waist. He missed the convenience of a void pocket, but Narlifex really hated being cooped up.

"We've docked on the *Hunter*. Major's asked everyone to report to the hangar. She's got some sort of big news." Crewes smacked his armored fists together. "Hope it's combat. 'Bout time, too. I get antsy sitting around too long."

Aran couldn't help but laugh at that. "You are the only Marine in the sector who hates days off." He buttoned his jacket, then followed the sergeant out of his quarters.

"Nah, that ain't it." Crewes shook his head. "The Krox

ain't takin' days off. They're out there killing and binding. Can't let 'em get complacent. I want them telling their hatchlings horror stories about us."

"Bord and Kez?" Aran asked as he stifled a yawn.

"I sent them ahead. I wanted to talk to you, private like." Crewes fell into step beside Aran. "You know I've got mad respect for you, right, LT? You've become a fine officer, and you keep us alive." They strode down the corridor into the *Talon*'s common space.

"Thanks. I sense a but, though." He paused and gave Crewes his full attention.

Crewes looked very uncomfortable. "I ain't gonna sugar coat this. I think you should quit. From the Confederacy, I mean."

"Now that I did not see coming." Aran leaned against the wall. He'd been preoccupied with Nara. What had he missed? Had he been neglecting his duties?

"It's just that I've been thinking. You ain't a follower, sir. Not like me." Crewes gave a half smile. "I'm thinking we could build something. We're all flush with scales after Virkon. That means we can all buy out our contracts. I think we should, sir. The major gave you the *Talon*, right? We could still fight the war, but then we could go where we wanted. Fight how we wanted. And then there ain't no suits tying us down with bullshit rules."

Aran considered that. It certainly sounded attractive. They had enough money to keep the *Talon* resupplied through an extended campaign, and he could probably get whatever supplies he needed at a discount through Kazon.

"The only thing I haven't figured out," Crewes continued, "is how to recruit. 'Cause we're gonna need more than just the handful of people we have."

Aran scratched his beard. "That would be easy enough

to handle, I think. I'd choose quality over quantity. We could make offers to anyone we meet that's a good fit. Maybe we could buy out Davidson's contract."

They exited the common room, and took the ramp out of the *Talon* into the *Hunter's* hangar. It couldn't have contrasted more with the first day Aran had seen it. The place flowed with life now. Techs ran various diagnostics on hovertanks. Marines drilled, or lounged about playing cards if their work was done. There was a relaxed readiness to everyone that Aran very much liked.

The largest concentration of people clustered at the base of Davidson's hovertank, which was parked against the far wall near the largest scry-screen Aran had ever seen. It covered the entire wall on that side of the hangar, from floor to ceiling.

"When did they find time to install that?" Crewes rumbled.

"And who paid for it?" Aran asked. It seemed more and more that Ternus was stepping in and taking a direct role with the *Hunter*. With Voria having moved to the *First Spellship*, there was no one to really oppose the takeover. This ship belonged to Ternus in all but name now.

They threaded past Marines, most of whom delivered respectful nods. Aran returned them as often as he was able. He'd heard what these men had done, the role they'd played in the battle on Virkonna. They were heroes in his book, every one.

"Aran!" Davidson called. He stood atop his tank, one arm draped over the spellcannon. "We're getting big news. I'm throwing it up on the scry-screen."

The lights dimmed a level and the wall lit. A grey-haired reporter floated in a suit of Ternus power armor. Behind her an orbital battle played out in the umbral shadow of a grey-green world.

A gargantuan Fissure split the whole of the night sky, and Krox forces were pouring out. Dozens of troop carriers, flanked by winged forms. It was a force many times what they'd faced on Virkon, though thankfully most of the Krox numbers seemed to be carriers, and not Wyrms. Aran had personally accounted for many of their kind, and hoped that he'd managed to thin their numbers. He wasn't sure how much it would matter. The stream of Krox was endless.

The reporter winced and covered her head as a starship detonated behind her, but straightened immediately after the glow faded. "This is Erica Tharn, reporting live. As you can see, the Krox have arrived at New Texas, and are quickly overrunning the defenders."

The first wave of carriers approached the planet, which had considerable defenses. This was no Shayan world to rely on magic. No, these people trusted steel. Dozens of orbital defense platforms hovered between the approaching fleet and the world they protected, each close enough to support the others. They formed a loose defensive net, a clever defensive feature.

Ternus warships, small frigates and cruisers mostly, flitted between the stations. They were perfect for rapid response, and would allow the Ternus defenders to focus fire on weakened ships. Unfortunately, he only saw a handful of battleships stiffening the Ternus ranks. Those lurked behind the defensive screen, which was probably how Aran would have deployed them too. If the Krox broke through, those ships would be needed to hold the line.

All of a sudden, the closest rank of Krox carriers were wreathed in explosions, all along their hulls. The damage seemed superficial, until it wasn't. The first carrier imploded, followed by a half dozen others.

"What the depths took out those ships?" Aran asked Crewes.

"Micromines. Ternus loves 'em," the sergeant explained. His gaze hadn't left the scry-screen. "They'll swarm a target and explode near sensitive areas. Each mine discharges a pod of nanites, and the little bastards dismantle the closest system to the impact point. I hear they're crazy expensive, but looks like they're worth it."

The next wave of carriers met with a similar fate, as did the one after. The Krox lost at least twenty carriers before the first rank reached the orbital stations. Curiously, they didn't attack. The stations lit them up, and that rank exploded spectacularly.

Aran shook his head. What were the Krox thinking? There had to be a method to their attack.

Then it hit him. "It's a distraction. Those ships are illusions. I'm betting only the first rank was real."

As if on cue, an entire Krox fleet decloaked on the far side of the planet. They'd slipped around the defensive net, and were beginning to make landfall. Each one descended toward a different city, and Aran's blood ran cold when he realized none of the Ternus defenders would be able to stop them before they grounded their troops.

Once binders reached the surface, they could hide and keep harrying defenders with animated corpses or enslaved megafauna. They'd be nearly impossible to root out, and the longer they were left unchecked the larger their respective armies would grow.

The viewpoint shifted back to orbit, and showed the Krox retreating from the Fissure. It closed in their wake, and the rest of their fleet moved to a spot behind the largest of three moons. That put them well out of range of the orbital stations, and the Ternus defenders clearly didn't have enough firepower to pursue.

The screen winked out, and dozens of conversations broke out all at once.

Davidson hopped down from his tank and strode deliberately toward Aran. He eyed Aran searchingly. "We have to stop this, man. We're the only ones who can."

"The *Spellship* isn't ready," Aran pointed out.

"Screw the *Spellship*. The *Hunter* can fly, and so can the *Talon*. My people are about to have to deal with binders, and I can tell you right now they aren't prepared." Davidson's features softened. "Please, Aran. You kill binders. It's what you do. My people need you."

Aran thought carefully about his answer, but in the end there was only one possible conclusion. Davidson was right. "We were already talking about mustering out of the Confederacy. I can do that right now, and have the *Talon* ready to fly in about four hours. After that, we're all yours."

As if on cue, the *Talon*'s spelldrive began to hum. Aran turned curiously toward his ship, wondering if some sort of internal mechanism had activated. The vessel lifted gracefully from the deck, then glided through the membrane separating the hangar from empty space outside.

"Uh, sir, I think someone just jacked our ride," Crewes boomed, "and my GODS' DAMNED ARMOR with it!"

"Yeah, I can see that." Aran stared after the *Talon*. There was only one person with the access and magic to take his ship.

Nara had just proved Kheross right.

11

CHOICES

When Nara resumed control of her body, she found herself standing in the *Talon*'s central matrix. There was an odd moment where her body and mind seemed to catch up, and she remembered the actions her body had taken while she'd been mired in Talifax's spell.

Her heart thundered in her chest as she prayed to gods she didn't truly worship. *Please let her friends be okay.*

Memory-Nara stepped into the *Talon*'s matrix and tapped the initialization sequence. A whiff of *fire* flowed into the vessel, and she felt an awareness of the vessel occupy a part of her head.

She guided it dispassionately into the air, and focused on the ship's external sensors so she could get her bearings. Davidson's startled-looking battalion stared up at her, and not far away stood her friends. She caught the shocked expression on Aran's face as she sped away. The *Talon* burst out of the *Spellship*'s cargo bay, and zipped effortlessly into the atmosphere.

They shot into the sky over Shaya, quickly leaving the

Spellship where it hovered next to the third branch. Memory-Nara poured *fire* into the drive to increase thrust. The *Talon* responded instantly and the world quickly fell away below them. She tapped the *void* sigil on all three rings, and switched to gravity magic as a power source once they departed Shaya's protective dome.

A squadron of golden spellfighters glittered on the horizon, and instantly shifted course to make for her position. That was hardly surprising. A vessel flying like a bat out of a dragon's maw had to be running for a reason, and Shayan war mages loved hunting down the guilty. At least it seemed unlikely that Ree would be one of them.

Memory-Nara altered her course to swing wide around the fighters, but they adjusted course to match. She used the abilities Neith had gifted her, and calculated their relative courses and speeds. They would reach her before she could open a Fissure. That meant either she fled deeper into the system and found another umbral shadow or she stood and fought them.

And then, just like that, the memory ended and Nara was back in the present. She stood in the *Talon*'s matrix, enmeshed in a situation created by Talifax. She'd stolen the Talon and run with it. She'd done so in full view of all Shayan forces, and their conclusion was inescapable. Nara was either working with binders or bound herself.

Ree's smug voice echoed through the bridge as the *Talon* automatically accepted a missive. "Hello, Pirate Girl. Where are you off to in such a hurry, I wonder?"

"I'm not really in the mood for your bullshit, Ree." Nara focused on flying as she desperately sought a way out of this that didn't end with her dead or imprisoned. *Well played, Talifax.*

She was faster than the spellfighters, and could probably

evade them long enough to disappear deeper in system. Unfortunately, that would give Voria time to respond and the *Spellship* might be able to catch her. That would be catastrophic, because it was exactly what Talifax wanted.

Nara could see it now. Voria catching her, and her tearfully explaining exactly what had happened. How long until Voria lowered her guard, and Nara assassinated her? No, staying meant killing her friends. Talifax had already shown her that.

Of course, he'd also put her in her current predicament. Why did he want her here? Because he knew she'd run. It was in her nature. If he wanted that, did that mean she should do the opposite? Should she stay?

A shiver worked its icy fingers down her spine as she remembered stroking the trigger and watching Voria's lifeless body slump to her chamber floor.

Staying was not an option. Running was, but not if it meant doing what Talifax expected. She wasn't going to be anyone's puppet, not even a god's.

She needed the safety of the umbral depths, and that meant she couldn't afford to be trapped here. She gave a frustrated sigh, then tried one last time to convince Ree. "Go back to Shaya, and we can pretend we never saw each other."

"Now, why would I do that, when I can run you down like the traitor you are?" Ree gave a musical laugh. "I'm going to catch you, Pirate Girl. And after I blast that ship out from under you, I'm going to drag you back in chains to stand trial."

"Last warning, Ree. Turn back." Nara didn't stiffen the argument any further. She knew Ree wouldn't turn around. At least this way she eased her own conscience for what was about to follow.

As expected, Ree and her fighters pursued Nara in the most direct course possible. That put them in a neat, nearly single-file line. The further they got from Shaya, the tighter that line became. Nara smiled wickedly as she performed the calculations in her head.

Ree was going to be so pissed, and while part of her felt a little guilt, she immensely enjoyed what came next.

Nara had nearly reached Fissure range when she flipped the ship and began casting her first defensive spell. Nara began with an images spell that created several identical clones, all springing up around the real ship. They were indistinguishable and would distract the initial volley. Then, rather than attempt to open a Fissure, Nara cast an invisibility and cloaked the ship. Only the false images remained.

She guided the *Talon* back toward the spellfighters while the illusions continued toward the umbral shadow, and angled her flight on an intercept course. Just before the spellfighters reached range of her illusions, Nara fired. She poured *void* into the spellcannon, and sent a level three void bolt directly at Ree's engines from close range. The spell hit the casing beside the right engine, which detonated spectacularly. Ree's wounded craft spun out of control, and her companions were forced to dodge.

By the time they'd recovered, Nara had already cloaked the ship again.

Ree's voice would have chilled the void. "If you want to fight, then show yourself and we'll give you a fight."

"Goodbye, Ree." Nara guided the ship back toward the umbral shadow as the fighters launched a withering hail of light bolts at her illusions.

"We will hunt you, *traitor*," Ree hissed. "Aran will hunt you."

Nara flinched at those last words, but anger quickly

overrode her guilt. "Maybe, but at least in your case I'm not too worried about you finding me. You've demonstrated today that you're as bad at your job as I always assumed. First Frit escaped, and now me. You're outclassed, little war mage. And I'm only going to warn you once. If you come after me again, I will shoot to kill, and it will be the last time you come after anyone."

Ree's response was a wordless cry of rage that would no doubt have shocked her sensible superiors.

Nara's own anger faded, leaving her suddenly empty. She shivered, and began casting a Fissure. Her vessel didn't appear until the moment the Fissure veined across the sky, and by the time the enemy fighters were aware of it, she'd already piloted the *Talon* through. She cast a final invisibility, then made the rudest gesture she could think of at Ree's disabled fighter.

"Hear me, Pirate Girl." Ree's voice was deadly calm now, barely louder than a whisper. Intimate somehow. "I will kill you for this. No matter what it takes."

Nara ignored her as the Fissure snapped shut behind her, sealing her in the depths. She began plotting a course using the maps that had come with the *Talon*. An illusion appeared over the scry-screen, and she studied it until she found what she was looking for. There it was, in an otherwise unremarkable system.

She had no idea what to expect at the Zephyr research facility, but at the very least it would contain more answers about her past. From there she could make some decisions about how best to thwart Talifax.

12

RESIGNATION

Aran knew he was a mess as he stepped off the transport and walked into Confederate HQ, such as it was. He didn't know where Nara had gone, or why. Her sudden departure was out of character, or out of character for the woman he'd thought he'd known. He refused to believe she'd been lying the whole time. Something had changed for her on Virkon, but he'd be damned if he could figure out what it was. He just wished she'd trusted him enough to share whatever she was going through.

There was no way to track the *Talon*. Nara had used wards to disguise her passage, and even Voria hadn't been able to locate her. That meant that, for the time being at least, there was nothing he could do about it.

He took a deep breath, then approached the receptionist. A plastic blonde sat in a comfortable chair with her knees tucked under her, and held a datapad in her lap. Not a scry-pad, but one of the devices Pickus used. Evidence of similar technology was all around them. The lights were fluorescent instead of magical. The soft music in the room came from artfully hidden speakers, and not the air itself.

It was rather refreshing to see a people who didn't use magic for everything they possibly could. Aran might not understand Ternus tech, but most of the principles didn't seem at all different than magic, except with a different power source.

"Ahh, welcome, Lieutenant," the receptionist called with a wave and a practiced smile. Her drawl drew a half smile. "The admiral is expecting you. He's right through that door."

She nodded to the office on the left, though he probably could have figured that out since the only other door was the bathroom on the right side. How frightening was it that the 'Confederate Headquarters' was nothing more than a single office with a receptionist and an officer?

"Thank you." Aran nodded gratefully as he passed and strode confidently into the admiral's office. It was a whole different feeling than the last time he'd been on Shaya. He knew who he was now, and what he could do. He knew his role in things, and no longer needed to answer to people like this.

"Have a seat, son," groused a steel-faced man who sat behind the desk. His posture was immaculate, as was his olive Ternus uniform. Despite pushing seventy, his physique revealed a lifelong gym habit.

Aran did as asked, and sat. "Thank you, Admiral."

"What did you want to see me about?" The admiral eyed him hawkishly over steepled fingers.

"I'm here to resign my commission." Aran reached into his jacket and removed a stack of blue scales. The idea that his entire future could be purchased with a handful repelled him. He set the scales on the desk and slid them across. "The rest of my unit will be resigning as well, and I will be buying out their enlistments."

The admiral leaned back in his chair and exhaled a long, slow breath. "Son, I've had a devil of a week. I've got supply problems of every kind. We're short on men and material. I have to be on a transport to the front in three hours. We have no—"

"Let me stop you right there, Admiral," Aran interrupted. "I apologize if I gave you the impression we weren't invested in the war. My men are forming a—I guess—a mercenary unit of sorts. We're resigning because we're tired of Confederate bullshit. That doesn't mean we aren't going to prosecute this war to the best of our abilities."

Nimitz eyed him searchingly for several uncomfortable moments.

"What are you are saying, son?" The admiral raised a snowy eyebrow.

"I'm saying that if Ternus were looking to hire a mercenary unit to, say, hunt binders on New Texas, that we're looking for work." Aran relaxed back into his chair. The words released a tension he hadn't realized he'd been holding. This was the right path.

The admiral's weathered face split into a grin. "I knew I liked you, son. You're a good soldier, unlike that arrogant woman you served under. I'll have the papers drawn up immediately. We can even grant you a line of credit to purchase gear before you head to the front. You've got that fancy ship, right? Think you can get there pretty quick?"

Aran's shoulders slumped. "We won't have access to the *Talon*," he admitted. That hurt, for obvious reasons.

"I see." The smile vanished, replaced by a slight frown. "How do you intend to get to the front then, son?"

"I understand you're not a fan of Major Voria, but I have a lot of respect for her, and with good reason." Aran raised a hand to forestall the admiral when he began to object.

"Hear me out. She's going to the Tender right now to get Shaya to commit to helping New Texas. We can hitch a ride on one of the vessels she sends."

"You know those self-important slits aren't going to help," the admiral snapped. "Eros is too paranoid to send so much as a single ship, so you're not going to find help there."

"I'm aware of that possibility, and I've come armed with a contingency plan. Sir, it's safe to say that the *Wyrm Hunter* wouldn't be flying if not for the Ternus Marines on Virkonna, and Davidson specifically." Aran gave the man a conspiratorial smile. "We're in complete control of that vessel, and it's doing no good parked in a berth on Shaya."

"Are you suggesting I look the other way while you and Davidson steal a Confederate warship?" The admiral's face had gone neutral, and Aran had no idea if he approved or not. Too late to back down now.

He took a chance. "That's exactly what I'm saying." Aran held the man's gaze.

"You've got some weighty, brass balls, son." The admiral relaxed back into his chair. He reached into his desk drawer and removed a foil-wrapped bar. He unwrapped a bit. "Chocolate?"

"Sure." Aran accepted a piece of the hard, brown candy. He'd never tried chocolate, but Kazon had mentioned it often. Aran tried a nibble, and his eyed widened in surprise. He gobbled down the rest.

The admiral smiled grimly. "Tell you what, son. If the major you're so loyal to can't get these slits to help, then I might just find myself otherwise occupied when the *Hunter* lifts off. Would be a real shame if someone made off with it."

13

HONOR YOUR OATH

Voria would never have admitted it aloud, but she was proud to carry Ikadra into the Chamber of the First. She wore her dress uniform, but she'd added her satchel and tome. She was an officer, but she was also a mage, and she wouldn't let these people forget it.

Seven people waited in a half circle around the Pool of Shaya, and their adversarial stance wasn't lost on her. She was still the outsider. She always would be.

"Shall we skip the preamble, Eros?" she called as she approached. She thumped Ikadra on the floor with every step, resisting the urge to smirk when several of the Caretakers gawked at the ancient eldimagus.

"Aww," Ikadra pulsed, "that staff is about to celebrate its first millennium. It's fully sentient. Hey there, little guy." She knew which staff Ikadra meant. Eros's right hand was wrapped around a midnight haft that drank in the light around it. The tip was an oval diamond that studied her as surely as she was studying it.

"You know I share your distaste for protocol," Eros allowed, but then gave a reluctant sigh. "However, some protocol is warranted, in honor of my esteemed colleagues. Why have you come before us, Child of Shaya?"

"Because the Krox have invaded New Texas." She met his gaze evenly, ignoring Ducius and the other Caretakers. "The hammer has fallen. If we don't react, and react now, then Ternus will cede from the Confederacy. If that happens, the farce is over. There will be no more cooperation. We will stand alone against the Krox."

Eros's eyes flashed and his face twisted into a parody of itself. "We already stand alone against Krox. Have you forgotten that they attacked the Tree itself? If not for Lieutenant Aran we'd have lost an entire district. They struck at us in the heart of our power, Voria. They will do it again, and soon. I have seen it. You play at being a flame reader. Surely you can see the possibility I've dreamt of."

Ikadra began to pulse. "Hey, uh, the metrosexual guy with the long hair—that's Eros right?" His voice was loud enough to carry, and doused all conversation.

After a long moment of silence Eros finally spoke. "I assume you mean me?"

"Yeah," Ikadra allowed. "Sorry if that was insulting, but you do look like you're prepping for a shampoo commercial."

Eros's nostrils flared. "Out of deference for your immense age I will tolerate your...eccentricities. For now. Are you circling a point, staff?"

"Oh yeah, sorry," Ikadra pulsed. "I just wanted to correct you. You said that Voria is playing at flame reading. She's been gifted with full godsight. She isn't playing at anything."

"Godsight?" Ducius demanded. "Explain yourself. Quickly. This is a sacred place and I will not have it profaned by your...poo jokes."

That drew a smile from Voria. "Word of your humor has apparently preceded our arrival."

"I'm famous!" Ikadra pulsed rapidly.

"The point you were getting to?" Eros snapped.

"Godsight is the ability to perceive potential realities that stem from this one." Ikadra pulsed thoughtfully. "You call it flame reading, but they aren't the same thing. Flame reading allows you to perceive a single reality. You'd know the difference, if your goddess were still alive. Voria's goddess *is* alive, and gave her the full ability. So I guess what I'm saying is that...well, your magic kind of sucks. Sorry, bro. No offense. Don't you hate how people say that to soften things right after they say something offensive?"

Voria had never loved a man as much as she loved Ikadra in that moment. He'd ridden to the defense of her honor like a knight riding to war. Eros's expression darkened.

"I apologize for the interruption." Voria gave a respectful bow. "I understand your fear of another invasion. I'm not suggesting you strip our world of defenses, but we must send aid. At the very least we should dispatch the *Wyrm Hunter*, the *Spellship*, and a division of your finest spellfighters. These people are not equipped to battle binders, and you know it. All of you know it. They need us."

A few had the self-awareness to understand her arguments, but it was clear by their expressions that most did not. Most could not see beyond their own system, and hadn't left this world in decades. They had all they needed here, after all. Their precious bubble, provided by Shaya.

"Let the Krox spend themselves against Ternus," Ducius finally called. A few others murmured their approval, though thankfully Eros was not one of them. Ducius was emboldened by the response, and his voice was louder as he continued. "I have nothing but respect for our allies, but we must be pragmatic. We know the Krox are coming. We can either spend time fortifying our world, or we can spend our strength to prolong the defeat of our most esteemed ally."

"Eros?" Voria demanded. She locked eyes with him.

"My predecessor signed the Confederacy into law," Eros said. His voice was icy, but his eyes blazed. "She is dead. The accord she created died with her. I have a responsibility not only to this world, but to the mother of us all. What I speak of now cannot leave this room. Literally."

Eros raised a hand and began deftly sketching a complex sea of sigils. The speed and dexterity were peerless, at least from a mortal. Voria certainly couldn't have duplicated it. Within moments the spell came together, and a wave of invisible energy pulsed through the room. Her skin tingled as it passed, and some sort of effect settled over her.

"There, we can speak freely now. For millennia we have sent our mages out into the sector to gain strength from other Catalysts. We have slowly gathered power, and at the twilight of their life each mage poured that magic into the Pool of Shaya. All this, thousands of years of dedicated effort, with the intent of resurrecting our goddess." Eros licked his lips, and stared down at the Pool of Life. "The time of her rebirth nears. We have very nearly procured enough energy. That was Aurelia's great secret. That was the reason she focused all her attention on Shaya, instead of helping the Confederacy in a more active way."

Ducius grinned suddenly, and his excitement infected his neighbors. "If we can raise the Mother, then she can oppose Krox directly. We'll have a goddess to fight their god!"

"Wow, Shaya would be really embarrassed to see this,"

Ikadra pulsed. His words snuffed out Ducius's excitement, leaving a cloud of anger in its wake.

"If that thing speaks of our Mother again—"

"You'll what? Cast a third level spell? Oh, no. Save me, Voria," Ikadra taunted. "I could disintegrate you before you started mangling whatever spell you were about to cast. I *knew* Shaya. Not this tree we planted over her grave. She'd be embarrassed by this display."

Voria expected an explosive response, but instead Ducius's eyed widened. His mouth worked, but he seemed unable to summon words.

"You knew Shaya?" Eros choked out.

"Yeah, and more importantly I know how she died." Ikadra's pulses came faster now. "Krox killed her. And many others. You act like a god is a fixed concept. It isn't. Gods come in all sizes and strengths, and Krox is a greater god. Shaya was a lesser god, even when she was at her peak. If you bring her back she'll be weaker than she was."

"If Krox comes back he will likewise be weaker," Voria pointed out. "But your point is taken." Her gaze touched each Caretaker as she continued, "I've met a living goddess. I've seen her strength. She's terrified of Krox, so much so that she won't intervene directly. She's stricken all memory of her name from every possibility, just to prevent Krox from finding her. Raising Shaya is a noble goal, but we cannot count on our Mother to stop Krox. We need to work with the resources and the allies that we have right now. We need to act, gentlemen. Send the *Hunter*. Send the *Spellship*. Keep your fighters if you must, though I doubt those will do anything to stop Krox if he should come for us."

"Eros, you can't allow yourself to be bullied," Ducius roared. "Send nothing. Your Caretakers forbid it."

"You speak for all of them now, do you?" Eros asked

sourly. He turned back to her. "The *Hunter* stays here. The *Spellship* stays here. I know I can't stop you leaving, of course, but I can recall my mages and you can find someone else to cleanse the vessel."

"I see." Voria squared her shoulders. She briefly considered a protest, but there was little point. "Well then, thank you for your time."

She turned on her heel and strode from the Chamber of the First. There was silence in her wake, though she heard low voices once she exited the room. She'd certainly given them a lot to consider. Hopefully enough to keep them busy arguing while she took both the *Spellship* and the *Hunter* and left this wretched world.

Their world had sworn an oath to the Confederacy, and by all the gods living and dead, Voria would see that Shaya lived up to it.

14

NEED A NAME

Aran dropped his pack in the corner of the officer's quarters Davidson had graciously offered. It beat bunking in the barracks, though he'd definitely grown spoiled during his time on the *Talon*. He considered laying down for an hour, but there was just too much to do. Voria had set a strict time table, and he needed to secure some equipment before he met with the crew to finalize their prep.

He sketched a *fire* sigil and the small scry-screen on the wall activated. It took several seconds until the missive was accepted, then Kazon's bearded face filled the screen. "Brother, your timing couldn't be worse. I only have moments. What can I do for you?"

"I resigned my commission today," he began, then paused as he considered the swiftest way to ask for what he needed, "I've decided to start a mercenary company, and Ternus has already offered us a job. I've got a line of credit, plus a fairly big pile of scales from Virkon."

"...And you need equipment. That I can do. Send a list to my secretary. We have a Shayan depot, and I can have anything you need delivered to the *Hunter*." Kazon frowned. He licked his lips, and his expression softened. "Brother, I know you have many concerns and I do not seek to add to them, but...I am worried. We are flying blind in the depths, and we are hunted. Stay safe. I will contact you when I can."

The screen went dark. Aran was more than a little shocked. Kazon had always been jovial when they'd spoken, but he seemed distracted and...well, frightened. What had rattled the big man? He hated this cryptic crap. If only he had more time. It looked like Kazon needed help, and he wished he were in a position to provide it.

Aran sighed. At least he'd secured the equipment—well, theoretically at least.

He exited his quarters and headed into the neighboring barracks, where the rest of the squad was bunked. Crewes still managed menacing in his fatigues, but definitely looked odd outside of his armor. Bord and Kezia were using an empty bunk as a makeshift table, and were playing Kem'Hedj.

"Crewes, did you have time to get a list of gear requirements together?" Aran asked as he flopped down on the bunk next to the sergeant.

"First thing I took care of, LT. You know how much I hate being without armor. It's bullshit enough that Nara made off with our ride, but taking our armor too? That's low." Crewes's frown was more disappointed than angry. He shook his head sadly, then continued, "Anyway, enough of the pity party. I ordered us four suits of Mark XI, each customized to match the pilot. I added a couple new spellrifles, and the conventional ordinance. Still not sure why you think we'll need that non-magical stuff." The sergeant bit into an apple and chewed thoughtfully.

"Even after all this time and training, we run out of

spells quickly," Aran pointed out. "Ternus makes some pretty nasty explosive rounds. The kind of stuff that might stop an enforcer, if you hit it right. I want us to start practicing using both, to prolong our combat effectiveness."

"Can't we just drink potions?" Bord raised an eyebrow. "Last time I tried using a gun the thing jammed."

"It jammed because you ran out of bullets." Kezia punched Bord in the arm. She looked to Aran with a smirk. "He's occasionally right, though, and this happens to be one of those times. We have more potions than I can count. I put out the word to the drifters, and they'll do anything to help you after you saved the Dims. We have enough beer for months."

"I'll have Davidson assign someone to tutor us once we get the guns." Aran climbed back to his feet with a grunt.

"Hey, Aran," Bord ventured. He didn't look Aran in the eye. "Are we, ah, gonna talk about Nara?"

Aran sat back down on the bunk, pushed down by the weight of Bord's words. He'd been so busy, he'd managed not to think about the situation.

"Yeah, we should do that," he said. There was no sense sugar-coating it. He scrubbed at his beard, which badly needed a trim. "Nara stole the *Talon*. Voria tried to locate her, and failed. We have no idea why, or where Nara's going." He closed his eyes and exhaled slowly. "She's been acting strangely for the past couple weeks, but I refuse to believe she's betrayed us. Until we learn otherwise, I'm giving her the benefit of the doubt."

"Respectfully, sir, fuck her," Crewes snapped. Aran had rarely seen that kind of fury in his eyes. "She walked out on us right before we're going to war, and she stole our damned ride. If she needed a ship, she could have taken Ree's spellfighter or something. Not screwed us."

Aran hated admitting it, but Crewes had a point. Nara *had* screwed them, with no explanation.

"I'm not giving up on her." Kez bristled up at the sergeant. "We don't know why she left. Yeah, it was shitty. But we have enough problems to focus on without laying them all at her doorstep."

"Whatever the situation with Nara, we've got more important business." Aran took control of the conversation again. "We've agreed to form this new outfit, but it isn't official until we have a name. Anyone have a suggestion?"

"Bord's Harem. We could recruit only women, and—ow!" Bord cut himself off as Kezia raised a fist.

"I didn't even hit you that time." Kezia eyed him sidelong.

"It's a reflex now." Bord grinned.

"Aran's Marauders," Crewes suggested. "Aran's got a name now. People know him on Shaya, and even on Virkon. We should use that."

Bord frowned. "He's already in charge. He doesn't have to be in the freaking name too."

"No, I think it's a good idea," Kezia said. "Sarge is right. We can't joost assume Ternus will keep paying us. We've got a pretty good pile of cash, but that could run dry, eventually. We need to make a name for ourselves, and being associated with the stuff Aran's already done is a good thing."

Aran shook his head. "I don't like it. Mostly the marauder part. I get that having my name makes sense, even if it does make me feel as pompous as Thalas."

"Yeah, marauder doesn't make too much sense I guess," Crewes allowed. "We don't do too much marauding. Maybe something more like defenders. Or scouters. Or like, ass kickers."

"We could be Aran's Handsome Band," Bord said. No one dignified it with a reply.

Kezia snapped her fingers. "I've got it. Aran's Outriders."

"That will piss off the Wyrms back on Virkon," Bord cautioned.

"Good point." Aran found a smile growing as he considered how the Wyrms would react to hearing him use the title without serving them. "Aran's Outriders it is."

15

UNPLEASANT DUTY

Aran dreaded his next task, but like it or not, it had to be done. He waited in the *Hunter*'s aft hangar bay, which was completely empty at the moment. A golden spellfighter screamed into the hangar, zipping through the blue membrane and landing within two meters of Aran.

He didn't flinch. He merely waited until the translucent blue steps descended from the cockpit. A helmet-less Ree appeared a moment later, scarlet hair spilling down the same armor from the fight with Kheross, despite the damage. The scorching and dents were mostly superficial, but he'd have expected her to have dealt with it by now.

"Let's make this quick, Mongrel." Ree glided imperiously down the steps. "You want something. Much as I hate to admit it, I still owe you for the Dims, and for Erika. I want to be out of your debt as soon as possible. So let's hear it."

He enjoyed how blunt she could be, even if her delivery usually made mockery of him.

"Fair enough. Ternus is getting hammered. I know you've seen the missive." Aran wrapped his hand around

Narlifex's hilt, and the blade thrummed a greeting. "If we don't help them, they're done, and you know it."

"The Caretakers have forbidden us from leaving this world." Ree shook her head sympathetically. "It isn't that I don't want to help, but this I cannot do, Aran. If I leave, much less ask others to go too, they'll strip me of rank and title. They'll take my fighter."

"Damn the rules, Ree. In order for them to take your fighter they'd have to send forces to Ternus to claim it." Aran could feel his temper rising, and fought to keep it in check. "While they're there, maybe they could, oh, I don't know, kill some Krox. You realize that after Ternus, you're next, right?"

Ree blinked. "You're? Not we're?" she seemed taken aback.

"I resigned my commission this morning. I've got no reason to stay here, not when the war is being fought elsewhere." He had no particular loyalty to Shaya, though he also held no animosity for it. He just didn't need to be here any more.

"You've got no way off world from what I hear." Ree gave a very self-satisfied smile. "I guess I was right about Pirate Girl after all. She stole one of the most valuable ships in the sector, and you didn't suspect a thing. Let me guess. First she slept with you. You lowered your guard, and bam...she took off with the most valuable starship in the sector."

That kicked him in the gut. Hard.

"Yeah, that's pretty much how it went down," Aran admitted. It hurt, but he kept probing the wound, the way you kept touching a scab. "If you come with us you can taunt me about it the entire way. And I'll admit you were right, every time."

Ree deflated a little, probably because she wasn't getting the reaction she wanted.

Her expression softened, and she brushed a lock of scarlet over her shoulder. "I wish I could help, Aran. I do." She shook her head. "I just can't."

He closed his eyes, just for a moment. He knew exactly how Nara would respond, and he didn't like it. This kind of manipulation wasn't his forte, but there was a lot riding on the outcome.

"Where do you think Frit went?" he demanded, opening his eyes and fixing them on Ree.

Her beautiful face twisted into a snarl at the name. She glared hard at Aran. "Into the depths, for all I care."

"I think you *do* care. Frit is a powerful true mage. I've seen her melt defending units. She escaped with, what, forty more Ifrit? That's a hell of an artillery squad, don't you think?" Aran met Ree's gaze without flinching.

"And you think I'm responsible for the damage they'll do to Ternus." Ree's hand tightened around the hilt of her spellblade until the knuckles went white. She fought some internal war, and her gaze dropped as she spoke. "And you're right. I am responsible. And yes, she will probably be at New Texas. Dammit, Aran, they will take my command if I do this. They'll take everything."

Aran reached out slowly and rested a hand on her shoulder. "I realize what I'm asking, Ree. I know how important your people are to you, and I know what your place among them means. But your leaders are wrong. They're scared, and that fear is blinding them. If Ternus falls, this war is over. This is our last chance to resist. Our last chance to save everyone we love."

Ree's eyes shone with unshed tears and she gazed wildly around the hangar.

"I don't know what to do," she whispered, a tear finally breaking free. "If I stay, I have to watch as that traitorous Ifrit murders her way through our sworn allies. But if I go, there is no coming back."

Aran didn't envy her the choice, and he knew that further words from him would only cloud the issue. She needed the mental space to make her own decision, so he stood there silently and waited. Almost a minute passed before she finally looked up at him. The tears were gone. The strength had returned.

She mounted the first step to her fighter. "I'll speak to every Kamiza. I'll explain the need. I can't promise anyone will answer, but even if no one else comes I will be there with you when you leave for New Texas. Frit is my responsibility, and I'm going to make sure she never hurts anyone again."

16

TO WAR

Aran strode onto the *Wyrm Hunter*'s bridge for the first time in what felt like several lifetimes. After spending so much time on the *Talon*, the limited matrices were strange. He missed the comfortable chairs, and found standing...odd.

"Crewes, you've got the offensive matrix. Get our scryscreen up," he ordered as he walked toward the central matrix. "Bord, you're on defensive."

"Sure thing." The shorter man ducked into the spinning rings. "Yeah, that's right, I ain't calling you *sir*, neither."

"Bord," Crewes snapped. The dark-skinned Marine stared Bored down from the offensive matrix. "I will literally fry you."

"Looks like your crew is just as colorful as ever," Davidson said as he strode onto the bridge behind them. "We're all buttoned up below. You ready to do this?"

"The sooner we're off this rock, the sooner we can get into the fight," Aran said. He tapped the first *fire* sigil, then the second and third in quick succession. "They probably won't challenge us until we're airborne, but if they do we should be able to get away without much trouble. Bord, I want you ready with a ward just in case. Hopefully Voria keeps them busy."

"I'll stand by, sir." Bord eyed Crewes fearfully.

Crewes tapped a sigil and the scry-screen flared to life. "They ain't even noticed us. Looks like they're all focused on the major. Can't say I blame 'em."

High above them, Aran watched as the *Spellship* lifted slowly into the air and began drifting skyward. The pitted hull was far from pristine, but the dark stains were gone. It looked like they'd finished cleansing the outside at least.

She was long and sleek, and glittered in the sun as she pulled away from Shaya. Only when the *Spellship* passed by the rest of the Shayan war fleet did it become clear how much larger she was than any other vessel present.

"So how do you want to handle your prisoner?" Davidson asked, drawing Aran's attention from the *Spellship*. "That Kheross guy creeps me out in a bad way. The last thing we need is him breaking loose while we're dealing with the Krox."

"Let's make him my problem," Aran suggested, though he was mostly focused on piloting. Kheross was going to be pissed when he found out about Rhea being left behind with Eros.

"Sir," Crewes called again. "We've got squadrons of fighters lifting off from the fourth, seventh, and eighth branches."

The screen shifted to show three clusters of golden spell-fighters rising from the tree and streaking in their direction.

"Send a missive to the lead fighter," Aran ordered. He hoped he was right, because if those ships were hostile, the *Hunter* would be hard pressed to keep them at bay long enough to escape. They were light, fast, and could deliver a lot of punishment when backed with the kind of firepower Shayan war mages could bring to bear.

The scry-screen shifted to show the inside of a cockpit, with Ree's face taking up most of the screen. Her expression was pained, but she spoke with confidence. "I've spoken to everyone I trusted, including Erika. She spoke on your behalf, and it was that more than anything else that convinced the others to come."

"Wait, those fighters are coming with us?" Davidson blinked at Aran.

Aran shot him a smile, but spoke to Ree. "You can dock in the aft hangar where we met. That's all yours. We'll stay out of there. You can set it up however you want. Just send a missive to Major Davidson here, and I'm sure he'd be happy to get you whatever supplies you need."

"Thank you so much for coming, uh, what's your title?" Davidson asked.

"Master Reekala." Ree straightened proudly.

"Well thank you, Master Reekala. We're grateful for the help."

"It isn't free," Ree said. "I have a condition. If the chance arises to kill any or all of the Ifrit who left Shaya, then I want free rein to hunt them. Do we have a deal?"

"Davidson?" Aran asked. He certainly had no problem with that. He'd liked Frit from the little he'd seen, and he understood the desire for a slave to be free. Better than anyone. But that didn't excuse her working with the Krox. That he couldn't forgive.

"Agreed. I'll see that you have whatever you need. If you can counter the Ifrit, that will help tremendously." He nodded gratefully.

"Now all we have to do is escape Shaya," Aran said. "Get

to your stations everyone. We're making for the Umbral Shadow. Let's hope Voria can keep them busy."

17

THEY'RE GOING TO FIGHT

Voria strode onto the bridge of the *Spellship*, and was immensely pleased by what she saw. The silvery walls were pristine, the halls well lit from the soft, magical glow of the ceilings. The entire ship pulsed with clean power and her song—if it wasn't just Voria's imagination—seemed to be...whole.

Unlike the bridge of every other vessel, there was no visible matrix. Instead, there was a wall-length scry-screen that showed Shaya slowly falling away as they gained altitude.

"Ikadra, I understand I can fly the ship using you as a matrix, but there must be an alternative. Where is the backup matrix?" She walked to the screen and peered down at the gigantic redwood.

"The whole room is the matrix," Ikadra pulsed happily. "If you look at the walls, all the sigils you'd normally see on your primitive rings are present. The magic emanates from this room. But the vessel is different in a lot more ways. She's alive." The pulsing slowed. "And she thinks I'm a child. With a 'juvenile' sense of humor. How rude."

"I think she and I are going to get along." Voria allowed a smile. She reached out experimentally with her senses and felt the magic in the walls. There it was, the matrix. But it wasn't like any other matrix she'd worked with. It was... more. "Ikadra, what does the fourth ring do?"

"That's the temporal ring," he pulsed. "It will link directly to your godsight, and allow you to inspect, and journey to, possibilities you can perceive. I'd be careful. There is a literal planet of poo out there."

"Noted." Voria looked down on Shaya. This wasn't going to be easy, but it had to be done. She was about to break her people. "Ikadra, I'm going to need something flashy. I want to project an illusion in the sky over Shaya. It needs to possess both light and sound. I want every citizen on that tree to see and hear this message."

"Oh, that's easy. You can simply cast a standard illusion through the matrix, and the *Spellship* will amplify it."

Well, that was handy. Voria licked her lips and considered what she was going to say. She raised her hand, but rather than touch the wall, she willed each sigil to activate. *Dream, dream, air, dream, air, fire.*

The ship vibrated and a wave of magic rolled outward. It drew on her reserves, but less than she'd have expected. The ship was providing most of the magic, which might be its most impressive capability to date. Magical battles were determined by who ran out of magic first. The *Spellship*'s reserves meant that it would almost always be her opponent.

A towering ethereal version of herself appeared over the planet, like some benevolent goddess, with bad hair and a tiny mustard stain on her sleeve.

"People of Shaya, I apologize for the unconventional manner of my request, but I must ask a great sacrifice." She paused then, staring down at the world where she'd been born. What would these people think of her now? Did this prove she was as arrogant as they claimed? Perhaps. "Our ally, Ternus, is under assault by the Krox. We failed them at Vakera. We failed them at Starn. But at Marid we held the line. We pushed the Krox back. Now, our allies are being tested as never before. Our leaders demand we do nothing, that we huddle here under our mother and hope that the nasty Krox go away. Ask yourself what Shaya would do. What Shaya *did*. She sacrificed her life for a cause she believed in."

She paused then, considering her next words. She didn't want to cause any more division than she had to.

"I understand the Tender's reasoning, but we cannot let our fear prevent us from living up to our obligations," she continued, her resolve building with each word. "We must push the Krox back. We must save our allies. To that end, I officially resign my commission in the Confederate military. I am taking my ship—this ship—and departing to aid Ternus. I call upon all brave Shayans, all brave Drifters, and anyone else willing to stop the Krox. We leave in two hours. All who wish to join us will be given a berth on my vessel."

She waved a hand and the illusionary version of her disappeared. Now all she could do was wait.

"Do you think anyone will come?" Ikadra asked.

"I don't know," she admitted. "A few will, certainly. But enough? I doubt it. The only thing we can count on is the *Hunter*, and Aran's company. Beyond that? We wait and see."

Ikadra lapsed into uncharacteristic silence.

Within a few minutes a small cloud of ships rose from the lower branches, and from the dims. More vessels joined it, a few from the higher branches. That cloud began moving in their direction, and as the glittering ships rose so too did her spirits. More and more followed, a steady stream all flowing toward her.

"They're coming." She didn't realize she was crying until the first tear slid down her cheek. "They're going to fight."

The largest speck rocketed past the others, and she instantly recognized the *Hunter*'s silhouette. It flew far more quickly than she'd ever be able to manage, which told her exactly who was at the helm. The *Hunter* broke off from the rest of the fleet and began making for the planet's umbral shadow.

Voria sketched a missive, and the scry-screen flashed red as it waited for Aran to accept it. A moment later the *Hunter*'s familiar bridge leapt into a strange clarity she'd never seen from a scry-screen. It possessed depth in a way a normal scry-screen failed to capture.

Aran wore a mischievous smile, mirrored by Crewes and Davidson. She couldn't help but return it.

"You certainly know how to make an impression, Major," Aran said. "You know Eros isn't going to take this lying down."

"Of course not. I'll deal with his tantrum. You need to get out of here, and get to New Texas. Relieve them, Lieutenant." She caught herself. "I suppose that title isn't applicable any longer. Good luck, Aran. Major Davidson. Do us proud."

Davidson's relaxed expression darkened. "Do us proud? What the depths does that mean? What will you be doing?" Davidson demanded. "You're going to be following us, right?"

"No." Voria met his stare with equal weight. "Nebiat is far craftier than you give her credit for. New Texas is an important battle, but I believe it to be a mere distraction. She hopes to misdirect us from her true target."

Davidson stared incredulously at her. "What could possibly be a more important target than the shipyards at New Texas?"

"I can't say with certainty, and it terrifies me. My best guess right now is Ternus itself." Voria shifted her attention to Aran. "We are beset from all sides. If we move in strength to relieve New Texas, and Nebiat also attacks Ternus or Colony 3, then those worlds will be unable to defend themselves. If I'm right, I need to be there when the hammer falls. That means you're on your own with New Texas."

Davidson eyed her darkly, but gave a grudging nod. She wished she could persuade him that she was right, but time would vindicate her actions. She was certain of it.

"We'll do you proud, sir." Aran snapped a tight salute, perhaps the last she would ever receive now that she was no longer enlisted.

The screen went dark, then shifted back to a view of the world below. Eros would be coming.

18

GET OFF MY SHIP

Voria hurried down to one of the *Spellship*'s larger hangars, and arrived just in time to receive the first batch of ships. The first trio were rickety cruisers held together with glue and duct tape as much as anything else. The nearest transport wobbled to a halt, and the hatch opened with a creak.

A dense cloud of greenish smoke burst out, and a drifter tumbled out. He landed heavily on the deck, and lay there stunned for several moments before wobbling to his feet. His eyes were bloodshot, and he wore a beatific smile.

"Yer speech wuz wonaful. Come ta sign oop." He promptly passed out in a heap.

Other drifters began emerging, each carrying a backpack and one or more kegs of beer. An older man with a beard, shorter than the rest, came to stand near her feet. "Herd good tings aboutcha. Come to join up, 'n all. Where should we set up?"

Voria pointed at a wide hallway leading deeper into the ship. "There are empty rooms all along that side of the ship. You're welcome to set up where you'd like, but I ask that you stay close together and don't venture too far from this hangar until we see how much space everyone will need."

"Done." The drifter spat in his palm and offered it to her. She spat in her hand and accepted it.

Her attention was drawn by movement, and she saw that the next ship to land was a golden shuttle. The kind of shuttle no drifter, and no lesser noble, could afford. The kind of shuttle a Tender might use.

A trail of shimmering, blue steps led from the ship's airlock down to the deck, and the door opened to disgorge a quartet of war mages encased in Mark XI armor. They moved to flank the steps, and a moment later Eros strode imperiously down them.

Voria was mildly surprised he'd come in person rather than send a missive, which attested to the gravity of the situation. If Eros was willing to leave his bolt hole, then he must see this as being of the utmost importance. She needed to be wary in dealing with him. It was possible he might even try to overpower her.

Ordinarily that would be easy for him, but here she was connected to the ship. Combined with Ikadra she might be able to force him back, though she doubted she could best him.

"Welcome to the *First Spellship*, Tender. *My* ship. What do you want?" Voria tightened her grip around Ikadra, and prepared to cast if needed.

Eros frowned, but said nothing. He walked closer, and didn't stop until he stood uncomfortably close. He leaned in, and dropped his voice to a near whisper. "Voria, please. Stop this. You are destroying our people. Fully a quarter of our ships are joining your mad quest."

"None of them warships," she countered. "You're losing

shuttles, transports, and old frigates. Nothing of any significant worth. You hate the drifters anyway, don't you?"

"Ree's taken a third of our spellfighters," Eros snarled, his eyes flashing. "Over a dozen of our finest war mages followed her, with Erika's blessing. We have no more than twenty fighters left to defend our world, and none of them will be piloted by our best."

The chaos around them drowned out their words, shielding their conversation as effectively as any ward. Voria was aware of countless possibilities, from which room each drifter would choose, to countless variations of Eros's next words.

"I'm sorry." Voria took Eros's hand in hers. Not in any sort of romantic way, but as a comrade in arms. She gave it a squeeze. "You've been asked to shepherd our people through the worst crisis since the death of Shaya. I understand your fears, and that you must do what you think is right."

"I don't understand," Eros choked out. He eyed her searchingly. "How can you walk away from our goddess? We're all she has, Voria. And you know how close she is to rising."

"Close is relative, old friend." She shook her head and released his hand. "It could be decades. If we're lucky we're still talking years. She won't be here tomorrow, barring a miracle. She won't be here in time to stop Krox, and you know it. We have to do this ourselves, and we can't do it by hiding on this moon while we wait for them to come to us. We have to play the game on our own terms, while there are still pieces in play."

"This is no game," he snarled. "This is the survival of our species, of our goddess. Our Mother, Voria."

She narrowed her eyes. "Do not mistake my analogy for

a lack of gravity, Tender. I'm playing for bigger stakes. I'm playing for the entire sector, not just our world. We cannot stand alone, Eros. If we try, we will fall, and so will everyone else. Krox wins, and Shaya dies a final death."

"No!" He raised a hand as if to strike her.

Voria wasn't certain how she'd have reacted. She liked to think she'd have blocked the blow, but not struck back. She had too much empathy for the pressures Eros was under.

"Oh, hell, no, god-boy." Ikadra's sapphire flared and bands of matching energy snapped into place around Eros, pinning his arms and legs. "Please, please, please let me launch him into the sun. Shaya will just pick another Tender. We won't lose much, and think about how satisfying—"

"Release him, Ikadra," Voria demanded coldly. She sighed, and moderated her tone. "I'm sorry, Eros. For everything. I am sorry you cannot see things as I can, but trust me when I say that if I do not follow my instincts in all this, nothing of our people were survive."

"If you do this," Eros whispered menacingly, rubbing at his sleeve where the band had restrained him, "you will never be allowed home again. I swear it."

Voria shook her head. "And that's what you don't understand, Eros. I am home. Now get off my ship."

19

NO HELP FROM ANY QUARTER

Kazon was still preoccupied by the thought of Skare's gaunt, angular face. He didn't mind admitting to a healthy dose of fear, and he wondered if that fear wasn't part of the reason for the man's appearance. Skare knew it unsettled people, and in a culture where everyone was beautiful, Kazon had finally realized why his enemy valued that. Being ugly became its own form of beauty, because it made you significant.

It was one more way Skare had demonstrated his fiendish intelligence, and Kazon found it deeply unsettling. The man was always so many steps ahead.

"Are you even listening?" Jolene snapped. Kazon's eyes rose to find his mother eyeing him hawkishly across the broad expanse of her desk. The entire wall behind her was a scry-screen, and currently displayed hundreds of ships in neat, clean lanes as they maneuvered through the fleet. "I asked what you were hoping to accomplish by being so blunt. Did you expect he'd simply tell you where the metal came from?"

Kazon squirmed on the hovercouch, struggling to find a

comfortable position. "Respectfully, Mother, have all your stratagems produced any better intelligence? What was lost in me asking?"

Jolene tapped her lip absently with one finger as she studied him. "You may have a point. At worst he thinks you an imbecile. And he might waste time looking for some sort of hidden motive or plan, I suppose." She leaned across the table, her eyes flashing. "It doesn't excuse your actions. Nor am I convinced you understand the threat Skare poses."

Kazon inhaled slowly through his nostrils, a memory of the Skull of Xal rising involuntarily when she'd said the word threat. His teeth chattered as, just for an instant, he was back on that rotting Catalyst.

"I can see he is not the only one who believes me an imbecile," Kazon snapped. He immediately regretted the lapse, and pushed the image of the Skull from his mind. It wasn't easy. Xal was part of him now. "I understand the threat, I assure you. You are concerned that Skare's market share is up, his influence is up, and most of the board will quite literally sell their own soul to discover his secret."

Jolene folded her arms and eyed him primly. She said nothing, so he continued.

"I don't think you understand *my* concern." Now it was Kazon's turn to lean across the desk. He removed the bracelet Aran had sent him from his pocket, and pushed it across the table at Jolene. "Look at it, Mother. Look at the complexity of the runes. Skare might not believe that it was created by a goddess, but you know better. None of our mages, not even our best ones, can produce a spell of this magnitude. We've identified it as a binding, but can't even tease out the spell's real purpose or limitations."

Jolene picked up the bracelet. She peered down at the oily metal, fixed on it. "Yes, yes, you've told me. Bound by a goddess." She finally set the bracelet down and frowned at him. She exhaled through her nostrils, and closed her eyes for a moment before speaking. "I don't think you an imbecile, though you are certainly more impulsive since your... accident. Nor do you seem to grasp the complexities of Inuran politics you were once so adept at navigating. There is a very real chance that Skare has already won. If he were to assassinate me tomorrow—"

"The board—"

"Would do *nothing*," she snarled, seizing the conversation once more. "Not while Skare controls the secret to this metal. We are not safe until we have it, and Skare knows it. He's flaunting it. That's why he was involved in your sister's trial. That particular bit of theater was an insult. A calculated one."

Kazon wondered if that were really true, but he wondered privately. He'd seen his mother explode several times when Voria's trial had come up, and he'd come to realize that Jolene's anger was attached to Dirk's death. He didn't know the nature of their relationship, beyond that they'd fathered Voria together several decades ago. But, whatever her feelings had been, she was still grieving.

"How do you suggest we proceed then, Mother?" Kazon kept his tone respectful, playing the dutiful son. The role did not fit very well, but he'd wear it if he had to.

"I don't know." She heaved a heavy sigh and rose from her desk to move to the scry-screen. She folded her arms as she stared out at the Inuran fleet. "Right now we're playing his game, on his terms. And that terrifies me."

It terrified Kazon, for different reasons. She didn't see the threat. She didn't understand that this metal was something terrible. Even if she somehow overcame Skare she'd merely assume his place, and do everything she could to expedite production. That left him with a very difficult choice.

Kazon picked up the bracelet from Jolene's desk, and quietly left the room. She'd already forgotten his presence. As he exited, the pair of guards outside subtly shifted their stances to angle their spellrifles in his direction. Each wore a set of midnight spellarmor, and they studied him through those unreadable faceplates.

He hadn't really understood what he was giving up when he passed his voting rights to his mother. These men were loyal to her, assuming they were loyal to anyone. He might be rich, but he had no power here.

Kazon squared his shoulders and walked slowly past them, forcing himself not to pay them any mind. Instead, he turned his mind back to the riddle he'd apparently been trying to solve before his mindwipe.

Whoever had founded the Inuran Consortium had gone to painstaking lengths to remove all traces of their involvement. The few scraps Kazon had found hinted that this creator had divine origins, which certainly made sense if they'd somehow removed themselves from history.

If ever there were a time for that founder to make themselves known, it was now. Kazon's only hope lay in finding them and convincing them to help him stop Skare.

20

THE BEST-LAID TRAP

Skare had baited his trap with the utmost care, as he always did. It was simply a matter of giving your prey exactly what they most wanted. They knew the trap was there, but they came anyway, hoping to somehow evade it because they were aware of it.

"Please, come in, Jolene." Skare rose from his hovercouch and moved to embrace his greatest rival.

"Don't touch me," the taller woman snapped, pushing him back with a single finger against his chest. "I came, Skare, but my trust is vanishingly rare. Let's hear whatever scheme you've cooked up, because I know you're not really giving me the secret to your new alloy."

Skare allowed a smile—well, more of a grimace, really—to slide across his features. Jolene recoiled a few millimeters, though she tried to hide it. The fact that his appearance still gave her discomfort was a source of immense pride.

"Very well, we'll skip the preamble." He swirled the contents of his glass, then fished a vial from his pocket. The glass holding the dark liquid had been triply enchanted, and was as close to unbreakable as he could create. He held it up to the light to expose its precious contents, nearly a quarter of what he possessed. "This liquid is the blood of a goddess. A very rare goddess. Through a lengthly process this tiny amount can be enchanted to infuse a near infinite amount of metal."

Jolene's eyes smoldered with hunger, and were fixed upon the vial as she spoke. "And you are showing it to me why?"

Skare crooked his free hand and a second cup winked into existence next to the first. It rapidly filled of its own accord. He touched the surface of the vial to remove the cap, and dumped precisely half into each goblet.

"This liquid is infinitely valuable," Skare explained, as if Jolene hadn't spoken. He handed her a cup, which she accepted with a good deal of suspicion. "And the amount I poured into each cup could purchase a colony. More, if you could find a buyer who could afford it."

Skare sipped his wine, enjoying the rush of dark power that slid down his throat. He savored another gulp, and before he realized it he was licking the inside of the glass clean. He looked up to find Jolene studying him, her face twisted into horrified disbelief.

"You seem reluctant to try it." He forced himself to set the cup back on his desk. "Is that because of my physical reaction?" Skare wiped his sleeve across his mouth, and then licked the stain.

"You're clearly an addict." Jolene scooted backward into her chair, away from the cup, which she'd set on the edge of the table, as far from her as she could. "What makes you think I'd want to start down the same path? And why would you waste such a precious resource?" She eyed the cup, though, with a hint of longing.

"You know why." He smiled magnanimously. "Money is

pointless. Fame is pointless. Beauty, pointless. You know better than nearly any other person in the sector what isn't. Power, Jolene. It's the thing we both understand that so many of our rivals did not. Power is everything. Why should you drink it, Jolene? Why, while knowing that it will create a longing in you for more?" He leaned across his desk and his smile became ghastly. "Power as you have never known. My magic is infinitely stronger. My immortal life, secured. You? You might be able to live a few more centuries by pillaging magic from Catalysts. If you're lucky. But me? I am truly immortal, Jolene. And I will become a demigod. In enough time, who knows? I might become a full god."

The rush of power was upon him now, and he longed to demonstrate it. He knew that doing so would have an adverse effect though. Her curiosity needed time to grow, to germinate within the field of doubts he'd sewn.

"If this liquid is so powerful, and you crave it so much, why would you offer a portion to me?" She cocked her head, then shook it suddenly with a self-deprecating laugh. "I am impressed by the trap, Skare. Very impressed. The bait is nearly irresistible, as you know I seek to prolong my life as long as possible. But I'm not going to drink this. I'm going to have it analyzed."

He shook his head slightly. "No. The liquid does not leave this room. If you wish to drink it, you may. If not..." He reached for the cup.

To his surprise Jolene snatched it up, and downed the contents in three quick gulps. She eyed him a challenge as she wiped the back of her hand across her lips. "A devil's bargain then. Very well, I've accepted the bait. I've done it knowing you will use it to hang me."

"Then why do it?" He asked. His entire body burned, in the most wonderful way.

"Because you reminded me of something." She leaned forward and her features hardened. "I have been at the bottom before. Many times. But I have always clawed my way back up. And one day, I will find a way to use this to my advantage. I will unseat you, Skare."

He began to laugh, then settled into his couch and watched. As expected, Jolene's pupils dilated. Her mouth went slack. She was no longer in the present moment, but instead seeing the world as a goddess saw it. Learning that the universe wasn't a static thing, as their limited understanding of magic painted it to be. It was fluid, possibilities spinning off in every direction.

Skare rose to his feet. "I have business to be about. Your...transformation, for lack of a better word, will be brief. No more than a half hour. When it is over do whatever you wish, Jolene. I know you think there is a hidden hook in all this, but in time you'll understand that we are very much on the same side."

He strode from his quarters, smiling. The best way to deal with an enemy was to give them a vested interest in your success. Jolene had that now, even if she didn't fully understand yet. She was a part of Nefarius, and in time would learn the awful price.

They were allies now, bound by the same hellish pact.

21

X-3

Nara had six eternal days to live with her choices. They made what would have been a cavernously empty ship positively claustrophobic, and she saw her abandoned friends everywhere. She'd taken one of the most potent weapons in the sector at a time when it was needed to battle the Krox, and she'd done it out of pure selfish need. What did that say about her?

During her many sleepless nights she examined the returning memories, and took some small solace there, at least. She'd yet to see much of the woman she became under Yorrak's control, but as a Zephyr she hadn't been appallingly muhaha evil or anything. She might have been cold, but she didn't seem any more callous than most soldiers. Whatever she'd become must have happened later, after the first mind-wipe.

That meant that the woman she'd originally been, X-3, had been a good person. Or better than the woman Aran had briefly known. And if that were the case, didn't that mean that the real Nara lay somewhere in the middle? She turned the questions over and over in her mind, because there was little else to do.

By the time Nara reached the unmarked Ternus system she'd started to go a bit stir crazy. "Come on, come on." She tapped her fingers along the stabilizing ring as she waited for the Fissure to finish opening.

The very instant it was wide enough, Nara guided the *Talon* through. They emerged behind a truly massive gas giant with a roiling orange storm covering its entire surface. "I guess the facility must be deeper in the system."

She piloted mostly by instinct and returning memory, and slowly curved around the apex of the planet. In the distance she saw rocks glittering in the sun, and the image strummed a memory. She'd been here before. Many times. This had been, for many years, home.

Nara guided the *Talon* forward, but took a moment to tap a *dream*, then an *air* sigil. The ship quivered, and the invisibility spell cloaked them from enemy detection. No sense taking any chances.

She guided the ship around the edge of the asteroid field, and spent a good twenty minutes scouting before she located the installation. It had been mounted to the back of one of the larger asteroids, and while it wasn't evident from looking at it she remembered they'd had mounted thrusters throughout the rocky caves that helped them maneuver the asteroid wherever they needed it to be.

That level of security had protected them for years, until they'd drawn the ire of a god, apparently. Assuming that's even what Talifax was. Nara had no idea where he stood in relation to a goddess like Neith, but she was fairly certain that the spider-goddess had made a very wise decision by remaining hidden. Talifax was the only being she'd seen able to utter Neith's name aloud, which only underscored the terror.

Nara flew toward the docking area and landed in berth six, as she always had. The surrounding berths were empty, and the outer station walls were scored and dented from repeated asteroid impacts. During her time, they'd had point defense lasers designed to deflect such rocks, but if the system was down, it would explain the damage.

She hurried down to the *Talon*'s cargo bay, where they kept their spellarmor and weapons. A sudden surge of guilt washed over her as she walked past first Crewes's armor, then Kez's. They'd need that armor, but she'd stolen it.

Nara forced herself past it, and sketched a *void* sigil before her own battered Mark V. Unlike Aran, she'd been flying the same suit since the beginning, and it hadn't been in great shape to start out with. But it was familiar, and was the possession she'd owned the longest.

She slipped into the worn interior, and inhaled the tangy, sweat smell that had once bothered her so much. Nara willed the armor into the air, and drifted through the cargo bay's protective membrane and out into the void. She drifted slowly toward the station, and noted that the docking arm that would normally extend to approaching ships had been damaged.

Nara sketched a blink spell and appeared inside the arm's airlock. The corridor inside was dark, so she sketched a *fire* sigil and a globe of flame appeared over her, enough to cast long shadows around her. The walls had been scored by something sharp, and bore a number of dents. That seemed consistent with the rock spiders she'd seen in her memory.

She moved down the corridor and into the mess. Two skeletal bodies lay against opposite walls. Both wore the suits from her memory, each shredded by the rock spiders. They hadn't had a chance against a summoned creature like that. Their spells were their best weapons, but they'd been trained to only fire those on command. The very mechanism of control Ternus had used had prevented their creations from defending themselves.

Nara paused long enough to retrieve her staff from her void pocket, then advanced further into the station. The place seemed completely devoid of life, but it didn't appear to have been looted. This place must have lain dormant ever since Yorrak had raided it, which meant that whatever Talifax intended her to find was probably still here.

"Indeed." Talifax's voice rumbled from the shadows up the corridor. She couldn't see his face, but his shadowed form loomed at the edge of the light cast by her globe of flame. "You will find the equipment you used for so many years, and now you possess the memories to properly utilize it. That, however, is not what I intended you to find here."

Nara's anger kept her warm inside the armor. "Clearly you aren't going to kill me since you need me for something. Before we go any further, I have to ask…why? Why the games? Why taunt me? What purpose could it possibly serve, other than ensuring I hate you?"

Talifax stepped into the light, yet the light still refused to touch him. He remained hazy and indistinct, as if not really here at all. "Such communication serves two purposes. First, it ensures you understand that I can reach you anywhere, at any time. That everything you do is at my behest. And second, it allows me to converse with another being, an indulgence I rarely have a chance to engage in."

This thing was…lonely?

Nara continued up the corridor and did her best to

ignore Talifax. That single admission robbed him of some of the terror, though Nara was still painfully aware that he could incinerate her at will if she didn't do exactly what he wanted.

It didn't take long to reach her room, and as she'd remembered, there was precious little of use. No diary. No teddy bear. Nothing to suggest a real person had lived here. Everything she'd possessed had been on the comm unit she'd used, and she still had no idea what had happened to that.

Nara left the room, Talifax's specter hovering behind her as she continued to explore. She vaguely remembered a training room, and made for that wing of the facility. The damage was less here, and there was almost no scoring along the walls as she reached a wide gymnasium.

"What you seek is along the far wall," Talifax rumbled quietly. He seemed content to observe, for the most part, and Nara saw no reason to dignify his words with a response. The best she could manage right now was ignoring him.

She drifted in that direction, the globe of light illuminating a swimming pool, and then a firing range. Finally she arrived at the far wall, which held a dozen tubes, each containing a set of the armor she'd worn when she served as a Zephyr.

Each suit was a muted grey covered in small bumps. She approached carefully and instinctively tapped in a sequence on the number pad. The tube hissed open, showing that this place had some power, at least. She leaned into the tube and noted the cable attached to the visor. That cable plugged directly into her spine, and she knew if she touched her neck she'd feel the scar.

"I assume you expect me to take this?" She half faced

Talifax. "I don't see why I would. It doesn't offer any advantages my Mark V doesn't already offer. That thing doesn't even have potion loaders."

Talifax's tone was amused. "Your current spellarmor does not possess the necessary technology to interface with Ternus computer systems. Nor will it interface with your implants."

Implants? She blinked as a piece of memory returned, a mask descending over her mouth, and then sudden unconsciousness. People moving around her, measuring vitals. Her awakening fully, to find every part of her body sore. She'd been unable to even walk for weeks. What had they done to her? What did these implants do?

"Besides," Talifax continued. "You miss the obvious. You can simply wear both."

Nara looked back up at the armor she'd worn as X-3 and realized he was right. It was form fitting, just like a flight suit. She could wear that, and then don her spellarmor as needed. That made this a pure upgrade, as well as a link to her past. Putting it on would be challenging, though, as while this place still had atmosphere, it had no heat. Nara opened her void pocket and began balling up the suit.

She'd just finished stuffing it inside when she heard voices in the distance. Light danced up one of the corridors, a layered illuminance as if cast by a flame. Mages then, whoever they were. What were the odds that they'd arrived at a remote, and very secret, facility at the precise moment she herself did?

"I assume whoever they are is what you really intended me to find?" Nara reached for the new rifle next to the suit and added that to the void pocket before sealing it. She could examine it later.

"Or rather, they who will find you." Talifax vanished.

The voices were growing closer, and Nara realized she recognized one of them. It was Kahotep, the hatchling she'd fought for the *Spellship*. It wasn't Kaho that scared her, though. It was the word he used. Mother.

Nebiat was here.

22

MAGIBOMBS

A great many unspoken things changed as Frit's ragged family crossed the umbral depths in search of whatever facility Nebiat intended to use them at. Very quickly the Ifrit settled into subservient roles. Nebiat never gave an order, but every one of her suggestions was obeyed without hesitation. It was becoming a habit, even for her, Frit realized.

Nebiat never asked them to do anything unreasonable. She never demanded. So it made it difficult to say no, especially when you were going to do whatever she asked you to do anyway.

They arrived at Ternus on the sixth day, and Frit was grateful, if for nothing other than the break in the monotony. She joined her sisters in the cargo bay, where Nebiat had asked them to gather. Nebiat was already there, though there was no sign of Kaho. Perhaps he was needed to fly the ship.

"Sisters," Nebiat called in a high, musical voice. "Your attention, if you please."

The Ifrit dutifully fell silent, and each watched her expectantly. Fritara stood the closest, which didn't surprise Frit in the least.

Nebiat pointed at the docking tube opposite the cargo bay where they stood. "This facility was once used by Ternus in a misbegotten attempt to harness magic. Like their failed experience in the umbral depths, it was eventually abandoned. However, I've recovered information that there may still be a weapon of considerable power here. One that could turn the tide of the war in our favor."

"And you want us to find the weapons?" Fritara gushed.

"Precisely." Nebiat smiled down at Fritara like she might a pet that had performed a trick, and Fritara gobbled up the praise. "Explore the station and bring anything useful back to this cargo bay. I will await your return here."

Frit turned without a word and kicked off the hull. The motion aimed her at the docking tube, and she sailed roughly down the middle until she reached the door at the other end. Her sisters were already landing behind her, each adopting the combat stances they'd been trained to use.

Frit punched the cycle button, and they crept inside the dead facility. There was no light, and no heat, except what they brought with them. Frit turned back to her sisters. "I'll head down this way. Spread out, and let's see if we can find what Nebiat is after."

Her sisters began splitting up, so Frit headed up a corridor at random. Being away from the others gave her room to think, which was damned nice. She always had her guard up around Nebiat, and increasingly around Fritara. How long before she feared other sisters too? This wasn't at all what she'd planned when she'd left Shaya.

Frit paused suddenly, as she caught the glint of something in the darkness. She looked up and realized it came from a doorway she'd otherwise have missed. She moved cautiously into the room, and bent to inspect the object. It was a spellpistol mounted on a rack where it was being fitted with some sort of scope.

Behind it lay a row of metal cylinders about waist high, each emblazoned with the Ternus biohazard symbol that she'd come to associate with their nuclear weapons. Frit's shoulders slumped. It figured that she'd be the one to find the weapon Nebiat needed, and to find it this quickly, when she'd have preferred it never be found at all. She approached a cylinder and bent to read the script on the side.

She'd been trained in several languages, and sector common—as Ternus called their language—was one of her favorites. "Magibombs, huh? Not a terribly inventive name," she mused aloud.

"But very descriptive," Nara's familiar voice came from behind her, and she realized the spellpistol was no longer mounted on the rack. "When did Nebiat bind you? The Frit I know would never use magical weapons like that, much less give them to Nebiat."

"Nara?" She asked, aware of the quiver in her voice. Frit spun to find Nara's Mark V spellarmor, its chrome mask covering her face. Both hands were wrapped around the spellpistol Nara had taken from the rack, and the barrel was aligned with Frit's face.

"Damn it." Nara dropped the barrel a few millimeters. "At least tell me why, Frit. Why are you working for Nebiat?"

"Nara, my sisters and I were slaves," she growled. Frit was surprised by the sudden rage welling within her. Where had that come from? "I had to get my people out. We deserve the right to determine our own future."

"Even if that future is serving as weapons for Nebiat, and

wiping out me and Aran, and anyone else Nebiat wants dead?"

"I don't care about Aran, you do." Frit snorted in derision. "And I don't care about anyone else on Shaya. Besides, if you're still loyal to the cause, what are you even doing here? And where is the rest of your company?"

Nara lowered the pistol entirely. "Okay, good point. I'm AWOL. I've got some problems of my own. My memories are returning." She bit her lip, then smiled. "It's good to see you, Frit. I've missed you terribly."

"You have no idea how badly I want to hug you right now." Frit took a step closer to her one friend in the sector.

Nara closed the gap and seized her in a fierce hug. "Gods, I missed you."

Frit dropped her words to a whisper as she disengaged. "I'm so scared, Nara. I needed Nebiat's help to get away from Shaya, and she hasn't asked us to do anything bad. Not until now. I know she's using us, and in a way it's even worse than Eros, because at least he was honest about it."

A metal rod rolled across the floor behind her, and Frit spun to face the door. Fritara stood there, watching them with an accusing frown. "How dare you, Frit? Nebiat has been nothing but kind to us, and you think she's worse than Eros? Worse than Shaya? I wonder what Nebiat will have to say about this, and about you aiding an enemy. That's Nara, right? The friend you went on so many binder hunting adventures with?" Her mouth twisted like she'd eaten something sour. "You make me sick. I can't believe you'd repay Nebiat's kindness with...with lies!"

Fritara's right hand tightened around the hilt of her spellblade, and Frit tensed. Fritara was one of the most gifted war mages among their ranks, and the thing she was most fabled for was speed. A true mage's worst enemy.

Frit spoke without thought. "Nara, run!"

Nara probably assumed she had the advantage because she was wearing spellarmor. She hadn't seen the fight with Ree when they'd fled Shaya. She had no idea what she was dealing with, and Frit had no way to intervene. No way to warn her.

Nara's spellpistol snapped up and the barrel began to glow a menacing purple-black, but Fritara was faster. Her smoldering leg whipped around in a high kick that caught Nara's wrist and sent the spellpistol spinning away, while also sending cracks spiderwebbing across the armored gauntlet.

Fritara lunged, and seized the back of Nara's helmet. She slammed Nara's face down into the pedestal that had held the spellpistol. Once, twice, and then a third time in quick succession. Each blow sent an audible crack through the room, and after the third, Nara's helmet shattered. Her gaze was unfocused, and her movements listless.

"That's enough." Frit took a threatening step forward, though there wasn't much she could do to intervene. "It isn't up to you, or to me, what happens to her. That's up to Nebiat. She'll want Nara alive, and you know it. Besides, I found the weapon Nebiat was after." She nodded at the canisters along the wall.

Fritara relaxed a hair, but her grip on Nara's helmet didn't slacken. "I still think you're a traitor, and I bet Nebiat will too."

Frit only hoped that there was some way to save Nara. She wouldn't put it past Nebiat to disintegrate her on the spot, but try as she might, she couldn't think of a way to intervene that wouldn't still end up getting her best friend killed. There was no choice but to play this out and hope for the best.

"Well?" Frit gestured at the corridor. "Let's go fetch Nebiat."

23

I DON'T UNDERSTAND

Nebiat inhaled a long, slow breath. She didn't need to breathe, but she enjoyed the momentary relaxation it provided. Waiting was the most difficult part of delegation, especially when you weren't at all certain that the delegate was interested in accomplishing the mission.

Frit had proven more resilient and more astute than Nebiat had bargained for. She's been the perfect tool to free the Ifrit, but now those same Ifrit looked up to their sister. They idolized Frit, and while they might be grateful to Nebiat, that only extended so far. If Frit rejected her, they would too.

Nebiat tapped her lips with a finger. She'd need to arrange for Frit to die heroically during the assault on Colony 3. That shouldn't be too difficult, as the resistance there was likely to be fierce.

The air near Nebiat began to warp and shift, gradually resolving into a missive showing her father's scaled visage. His scales glittered in the weak light of an unfamiliar star, absent the purple hue of the Erkadi Rift. Where was he?

"Daughter," Teodros rumbled, his eyes fixed on her. "I have been studying possibilities, and we near a confluence. These next moments are vital. Everything I have worked for is about to come to pass."

Nebiat schooled her features into a dutiful expression. "Of course, Father. What is it you wish me to do?" She hated that he could order her about, and she hated even more that she rarely understood his motives when forcing her to execute his will.

"You are about to be presented with one of your enemies," Teodros explained. His illusionary self loomed over her, just as his real-life counterpart would have. "Suppress your instincts. Do not kill her. Momentary satisfaction, in this instance, carries a very high cost."

She cocked her head, genuinely intrigued. Which enemy? And why were they here? "Of course. I will stay my hand."

"This prisoner possesses a vessel." Teodros paused, and bared his teeth in a way that had terrified her since she'd first hatched. "This vessel is not for you, and you will not claim it. Instead, you will give it to the Ifrit girl. You will give her command of the vessel, and you will entrust her with the weapon. She will destroy Colony 3."

Nebiat's hands curled into fists. "Father, we can't trust her. I'm not certain that she will even agree to destroy the world when asked to do so, and even if she will, do you really want to leave this to chance? I can ensure victory myself, and it will only cost a few days of my time."

"No!" Teodros snarled. His eyes flared with potent *spirit* magic, hinting at his near-divine power. "You will do as I order, and *only* as I order. You will place the Ifrit girl in charge of this mission, and you must send my treacherous grandson with her."

Nebiat closed her eyes, and took another deep breath. It didn't help. "Kaho will look out for his best interests, which introduces yet another point of failure in this plan." She opened her eyes. "I do not doubt your abilities, Father, but what you're proposing is the height of foolishness. Why would you remove your most potent pieces, and entrust critical tasks to those who you *absolutely* cannot trust?"

Teodros continued as if she hadn't spoken. "You will do one final thing. Allow the Ifrit girl to determine the fate of your prisoner. She will choose to keep this prisoner with her. This must be allowed to transpire. Do you understand me, daughter?"

Those last words had been delivered in his 'do not fail me' voice, and Nebiat gritted her teeth. "And what of me, Father? What will I be doing?"

"You will bring the rest of the Ifrit back to the Rift." Teodros's eyes glittered. "By the time you arrive, the pieces will all be in place."

The missive ended, leaving Nebiat with nothing but questions. Where was her father, and why had he finally left the Rift? Why entrust the fate of Colony 3, and potentially the entire Confederacy, to someone like Frit?

The possible answer terrified her. The only reason she could think of to ignore Colony 3 was if Teodros didn't care about the fate of the Confederacy. That made no sense. Why launch this entire war, why systematically dismantle the Confederacy, if you didn't really care about the outcome?

She shivered, and prayed that when she reached the Rift, her father finally made his plans clear.

24

SO IT BEGINS

A high-pitched ringing overlay everything around Nara, and she blinked several times to clear her vision. Fritara stood over her with her spellblade extended, the tip very nearly touching Nara's throat. The blade crackled with voidflame, close enough that she could feel the heat through the space where her faceplate had been.

"Remove the spellarmor," Fritara ordered. "Now. Or I'll risk upsetting Nebiat."

"Okay," Nara managed. She sketched a *void* sigil with her index finger, and she slid out the back of the armor. She began shivering violently as she landed behind it. "I won't survive long like this. I have another suit I can put on, if you're okay with it."

"Walk." Fritara pointed down the corridor with her blade.

"No." Frit stepped protectively in front of Nara. "She's no threat without her armor, and we need her alive. Let her get changed."

Fritara eyed Nara dubiously for a long moment. "Fine, but make it quick."

Nara opened her void pocket and fished out the X-3 uniform she'd taken. She put it on over her flight suit, and her teeth stopped chattering as the suit drew from her reserves of *fire*. She left the goggles in the void pocket. If she chanced them, there was a good chance that Fritara would confiscate them.

Frit nodded at the canisters along the wall. "We need to prove you can be useful. Can you use your gravity magic to bring those with us back to meet Nebiat?"

"Sure." Nara sketched a *void* sigil, then a second to reinforce the spell. Seven canisters rose into the air, and she guided them into a cloud near Frit. "Lead the way."

Frit took point, but her suspicious friend fell in behind her. "Don't think I'm falling for your act, Shayan. You may have Frit fooled because you gave her a pat on the head once, but I'm on to you. Resist again, and it ends with you dead." She prodded Nara in the back with the tip of her spellblade. "Move."

Nara didn't reply, and did her best to play the terrified prisoner. That was the surest way to get them to underestimate her, and if not, then to perhaps take pity on her. Nebiat was no fool. If Frit and others thought her a benevolent leader, she would need to act the part. If Nara were a repentant servant offering no resistance, then killing her would jeopardize her relationship with Frit and her people. Nara needed to use that to stay alive.

"And already it begins," Talifax whispered, his breath hot on her ear, despite being inside spellarmor.

Nara obediently guided the canisters up the corridor. The walk back to the airlock was short and tense and Frit did not glance back once. Finally they reached the airlock door, and all stepped inside. The doors cycled, and they were exposed to the void. Frit appeared untroubled, as did her companion.

They glided slowly across the gap from the docking arm to a large grey cruiser of unknown design. Whatever it was hadn't been made in this sector, or if so it had, then it had been constructed centuries past. The time to examine the ship passed quickly as they reached the cargo bay and passed through the blue membrane.

Frit landed first and gestured at the corner. "Set the canisters over there."

Fritara landed a moment later and watched eagerly. She probably hoped Nara would resist, so she could kill her. Not today. Not if Nara had anything to say about it.

"Of course." Nara deposited the canisters in an empty corner of the room, and then waited for her fate to be decided.

Nebiat ambled into the cargo bay, taking her time as she approached. A wide, friendly smile bloomed as she neared Nara. "Ah, I see you've succeeded. Well done, Frit. I knew my faith in you was well placed. And a prisoner, no less?" She stopped next to Frit, and nudged her playfully in the ribs. "Tell me."

"This is her friend, Nara," Fritara burst in, unable to contain the information apparently. "Frit was going to betray us. She said that you're using us, but the rest of us can't see it." It all came out in a rush, and Nara winced. Not just because of Fritara's utter lack of social skill, but also because the information could damn her friend.

Nebiat began a musical laugh. She walked gently over to Fritara and placed a hand on her shoulder. "Thank you, Fritara. I may have some specific questions later. For now, I'd like to speak to Nara and Frit alone if you don't mind."

Fritara gave a crestfallen nod, and shot Frit a venomous look as she stalked off. Nara wasn't sure Frit caught it, but it hardly mattered. Fritara wasn't exactly hiding her dislike.

"Nara, Nara, Nara," Nebiat purred. She leaned closer, and delivered a predatory smile. "You are going to sing me a pretty song, or I am going to devour you one limb at a time. I want to know how and why you came to be here. Now. Your vessel. Where is it? Are you alone?"

Nara burst into tears. They were real, though the loss of control wasn't. "I'm alone. I came in the *Talon*. It's berthed in bay six."

"You stole the *Talon*?" Nebiat seemed impressed. "For what purpose?"

Frit folded her arms, but said nothing. It wasn't lost on Nara that she hadn't said a word when Nebiat had suggested killing her. Was their friendship that far gone, or was Frit protecting herself?

"I needed answers." Nara took a deep breath, and channeled the intellect Neith had given her. What was the absolute minimum of the truth she could safely reveal? "My memories have started to return. Not all of them, but enough for me to have questions about who I was before. Apparently, this is a Ternus research facility and I was one of the test subjects." She shuddered as visibly as she could. "We were used as assassins. Tech mages, though the scientists here didn't know enough to call us that."

"I see." Nebiat tapped her lip with a finger, then cocked her head. "And you left with the *Talon*? Just like that?"

Nara's shoulders slumped from very real guilt. "Just like that. I was going to bring it back once I found answers. I mean, I was terrified, and...it was a mistake. But I've already made it."

Nebiat folded her arms, mirroring Frit's stance. "Tell me,

little sister. She's your friend. How would you handle the situation?"

"Collar her, just like we were collared back on Shaya," Frit delivered instantly. "And put her to work. She's a talented illusionist, and we're going to need that to deliver the magibombs to Colony 3."

"So you've decided to work with me then?" Nebiat's face split into a pleasant smile. "Splendid! I'm so glad you can see reason, Frit." She leaned in close and pecked Frit on the cheek. Her next words were a bare whisper, but they were loud enough for Nara to overhear. "Because if it turns out you are playing me, then I will make good on my threat. I will devour her whole, right in front of you. And then I will do the same to you. Do you think any of your sisters would stop me?"

"No," Frit whispered back, returning Nebiat's embrace. She breathed into the dreadlord's ear, also loud enough for Nara to overhear. "They worship you now. But remember this, creature. I will protect them, whether they want it or not. As long as I'm still breathing you'd better believe I will stop you from using them like Kem'Hedj pieces." She released Nebiat, and jerked a thumb at Nara. "As for her? I'm going to do exactly what I said. She won't be mistreated, but she's a weapon, a weapon we can use. But if you really worry that I'm just keeping her alive to betray you, then kill her. Depths, kill me. I won't stop you."

Nebiat's brow furrowed. "If you think I seek your death, then you've very much mistaken my intentions. Very well, child. I will remand Nara into your custody. I will even allow you to take the *Talon* for the mission on Colony 3. Succeed there, and you will have my trust. You may take Rita, Fritara, and Kaho with you. The rest of your sisters will remain with me, under my...guidance."

Nara could only gawk. Nebiat was their most canny opponent. She didn't make rookie villain mistakes. Somehow, though, she was not only agreeing to let Nara live, but also to let an underling take care of something as important as Colony 3? What was Nara missing?

Then she remembered Talifax's awful words and realized that even Wyrms of Nebiat's age could be manipulated.

25

INEVITABLE OUTCOME

Jolene stared down at the data feed scrolling across her desk's scry-screen. It provided her, theoretically, access to all accumulated knowledge. Unlike the Shayans, who relied on their own libraries, or Ternus, who relied on their sectornet, Jolene drew from both. She used everything offered by technology or magic, as her entire family had been bred to do going back dozens of generations. Maybe hundreds.

Yet none of that data shed even the slightest illumination on her current problem.

She'd been corrupted by a goddess, and could already feel it changing her. Terrible fire raced through her veins, the lingering after effects of the blood she'd accepted from Skare. Yet as terrible as the fire was, she'd have given anything for more. Anything to bring back that painful clarity, the ability to perceive countless realities at once.

The screen stopped as Jolene caught sight of an interesting file. It was a Ternus holoseries by an Erica Tharn, which attempted to catalogue gods, from a quick glance at the episode guide. She scanned the list and found the usual suspects, the ones everyone in the sector knew about. Virkonna. Krox. Xal. It was the last one that gave her pause, though. Nefarius.

She tapped the screen and a holographic video emerged from the desk. It showed a stately human woman of advanced age standing outside a temple on an unfamiliar world. The wind whipped at her clothing, and whorls of sand obscured a massive, stone structure behind her.

"I'm Erica Tharn, and you're looking at one of the oldest enigmas in the sector." The woman clutched at a wide, tan hat as a particularly strong gust of wind threatened to tug it loose. "The Temple of Xandun is one of three identical structures located over the past twenty years. Each temple lies hundreds of light years from the others, and it remains unclear how their societies were linked." She paused as the howling wind drowned out everything else. "As you can see, this world is quite inhospitable, but that wasn't always the case. As recently as four thousand years ago, this planet wasn't so different from Colony 3, and served as the home of a culture that has—"

Jolene waved impatiently and the video sped up. She slowed it again once the woman was inside the temple. "—Runes on the walls are a dialect of the language that, we believe, forms the foundation of magic itself. Apparently, they tell the story of the godswar, and it's this particular tidbit that justified flying all the way out to the edge of the sector."

The camera floated over to a section of the wall, which was covered in a sea of runes not unlike the sigils they cast for spells. Dotted in between were detailed pictograms, and the one the camera approached showed a shadowed, draconic face, complete with glowing eyes.

"Most gods," the old woman explained eagerly, "are

mentioned in many places. Their exploits are well documented, and cultures across many worlds often venerated the same gods. Yet this one is a mystery." She indicated a row of runes. "It identifies the god as Nefarius, who is usually referred to in the feminine, but occasionally in the masculine. Beyond that, we know little—"

"Clearly," Talifax rumbled from a previously empty chair, "I have miscalculated."

Jolene's heart thundered, but she used every iota of her business acumen to give her new master no visible reaction. It was a minor victory, but a victory nonetheless. "And how have you miscalculated, mighty Guardian of Nefarius?"

"In two, very minor ways." Talifax crossed his legs, and leaned his bulk back in the chair. "First, I missed the temple on Eleph. I should have scoured away all mention of our mistress. And second, I have allowed my own legend to be confused with hers. I have been mistaken for Nefarius."

Jolene knew patience was the smartest route, but something about this being's casual manner rubbed her wrong. If she was going to deal with him, then she should set the tenor now. "Enough of these games. Fine, you've caught me trying to learn more about Nefarius. And yes, I am looking for a way to avoid the kind of mental influence you seem to exert over Skare."

Talifax shook his helmeted head. "I do not have any influence over Skare. Any more than I do over you." He extended a large hand, and deposited a tiny vial on the corner of her desk. "The blood you ingest merely prepares you to properly serve our mistress. The amount in that vial is roughly equal to what I have given Skare. It will place you on more or less equal footing, though he will be unaware of it."

Interesting. That would allow her to continue to play a

subservient role, while seeking to turn the tables both on Skare, and later Talifax. "You have to know I'm planning on betraying you. I don't understand why you'd offer me still more power. Doesn't that make me a bigger threat?"

"Not to me." Talifax's tone suggested he was amused. "This vial represents more than simple power. It binds your fate to me, and to our mistress."

"How so?" Jolene slowly lifted the vial. It took everything she had not to instantly upend the contents into her mouth.

"Nefarius is not a tolerant goddess," Talifax explained. "Other gods know this, and know that they are fodder. They will destroy anyone and anything that bears her touch, for they realize that if they do not, sooner or later they will be devoured."

Jolene realized the extent of her folly in accepting the original gift. Nefarius had enemies across the sector. Krox. The Shayans. Ternus. And who knew who else. She could have aligned herself with any one of them, but now that choice was denied her. A simple, magical scan would reveal she was linked to their enemies, and they'd never believe anything she said about wanting to help them.

"It seems I have little choice then." Jolene upended the vial, and relaxed back into her chair as the tide of dark power surged through her, changing her.

"Yes," Talifax admitted, his voice distant. "There was only ever one inevitable outcome. You belong to her now, as we all do."

26

DESPERATE MEASURES

Aran dropped the tablet into his cup, and gave an eager sigh when it began to hiss and bubble. The smell of coffee wafted up, and the cup warmed in his hands. He took it over to the conference room table, and sat down near Crewes.

It wasn't any colder in the depths, but somehow it always felt as if it were. People bundled up more, and hot beverages were huddled over.

"Where are Bord and Kezia?" he asked as he took his first wonderful sip. Hopefully the caffeine kept him moving through the entire meeting. After that, he'd finally get a little sleep.

"Do you really want to know?" Crewes elbowed him and gave a chuckle. "They ain't had time to be a couple, and this is the last break we're gonna get before we're in the thick of it."

"Yeah, you're right, they should get what downtime they can." He took another sip, and found himself smiling. Bord and Kez finding each other amidst the chaos was proof that good things could survive, even when everything looked dire.

Davidson and several officers Aran didn't recognize threaded into the room and took up seats on the opposite side of the conference room table. Several carried thin map screens—sort of like translucent scry-screens—so people could see them from all directions. He rather liked the invention.

They set them up on the table, and pressed some of the buttons at the base. The maps sprang to life, showing a grey-green world. A series of tagged assets floated in orbit on one screen, while another showed the situation on the southern continent, where the Krox had broken through.

Angry red patches covered many of the cities on that continent, but the heaviest concentration all surrounded a relatively isolated area in a patch of mountains. That seemed odd, unless whatever that target was had immense strategic value. A command bunker for the world's leadership, maybe?

"Thank you for coming," Davidson began once the last map screen had been set up. "I was hoping that we might get your opinion on the tactical situation, and see if we can't come up with a plan on our arrival."

A woman in her early sixties stepped up next to Davidson. Her hair was pulled into a severe bun, and her uniform was immaculate. Her drawl was thicker than most he'd heard, "We'll stand alone, just like we always have. Truth told, we expected those arrogant slits to back out."

"Those arrogant slits," Ree growled from the doorway, "risked everything to be here. You called a tactical meeting and didn't include me?"

Davidson looked like a binder who'd just cast his last spell. "I apologize, Master Reekala." He gave her a low, graceful bow. Not the sort of thing Aran was used to seeing Davidson do. "It was a gross oversight on my part. We're grateful to have you here, and I'd love to get your opinion on the Krox's defensive posture."

Ree seemed mollified. She held her tongue at least, as she stalked over to stand next to Aran. He nodded a greeting, which she didn't return. She'd been even more surly than usual, and this time he couldn't blame her. He didn't really understand what she'd given up. He understood intellectually that he'd lost his home, but the mind-wipe meant he didn't really remember it. She remembered everything she'd sacrificed.

"It looks like the Krox haven't secured orbital superiority. Why?" Ree leaned in close to one of the maps. She studied the cluster of green tags Aran assumed must correspond to the orbital stations. "As long as you have these, they can never conquer the planet."

"They're not here to conquer," Aran observed. "They ignored the orbital defenses so they could raze the planet. If they keep the stations pinned in place, it won't matter if they never take them. They kill every person on your world, and then they leave."

"The stations would end up guarding a tomb." Davidson exhaled a long breath and scrubbed his fingers through his hair. "I don't see how we can stop them. We need to beat them on the ground, but our forces aren't equipped to deal with the Krox, not in those numbers."

"What kind of defenses do you have on the ground, around this place?" Aran tapped the map to indicate the concentration of Krox in the mountains. "And what are they after?"

"That's Fort Crockett. It's where our military leadership would retreat in the event of an invasion. It's equipped with our best tech, and the best magical defenses the Inurans were willing to sell. It's virtually impregnable, even to the Krox."

"Nothing is impregnable," Ree said. She moved over to inspect the map. "The Krox can teleport. They can disintegrate walls. Somehow, they will get inside."

Aran agreed, but saw no reason to drive the point home. "The fact that they've some sort of magical defenses is reassuring. It might not be sufficient to save them, but it could give us enough time to reach them, at least." Aran studied the map. "Assuming they do make it in, what will the Krox face inside?"

"Well trained Marines with our most updated hardware, but very little in the way of magic or magical defenses." Davidson shook his head. "We've got measures in place to detect binders or other casters, and those work great to keep a single binder from invading. But against these kind of numbers? All we can do is throw men at it. And, as you can see, that's not working here. The Krox have isolated Fort Crockett."

"And they're keeping your orbital forces busy, so you can't relieve them." Aran frowned. "Give it to me straight, Davidson. How important is that place? If the Krox take it, will your people keep fighting?"

"It's not a matter of losing our leadership." Davidson met Aran's gaze through the map, the glow painting his face scarlet. "That bunker controls all of our automated hardware. We're talking drones, tank busters, and most importantly, nukes. If they get that place, they could carpet bomb the planet, and use our own ordnance to do it."

"Gods," Aran breathed, "and they'd lose nothing. The Wyrms don't care about radiation, and irradiated corpses make great shock troops to use when they push Ternus directly. If we lose New Texas, they'll use it as a staging ground to take your capital."

"There only seems to be one real solution," Ree interjected. "You need to convince your command structure to sacrifice themselves. They can ground the explosion right over their facility. That will prevent the Krox from gaining control, and wipe out a significant portion of their current forces."

"Do you have any feelings at all?" Davidson snapped. He stabbed the map with his finger, and his drawl was thicker than usual when he spoke again. "We ain't got much arable land on this planet. This ain't Shaya. That plain, there—that's our breadbasket. It's downwind of the place you want to nuke. If we did this, our world would never recover. Even if we won, we're talking famine until we could secure enough food from Colony 3. If Voria's right about war on Ternus, then the capital is going to be snaking every last shipment. My people would die en masse."

"And that's better than letting the enemy carpet bomb the whole planet?" Ree shot back. Aran knew her well enough to know she'd never back down from a confrontation like this. Not if her pride was on the line.

"Respectfully," Aran interrupted. "Ree, you haven't fought the Krox. I have. They're not just after a military victory here. They want to crush morale. Davidson, if the Ternus leadership on this world commits suicide, how will Ternus react? How will the average citizens of your world deal with loss like that?"

"Shit." Davidson frowned. "Yeah, I see what you mean. We're an independent lot. If you take away our leadership, we'll break into a bunch of individual factions. Every faction will be focused on protecting their own territory. Easy pickings for the Krox. So what the depths do we do then?"

"The only thing we can." Aran touched Fort Crockett on the map. "You insert my company in there, and we keep those people alive until your people get us some help. As long as that facility survives, the Krox have no choice but to deal with it. We keep them pinned long enough for reinforcements to arrive."

"That's suicide," Ree protested. "You'll never survive against that kind of enemy force. They must have dozens of binders, and countless troops."

"I'll need a map of Fort Crockett so I can start planning defenses." Aran spoke as if Ree hadn't. "Ree's squadron can support the *Hunter*'s insertion run. You get us into low atmosphere, and let me do the rest."

Davidson gave a low whistle. "Man, you are even crazier than I thought. I'll get my people moving."

27

UNLIKELY ALLIES

Now that they had a plan, and that plan required the aid of every resource he could muster, Aran decided to deal with the thing he'd been most dreading since leaving Shaya. He needed to break the news about Rhea to Kheross. He briefly considered bringing Crewes, and possibly Ree. That sent the wrong message, though. It showed fear, and suggested Aran needed the backup.

Worse, it showed a lack of trust.

That made the decision for him. Aran decided to go alone, risky or not. He threaded a weary path through the *Hunter*'s narrow corridors, once again missing the spacious layout of the *Talon*. Which made him think of Nara. Which made him focus instead on the present, to prevent dealing with bullshit emotions. Emotions were stupid.

The area outside the brig was deserted, except for the pair of Marines guarding the doorway. They gave a Ternus salute as he approached, and Aran instinctively answered it with a Confederate version. Did that fit anymore?

He walked into the brig and over to the only occupied

cell. Kheross sat on the bench with one knee pulled up to his chest. He oozed relaxed arrogance. A predator in its lair.

"Have you finally encountered a threat that requires my strength?" Kheross gave a sharp smile. "I knew you'd come calling, but I didn't think it would happen this quickly."

"Yes, but I'm not here to release you." Aran rested a hand on Narlifex, and noted that Kheross's eyes flicked down. Good. "I have news, and you aren't going to like it. I'm asking you to remain calm, and hear me out."

"Oh I'm going to love this, aren't I?" The deep purple in his eyes flared, and the energy in Aran's chest sang out in answer. He didn't like the reminder of their shared power.

"Rhea isn't aboard," Aran began, "Eros, the Tender, refused to release her after they finished the cleansing ritual. She's in enforced, magical slumber." He left out that her mind was probably being delved by Eros's most powerful mages, as they attempted to extract every bit of her memory to learn if she was truly what she appeared to be.

Kheross eyed him calmly. "And you expect me to rage? You expect me to tear apart this cell, and then this ship—is that it?" He rose slowly to his feet and approached the bars. "I note that you came alone, despite knowing these bars aren't really an impediment. Why, if you thought I might fly into a berserker rage?"

"Because I need you," Aran admitted, as much to himself as to Kheross. "We're walking into a fight that we're unlikely to walk out of, and I can either leave you locked up here, or I can trust an enemy to preserve his own skin. The thing is, Kheross, I don't know you. I don't know what motivates you or what you want. And that makes it really difficult to trust you."

"Of course it does. You are a fool if you ever trust me." Kheross gave a languid smile. "*Void* is cold, Outrider. It is eternal. It is patient. Slowly, star by star, it is draining the universe of all life. All heat. All light. And I am of the *void*. You know what it is I mean. You have been touched by it."

"Not in the same way you have," Aran said. "*Void* is one of many aspects I use. A tool, no more or less important than any other. It certainly doesn't dominate me the way it does you."

"Perhaps. Or perhaps you don't realize it yet. *Void* is insidious." Kheross laughed, and slowly returned to his bench. "So you've come to ask if I'll help in this battle? Tell me of this conflict."

"The Krox have a fleet in orbit around our target," he explained. "They're pounding a facility in the mountains. We're going to run their blockade, and insert our team into that facility. I want you to use your Wyrm form to help us get in, and then stick around to help the defenders survive for as long as we can."

"A last stand?" Kheross raised an eyebrow.

"A holding action," Aran corrected. "We will receive reinforcements from Ternus. All we have to do is hold out for a few days."

Kheross gave a broad smile. "So long as I have a chance to kill Krox's progeny."

28

STIPULATION

Aran tapped the final *void* sigil, and the scry-screen showed a sharp, purple Fissure veining across the black. On the other side lay stars, and light, and life. All around him Aran noticed sighs of relief, from Crewes and from Bord. Nearly a full week in the depths had weighed heavily on all of them.

Yet he felt nothing. Then again, they hadn't been touched by a *void* Catalyst.

The *Hunter* passed through the Fissure, into the site of a recent battle. Hulks of shattered Krox carriers floated around their exit point, and Aran tensed, hoping none of them were faking. He accelerated rapidly away, guiding the *Hunter* toward the cluster of Ternus stations in low orbit around the planet.

The closer they came, the more the hulks were Ternus vessels, and not Krox. Both sides had paid a heavy price, it seemed. Thankfully the post-battle skirmishes appeared to have died down, and there was no sign of the Krox fleet, if it had survived.

"Davidson, this is your show," Aran said, turning to the

blonde major. Davidson stood near the offensive matrix, staring up at the scry-screen.

He scrubbed his fingers through his beard, eyes scanning back and forth. "Depths, we've just gotten clobbered. I've never seen this much devastation, not even at Starn." He turned to Aran. "We can link up with the brass, and get the lay of the land before we begin our run."

"Sir, we're getting an incoming missive. You want it on screen?" Crewes asked from the offensive matrix.

Aran nodded. The screen resolved into the back of a man's head. He was speaking to someone off screen, "Is this thing on? How do I know if he can hear me? Gods, but I hate this magic crap."

"Hello, Admiral Nimitz," Aran called.

The leathery officer turned back to the screen. "Ah, there you are. Davidson, you got a report, son? Where's Voria and her fancy ship?"

"I'm afraid this is it, sir," Davidson admitted. He folded his arms and took a step closer to the scry-screen. "We do have a division of Shayan spellfighters. They're every bit the equal of our special forces, and we've brought Aran and his company. They shouldn't be underestimated."

Nimitz's shoulders slumped, but only for a moment. Anger fueled his gaze suddenly, probably the only thing keeping him on his feet.

"I've read your reports from Shaya and Virkonna, and I agree." Nimitz eyed Aran soberly. "Here's the deal, son. We're losing on every front here. Attrition don't appear to be working in our favor. We've done for a lot of ships, but we have no idea how many more they've got. There's also a big fear back on the capital that this is merely a feint, so they can't spare any immediate relief."

Aran nodded. "That matches Voria's thinking. What's the situation on the ground, sir?"

"Binders have taken most of the cities on the southern continent. It was all too easy for the bastards. They just slaughter as many innocents as they can, and use them as fodder. They bleed us, and it costs them nothing but time." Nimitz rubbed his temples. "Short of scorching the areas where they're holed up we don't have an answer."

"We do now, sir," Davidson said. He nodded at Aran. "We've cooked up a plan. We think we can insert a team into Fort Crockett, and that they can at least prolong the defense. That might buy us enough time for Voria to arrive, or for Ternus to deploy."

"Ah, Major Voria." Nimitz rolled his eyes. "I don't have much faith in her. She's got a bad history of arriving in the eleventh hour, when most everyone else is already dead. She did it on Starn, and she did it on Marid. I expect we'll see the same here."

"Respectfully, sir, you can cram that right up your ass," Aran said, matter-of-factly. Crewes started to snicker, and Bord burst out into full laughter. Aran raised his voice to cover the commotion. "We're not part of the Confederate military any more, and neither is she. That means I get to speak freely. We've been fighting hard since day one, and the entire time we've dealt with Shayan arrogance and Ternus petulance. When Voria shows up and saves our collective asses again—and she will—I want you to remember this conversation. She's sacrificing everything to be here."

Nimitz's expression was unreadable, but he finally gave a short nod. "Your loyalty is commendable, son. Let's hope it isn't misplaced. I've got one more stipulation, and I'm not sure you're going to like it."

"What's that?" Aran asked cautiously.

"We'd like to attach a reporter to your unit. The brass back on Ternus thinks it's important for morale, and I agree," Nimitz explained. "I've seen combat footage of your unit in action. Our people need to see that kind of ferocity, and we need to be able to spin it like we've got a chance."

Aran frowned. "I don't have time to babysit a civvie in a war zone."

"She ain't a civvie, not really," Nimitz protested. "Her name is Archeologist Tharn, and she's been documenting war zones for decades. You let her tag along, and she'll take care of herself."

Aran turned to Davidson, since he could better contextualize what Nimitz was asking. "Is he right? Will she be able to take care of herself?"

"Tharn?" Davidson snorted. "She's even crazier than you are. She'll be fine."

He turned back to Nimitz. "Deal. Get her here quick if you're going to. We're going to start preparing our attack run."

Nimitz's face creased into a smile. "I'll order the fleet to assemble on your position. Let's kill some Krox, son."

29

ORBITAL ASSAULT

Today marked the largest operation Aran had ever been a part of. The Ternus fleet outnumbered the one at Marid, even after the enormous casualties they'd suffered. Six battleships, fourteen cruisers, and seven corvettes hugged the curve of the planet as they began their approach.

Their goal was to punch a hole through the enemy position, all to insert his team inside. Unfortunately, that enemy position was a tough nut to crack. The binders—Aran guessed at least three—had animated every corpse within a hundred kilometers. That included the pilots of Ternus armor, giving them several dozen hovertanks, and twice as many missile batteries.

A fat, white ball of light shot up from the surface and Aran gripped the stabilizing ring as he guided the *Hunter* into an ungainly turn. The hull groaned as the ship strained to obey his commands, and the white streak grew larger as it approached.

"Bord, get me a ward, just in case," Aran growled through gritted teeth.

"Yessir." Bord began tapping *life* sigils and a white latticework of energy sprang up around the ship.

Meter by meter, the *Hunter* pulled out of the way, and the ball zipped by less than a kilometer off their port side. It slammed into one of the battleships, and sank inside with no visible effect.

"All capital ships, focus fire on the *Ramada*," Nimitz's gravelly voice crackled over the radio installed in the console Davidson had added to the bridge. "Take her down. Now."

Aran remembered the dragon breath at Marid, and how quickly binders could animate a crew. "Ree, are you standing by?"

"Ready to launch," she replied in a calm, confident voice.

"Take down the *Ramada*, as quickly as you can," he ordered. "Do the same for any vessel affected by one of those white balls."

"*Spirit* magic?" she asked.

"The worst kind."

"Acknowledged. Fight well, Mongrel."

Aran turned his attention back to flying, and guided the *Hunter* into a steep dive. The hull shook and rattled as re-entry battered the ship. He badly missed the *Talon*, and cursed Nara under his breath.

"Crewes, get the *Ramada* on screen." Aran guided them lower, and the *Hunter* moved toward the vanguard with several of the cruisers.

Crewes tapped several *fire* sigils, and the screen shifted to show a Ternus battleship, isolated now that the other ships had left it behind. Ree's squadron raced toward it, a dozen piranha descending on an unwary fish. Bright golden spells shot from their spellcannons, and peppered the *Ramada's* engines.

The battleship's cannons suddenly went live and began returning fire. Two of the spellfighters died in the first volley, and they lost a third as it completed its attack run.

Aran winced as the last fighter exploded. A quarter of their spellfighters lost in moments.

The surviving fighters swarmed the engines, then the cannons that had savaged their brothers. They took it apart, and within seconds she was nothing but a floating wreck, doomed by the planet's gravity well.

As they descended into the atmosphere, more conventional fire lanced up from the ground, clusters of missiles and the occasional anti-air fire. All of it pinged off Bord's ward with no apparent impact, which was why he'd brought the *Hunter* into the vanguard. They wanted to be a target right now, because they could survive the alpha strike.

The Ternus cruisers around them did not. Explosions wreathed each of the other vessels, their hulls already reddened from re-entry. One by one, they exploded into debris, which rained down on the cities below.

More and more fire concentrated on the *Hunter*, and Bord gave a grunt from the defensive matrix. "This is startin' to cost me. Too bad we don't already have that reporter they mentioned. I want to look all heroic-like."

"I'll joost bet you do." Kezia eyed him sidelong.

"Focus, people," Aran snapped. He didn't know any of the men who'd just died, but he didn't need to. He gritted his teeth as he forced the *Hunter* lower into the atmosphere. Other vessels were riding his wake. It looked like most of the Ternus armada had survived re-entry.

"There." Davidson pointed at the scry-screen, indicating a small cluster of silver buildings nestled between two peaks. They were deep in the mountains, and would be unreachable by land.

Gauss cannons had been built throughout the mountains, each cannon in a protected location to prevent return fire. Together they provided total coverage, and allowed the defenders to savage attacking aircraft.

"Are those emplacements manned?" Aran asked as he turned to Davidson.

"No, all automated. They're controlled internally." Davidson gave a grim smile. "We learned early on that manned emplacements were too easy for them to subvert. There's nothing they can do about those cannons, and they'll detect ambient heat, so most illusion spells won't fool them."

A sea of black figures swarmed around the base of the facility. They covered every slope, and as they neared deployment range, Aran could pick out individual corpses. Most wore Ternus uniforms, and all were armed.

"What are they doing?" Crewes asked. "Ain't no way they'll ever make it through those blast doors with small arms fire."

"They're keeping them pinned in," Aran answered immediately. "The binders know they can't get in this way, but they can force the defenders to keep their attention on it while they find another way in."

"Any idea which way they'll use?" Davidson asked.

Aran thought back to the plans he'd studied. "If it were me? I'd burrow in. Most binders have access to *earth* magic. That means acid. They keep you pinned at all obvious entrances, then tunnel their way inside."

"Well I'm glad you need to deal with it, and not me." Davidson moved to stand outside the command matrix. "It's that time. You'd better get down to the hangar for your drop. Good luck, man." He offered Aran a hand, and Aran took it.

"Take care of yourself, man." Aran clapped Davidson on the back as he exited the matrix. He turned to Crewes, Bord, and Kezia. "Come on. We've got a planet to liberate."

30

COMBAT DROP

Aran smiled as he approached the Mark XI spellarmor. It wasn't the same as his old suit, this one was undeveloped as it hadn't yet been to a Catalyst. But in every other respect it was the same, and he'd badly missed the power and speed such a suit offered.

"I'm going to need to put you away while I fly," Aran explained to Narlifex as he unbuckled the sword. "Just until we hit combat."

Dark. The sword pulsed. *Don't like.*

"It's temporary." Aran opened the void pocket and slipped Narlifex inside, next to his rifle. "I can't buckle you around the armor. Too much risk you'd be knocked loose."

The blade said nothing, but Aran sensed its reluctant acceptance.

He sketched a *void* sigil before the chest and slid into the armor with a slight smile. The comfortable interior settled around his skin, and the HUD lit instantly. Many of the fancy features from the armor Kazon had given him were missing, but Aran didn't care.

There were six potion loaders, four full of shimmering

white healing potions, and the last two the trademark blue of counterspell.

"Sir," Crewes's voice boomed through the hangar, and Aran turned to see him entering. Crewes already wore his new, chromed armor, an updated version of his old Mark VI. The sergeant's spellcannon 'accidentally' aligned with Kheross, who stood idly next to him. "I brought ego the magic dragon. Rest of the squad is all suited up and waiting at bay 9 for the drop." He poked Kheross in the back with his spellcannon. "I'd love a chance to break in my new armor, if you want to resist. Tell me you want to resist."

Kheross merely eyed Crewes.

"Thanks, Sarge." Aran guided the armor into the air and drifted over to land next to the pair. He couldn't help but smile at the sense of invincibility the armor afforded. "Kheross, did anyone explain why I asked you here?"

"Asked?" Kheross snorted. "I had little choice in the matter, unless I wished to...protest." His eyes flared a deep purple as he eyed Crewes sidelong.

Sarge frowned back at the Wyrm. "You want to throw a tantrum I could always use another workout, scaly. If we're gonna, though, you should probably get that ugly-ass dragon form on. Otherwise the fight will be over too quick."

Kheross's jaw tightened. His eyes narrowed and his voice dropped to a near whisper. "Provoke me at your own peril, human."

"I ain't provoking," Sarge shot back as his cannon lowered. "I just want you to know the consequences if you want to—what did you call it—'protest'. This ain't a democracy. I say move, you move. You don't like that, well, my squad already put you down once."

Much as Aran sympathized with the sergeant's position,

he knew this wasn't doing anything but creating more bad blood.

"We worked with Thalas," Aran interrupted. Both men turned their attention to him. "We can deal with Kheross. Today we've got a near impossible job. We need to get inside that facility, and we need to keep those people alive. We're good, Sarge, but not that good. We're going to need the muscle Kheross can provide."

"Tell me of this...operation," Kheross demanded. The purple energy smoldered in his gaze. "I will not commit suicide, but if you offer the chance to kill the progeny of Krox I will take it."

"Holy shit," Crewes barked. "LT, I think I just fell in love. If this lizard will kill Krox...well, I think we're gonna get along just fine, aren't we, scaly?"

"Oh yes." Kheross's eyed narrowed further and he delivered a truly malicious smile. "Fast friends."

"Just don't kill each other until after we get inside Fort Crockett." Aran took a deep breath and guided the armor into the air.

The *Hunter* rumbled as something exploded outside.

"That's our cue," Aran growled. "Let's move."

He zipped through the hangar, toward a narrow corridor that led to a row of small airlock bays. They were used to deploy single squads, and the entire bay could be detached as an escape pod if necessary.

Bord and Kez waited outside the closest bay, each wearing their brand new spellarmor. Kezia's was a midnight blue, and the heavier plating made her tower over Bord's smaller scout model.

"Last minute checks," Aran called as he drifted to the airlock and cycled the outer door. "We deploy in twenty."

The rest of the squad followed him inside, and they

closed the airlock door behind them. Kheross wore a bored expression, though something sinister still lurked in those hellish eyes.

"Aran, do you copy?" Davidson's voice crackled through the comm his techs had installed in Aran's armor.

"I'm here. We're about to deploy." He moved to the far wall and rested his hand against the red button, but didn't press it. "What do you need?"

The ship shuddered again as another round of anti-air fire pounded into them.

"I need you to wait about thirty seconds." Davidson's voice was strained, probably from piloting the *Hunter*. "Ternus just teleported Archeologist Tharn aboard, and they want her on the drop."

"Are you even serious?" Sarge roared, slamming his armored fists together. "Sir, tell me you aren't gonna accept this crap."

"Send her down." Aran said over the comm. He moved to the inner airlock door and cycled it back open. "We'll wait."

"Roger that. Thanks, Aran. I owe you for this." The connection clicked off, and Aran turned toward the sergeant.

"What gives, LT?" Crewes protested. He flipped open the faceplate on his armor. "It's bad enough we're taking scaly here, but you want us to babysit a reporter too?"

"Trust me, I get it," Aran replied. "Here's the deal, Sergeant. This planet is getting pounded by the Krox. They have no hope of victory, and so far as they know they have no help. They've lost world after world to the Krox, and now those Krox are beating down their door. Their leadership is under siege, and their cities are burning. They're a hair's breadth from breaking. They need to see that we can fight back, and we're the only people on this rock that can do that. Doesn't do much good if they don't get to see us do it."

Crewes gave a grudging nod of understanding, but he said nothing, so Aran continued.

"If we pull off this drop, and if they record it, then they can show the whole planet that the Confederacy sent help." He shook his head sadly. "I know it's a sham. You know it's a sham. The Confederacy isn't worth crap, and we they aren't sending any real help. But these people don't. This is our chance to give them some hope."

"We saw what that did in the Dims, Sarge," Kez pointed out. "Aran's right. Bord and I will take care of the reporter. I'll keep her in sight, and Bord can get a ward up around her as needed."

Something metallic pounded up the deck in the hallway outside the airlock and the squad shifted instinctively into a defensive posture.

A moment later, a figure in Mark V spellarmor strode into view, then stopped just outside the door. A pair of small black drones zipped up in the suit's wake, their cameras whirring as they moved to circle the squad.

The figure popped off its helmet, and a river of white hair spilled out. It framed a face that had once been beautiful, and had aged gracefully into handsome. She eyed them hawkishly, her expression unreadable.

"Good morning, Captain." She gave Aran a grim smile. "I'm Erica Tharn. Combat reporter and archeologist of the First Order. I can't fight, but I assure you I can take care of myself. I'm pretty slippery."

"Lady, I don't mean any disrespect," Bord piped up, "but you've got to be pushing ninety. You should be on a couch somewhere knitting, not diving into enemy fire."

Tharn raised an eyebrow. "Your concern is touching. I

will be fine." She turned to Aran. "Captain, whenever you're ready."

The *Hunter* shook again.

"All right, you can go. Keep us between you and hostile targets, and don't do anything stupid that will get one of my people killed." Aran turned back to the outer door. "Cycle the door behind you. We need to get moving."

Tharn replaced her helmet, and the instant the airlock door slid shut behind them, Aran slapped the red button for the outer door. The door retracted into the ceiling, and screaming wind filled the room. Streamers of dense, black smoke billowed out around them, obscuring their view of the battle.

"Deploy." Aran leapt out the airlock, and into chaos.

31

NOT IN ALL MY YEARS

Aran burst into a hail of anti-air fire, white rounds streaking up from the ground below. He twisted to dodge as one passed through the space he'd just occupied, then winced when it slammed into the *Hunter*'s aft hull with a deafening explosion.

The Krox lines snaked through every ravine, coating every valley in the mountainous region below. Vacant, dead expressions stared up at them, from the corpses of soldiers who'd once served this world.

Here and there, towering monstrosities crushed their way through the ranks. Aran recognized them as rock elementals, primal creatures infused with *earth* magic. They were ponderously slow, but every footfall shook the ground enough to send corpses tumbling. They'd been animated from the local mountains, granite faces that had stood up and started laying waste to the land around them.

Aran spared a glance at his company, and relaxed a hair when he counted all four—five, if you included their new pet reporter.

"What's the plan, LT?" Crewes called over the comm. He

hovered not far from Kheross, his cannon 'accidentally' aimed at the Wyrm.

Kheross was still in human form, and Aran could feel the *void* magic keeping him aloft. He seemed unconcerned with Crewes, and instead his eyes scanned the area below.

"Follow me," Aran called back, "We'll stay low and hug those hills as we make for the facility. Don't use your spell amplification unless absolutely necessary. We want to save that."

Aran dropped into a steep dive, corkscrewing around enemy fire as he approached the hills below. He studied the enemy movements, and noticed that three of the rock elementals had moved into a tight cluster, next to an overhang that blocked his view.

"They're not moving like the others. Looks like they're shielding something," Aran said into the comm. "I'm betting that's their access point. If we can overwhelm them, maybe we can use their own tunnel to get inside."

"Contact!" Crewes barked.

Aran spun in midair, his training taking over. Three black-scaled Wyrms dove at them from above, gliding silently down on them. They weren't the largest they'd ever faced, but they were large enough to be a threat.

"Kheross, you wanted some Krox," Aran boomed over the suit's loudspeaker. "You're on."

"As you wish, Outrider." Kheross's form, which had been streaking toward the valley below, suddenly arrested all momentum. His body began to ripple, exactly as it had back in the hangar.

Aran tore his gaze away and focused on their attackers. Two of the dragons were already fixed on Kheross, perhaps because they recognized one of their own. The last dove toward Bord and Kez, ichor dripping from massive jaws as it flew closer.

Aran opened his void pocket and smoothly withdrew his rifle. Narlifex pulsed a greeting, but he left him inside as he closed the pocket. The rifle snapped to his shoulder almost of its own accord, and he sighted down the barrel at the Wyrm diving for Kezia.

She hovered in midair using the new M9 thruster Kazon had sent with the armor, her hammer clutched in both hands. Bord waited behind her, and their new reporter friend flew just past him. They were lined up perfectly for the Wyrm's breath attack.

Aran didn't give the Wyrm a chance to take advantage. He poured *fire*, *void*, and *air* into his rifle, and a moment later it kicked back into his shoulder. The barrel disgorged a pulsing ball of mixed magical energy that sailed into the Wyrm's back, right where the muscles attached to the wing.

It wasn't the first time Aran had used that move, but hey, why change what worked? He smiled grimly as the wing tore loose. The Wyrm screeched as it clawed frantically at the air around it.

A moment later its flight stabilized, and it whirled to fix a venomous glance on Aran. "I too have *void* magic, little human. I do not need wings to fly."

"They do make it easier to dodge though," Aran pointed out.

The Wyrm didn't see Crewes, who was approaching on the creature's six. The sergeant's cannon bucked and a spear of solid, blue ice pierced the creature's back, just over the lung. It screeched weakly, and began clawing at the ice lance it suddenly found jutting from its chest.

Aran risked a glance at Kheross, who dove and wheeled with the other two Wyrms. They snapped at each other like wolves, and thus far no one had established an advantage. Kheross was larger than either Krox, but they'd clearly worked together before and kept trying to flank him. Kheross was holding his own though, for now.

Aran turned back to his target, and chose the most expedient way to finish the dragon. He triggered the first counterspell potion, and a ball of sapphire streaked toward the Wyrm. It exploded into a cloud of crystals, which spun around the Wyrm, then disappeared.

The Wyrm began to fall once more, the *void* magic keeping it aloft violently stripped away. It picked up speed, and by the time it slammed into a handful of corpses in a ravine below, the detonation was large enough to trigger a massive wall of smoke and dust. That provided cover from the ground fire below, giving Aran the freedom to deal with the other two Wyrms.

He flipped around and willed the armor to maximum speed. Aran shot back up into the air, drawing level with Kheross and his two opponents. He opened his void pocket, dumped the rifle back inside, then seized Narlifex's hilt.

We. Kill. The words thrummed with pleasure.

"Yep, time for a little dragon murder, bud." Aran wrapped both armored hands around the hilt, but paused as a sudden thought occurred to him. Narlifex had grown back in the hangar, and his size made Aran want to adopt a two-handed style.

In spellarmor, however, Narlifex could still easily be wielded in one hand. Aran shifted the blade to his right hand, then snapped his left wrist down to activate the spellshield. He'd rarely used it on his last few suits of armor, because Drakkon style focused on offense. Now that he had his memories back and truly understood Drakkon style he could finally adapt it as he saw fit.

He zipped toward the trio of Wyrms, assessing the combat as he approached. The smallest Wyrm bled from a hideous gash in his chest, but the scales on Kheross's draconic face had been rent from a slash that had very nearly taken out his right eye.

Aran poured *void* into his armor to increase his mass, then streaked toward the closest Wyrm. He approached from the rear, and delivered a wicked slash to the dragon's tail. Narlifex burst into sudden flaming brilliance, and the blade sliced all the way through dense scales, flesh, and bone alike, severing the tail where it met the tailbone.

He flipped backwards, but not quickly enough. The enraged Wyrm twisted gracefully, and its snarling face whipped around in Aran's direction. The Wyrm was the smallest of the three, but those jaws were still large enough to swallow him whole.

Aran sent a surge of *air* magic into his spellshield, and the energy crackled around the spinning sigils. He slammed the dragon in the snout, and used the momentum to spin away. The jaws snapped shut in his wake, and both clawed hands were already moving to seize him.

Kheross's much larger jaws abruptly clamped down around the creature's neck from behind, and he shook it violently. The tail-less Wyrm screamed weakly, but Kheross's clawed hands ripped into its chest over the wound Crewes had inflicted, tearing out a still beating heart. Kheross snapped it up greedily, then released his dead opponent. The mutilated Wyrm fluttered into the storm of dust raised by its companion's demise.

Aran scanned the sky for the final Wyrm, and located his corpse on one of the rocky slopes below. "Looks like we're clear for now. Nice work, people. Let's get down to those rock elementals."

One of Tharn's drones whirred past, the camera clearly focused on him. Aran ignored it, and focused on the battle.

He guided his armor lower and hugged the ridgeline as he approached the rock elementals. Their size became evident as he closed, "These things are a good forty meters tall."

"Man they grow 'em big here," Sarge called over the comm. "What's the play, LT?"

"Kheross, you're got a breath weapon, right? One that uses *void* magic?" Aran asked. They were coming up fast, and he didn't have a lot of time left to form a plan.

"I do," Kheross roared. His shadow passed directly over Crewes. "If I unleash it I can envelop all three elementals."

Kheross didn't wait for an okay, instead dropping into a steep dive that carried him ahead of the rest of the company. His scaled chest swelled as he sucked in a breath, and he unleashed that breath when he'd reached the elementals. A river of darkness boiled out to completely envelop all three rocky figures. It briefly obscured them from view, and when it cleared they were simply...gone.

The power of it chilled Aran to the core. This monster had been living in their midst for weeks.

He shook himself back to the moment. "Follow me."

Aran dropped into a climb that mirrored Kheross, and sailed under the rocky outcrop the elementals had been shielding. A wide tunnel entrance led into the darkness. The sides were completely smooth, as if bored by magic. Where there was magic of this magnitude, there was also a mage.

He paused before the tunnel entrance as the squad arrived. He noticed that the reporter seemed to have no trouble keeping up. Both of her drones hovered near her, their lenses whirring as they recorded everything.

Aran focused on the tunnel mouth. "I'm betting there's a binder in there, probably with a few enforcers for defense. Let's play this cautiously. Kez, Bord, you're in the lead. Advance with a ward. Sarge, I want you to engage any defenders the binder has. I'll deal with the mage."

"And me?" Kheross roared as he landed next to them. Each sweep of his mighty wings kicked up a hail of grit, which pinged off Aran's armor.

"Rear guard. I want you to shift back to human form and make sure nothing follows us into the tunnel. The Krox will almost certainly respond to our incursion. Now let's move." Aran zipped into the tunnel without waiting for a response. Kezia sprinted past him with Bord on her shoulders.

Bord patted her shoulder as they passed. "It ain't the way I want to be mountin' you, love, but I'll take what I can get."

The pair fell silent when a ghostly, white glow appeared in the distance.

"Spirit magic," Kez said. "Looks like you were right, sir."

"There's probably two binders then. One using earth to tunnel, and the other standing guard with spirit. Let's blitz them, people."

Kezia burst into a loping run, and Bord raised both hands. A latticework of brilliant, white sigils exploded around him, protecting both him and Kezia behind a shimmering ward. They sprinted down the tunnel, and Aran sailed just behind them.

He considered grabbing his rifle again, since he could use Kezia as cover, but decided against it. Combat shifted quickly in close quarters and he wanted to be able to react.

A trio of ghostly balls shot up the tunnel and slammed into Bord's ward. They disappeared with a few discolored ripples, but had no other visible effect on the ward. Kezia redoubled her pace, and Aran increased his to match.

Light glittered off scales, perhaps twenty meters up the hall. Beyond that, he could see faint, fluorescent lights, the kind that Ternus used. The Krox must have broken into the facility.

"Now, Bord!" Kez yelled. Bord rolled off her shoulders, and came to his feet next to Kez.

She brought her hammer around in a tremendous swing, and a draconic scream echoed up the tunnel.

Aran plastered himself against the tunnel roof and zipped past Kezia, and past the enforcer she'd just crushed. He scanned the darkness, and sure enough, there were two binders. Both were focused on Kezia, though the closest did look up in time to see Aran.

We. KILL.

Aran brought Narlifex around in a sweeping slash. The blade smoldered as it met the Krox's throat, a streamer of smoke rising as the headless hatchling fell to the ground.

The final Krox binder raised a clawed hand and began expertly sketching *spirit* and *earth* sigils. Aran gave a savage grin as he triggered a second counterspell potion. A ball of blue shot from his armor, and shattered the Krox's spell.

Crewes pounded past Aran. "I got dibs on this stain." His cannon bucked, and a wave of superheated flame washed over the unfortunate Krox. The creature shrieked once, then its charred, smoking corpse collapsed to the ground.

Aran's frantic breathing began to slow. They'd done it. "All right people, let's get into the hole the Krox made." He turned back to the tunnel. "We'll have Kheross collapse it behind us."

The rest of the company filed by him into a chromed hallway. The last to pass was Tharn, and she paused next to him, her drones whirring in her wake. "In all my years, I've never seen anything like that. I'm already uploading my footage. I'm going to make you a gods' damned hero."

Aran didn't have the energy to reply. He knew this was just the beginning. The Krox had been unprepared for his assault, but they'd recover quickly.

A purple glow came up the tunnel and Kheross approached. "They followed. I...encouraged them to cease their pursuit."

"Can you collapse the tunnel in our wake?" Aran asked.

Kheross glanced up at the ceiling, then nodded.

"Do it." Aran stepped inside the facility.

32

TERNUS

"Good morning, Pickus." Voria inclined her head at the fiery-haired tech as he peered up over his glasses at her, his freckled face bathed by the portable computer terminal sitting in his lap. "What do we have today?"

She strode onto the bridge, which currently appeared to be the bridge of the *Big Texas*, the tiny ship Voria had flown into the depths in search of Neith. It was where she'd met the tech, and apparently it was the place he found most comfortable since the bridge automatically reflected the subconscious desires of the pilot. It harkened back to a world a great deal simpler than the one he'd so recently entered.

"Morning, ma'am." He inclined his head back, then his gaze shifted back to the computer screen. "We're making some real progress. The drifters are surprisingly industrious, especially considering the bad rap they seem to have back on Shaya. They're making short work of the corruption on decks A and B. We've cleared out all the habitable areas, and we ain't even reached Ternus yet. They've even set up a bar, apparently."

That eased something in Voria, a tension she hadn't realized she'd been laboring under. Leaving Shaya meant cutting off the aid from the *life* mages Eros had lent them. The drifters were powerful mages in their own right, and had gleefully taken to the task of cleaning up sludge.

"Anything else of note?" Voria asked as she moved to stand near the *Big Texas's* viewscreen, the technological equivalent of a scry-screen. The *First Spellship* had rendered the illusion perfectly, right down to the faint, musty smell that always pervaded the bridge of her short-lived vessel. The vessel that had, ultimately, led her here.

"I completed the resources report." Pickus looked up again, and his face split into a gap-toothed grin. "Ninety-six qualified tech mages came with us from Shaya, and at least one of every aspect is represented. Obviously it skews toward *life*, but that's probably a good thing given the war. We're staffed enough to be a mobile hospital at this point."

Ikadra's sapphire pulsed forlornly. "This ship was used as a hospital once before. Shaya was the vessel's caretaker."

Voria noted the dejected tone, which had been a constant since Nara had left with the *Talon*. No one had seen that coming, but Ikadra had been the hardest hit. Even harder than Aran, and he'd been the closest with the treacherous woman.

"And it will be again." Voria squared her shoulders. "Pickus, add an addendum to your report to Ternus High Command. Tell them we are opening the *Spellship* to all wounded for the duration of the crisis, and organize our life mages to support the initiative."

"Yes, ma'am."

She winced at that. "I am not your mother, Pickus. One does not address one's superior as ma'am in the Confederate Marines."

"Respectfully, ma'am, I ain't in yer confederate outfit. I'm here to fix the ship." He closed his laptop and rose with a stretch. "'Sides, if I didn't refer to you proper my ma would know. She can sense stuff like that."

"Your mother possesses magical abilities?" Voria asked, mildly surprised.

"Uh, no, ma'am." He grinned at her sheepishly as he set his laptop down next to his ancient co-pilot's chair. "She ain't been to a Catalyst so far as I know, but she's got her ways is all."

"I'm sure she does." Voria shook her head with a smile, then waved her hand. The bridge rippled, a stone tossed into a pond. When the ripples cleared, the bridge had become the *Wyrm Hunter*. "I hope you don't mind, but I prefer something a bit more sentimental."

She ducked inside the command matrix, a half smile curving her mouth as the rings rotated around her. The soft hum was, well, it was home.

"You know you don't need to actually use that matrix," Ikadra pointed out.

"I know, but I rather enjoy it." Voria tapped the *void* sigil on each ring, in quick succession. "Pickus, I'm relying on you to establish a connection to Ternus when we emerge from the Fissure."

Void magic rolled from her in waves, disappearing into her illusionary matrix, but fueling the ship in a real way. The spell began to manifest, and the unrelieved black was suddenly split by a violent crack, one that quickly widened into an opening back to the world of Ternus.

Pickus fished out his pocket comm and thumbed the screen. A moment later, the scry-screen shifted to show a connecting sigil with the familiar stylized T used by the Ternus government. Several moments later, the screen resolved into a uniformed officer—a fleet admiral, by the five bars on his shoulder. It took her a moment to realize that she recognized the man.

"Hello, Admiral Kerr, though I guess that title isn't applicable any longer." Another weight lifted. They'd sent a friendly face for her to deal with.

Kerr's weathered face darkened. "A lot has changed since we last spoke, Major. Though I guess that title isn't accurate anymore either, as I understand it. How should I address you?"

That was an excellent question, yet over the several sleepless nights she'd not once considered it. What was her appropriate title now? She cocked her head. "Let's go with Colonel. That's enough to command a regiment, and that's what I'm bringing to the field. Though, to be fair, that regiment is rather...unconventional."

Kerr shook his head in amusement. "With you it always is, but I'm not gonna complain, Colonel. You saved our bacon at Marid, and got me a promotion to boot. It's fleet admiral now." He removed his cap and set it somewhere off screen, then scrubbed his fingers through greying hair. "Unfortunately, the political situation here isn't great. It ain't as bad as Marid. I'm certain Governor Austin hasn't been bound, but he's enough trouble as it is."

Voria squared her shoulders as an imaginary weight settled back over her shoulders. "Gods save us from politicians. We're awfully vulnerable here in the depths, Fleet Admiral. May we enter the Ternus system?"

"Permission granted, Colonel. I'll have flight instructions

sent to your vessel, and we can meet in person at your earliest convenience." The fleet admiral paused. "If I could offer a bit of advice, unsolicited like, try to keep your temper in check when you meet the governor, Colonel."

She gave a wry smile. "I make no promises, Admiral."

33

WAIT AND SEE

Voria wasn't certain what to expect when she guided the *First Spellship* into Ternus space. The Fissure snapped shut behind her, and the scry-screen now displayed a dazzling array of weaponry, all pointed in their direction. Countless gauss rifles bristled on dozens of orbital stations, which formed a perfect sphere around the planet's umbral shadow.

"One moment, uh, Colonel," Pickus muttered as his eyes ceaselessly scanned the computer screen. "There we go. We're not yet authorized to move forward, not until they complete their scans."

"What kind of scans, precisely?" Voria drummed her fingers on the stabilizing ring. Despite having served the Confederacy for decades, she'd never been to Ternus, and the place unnerved her. The idea of so much technology seemed so...cold, and devoid of life.

Even from this distance she could see that the world was covered in massive, concentric rings. Cities. Continent-sized cities. No part of the world had escaped, at least none she could see from orbit.

Pickus withdrew a toothpick from his pocket and rolled it between two fingers. His eyes never left the screen. "They're running a broad-spectrum analysis, but beyond that I can't rightly say."

Voria shivered. Something prickled along the skin of the *First Spellship*, and her link to the vessel conveyed the feeling. "They're doing something magical as well."

Ikadra's sapphire flashed, and he thrummed in her grip. "I sense *fire*, mostly. I thought these guys were all anti-magic and stuff?"

Voria considered that as the scan completed. "They've got that reputation, but I've always wondered. Ternus has a lot of money, and the Inuran Consortium is happy to sell all sorts of magitech if the price is right. I suspect it was a wise investment."

"They just gave us the all clear sir. We've been given a course to the nadir point of the planet, over the southern continent." Pickus punched a few more buttons on his screen. "Apparently we'll be docking with Alamo Station, where Governor Austin will receive you."

"Acknowledged." Voria willed the *Spellship* in that direction, and the vessel followed. Unlike with the *Wyrm Hunter*, piloting was not an ongoing task, unless she wished it to be. Now that the vessel understood where she wanted to go it would pick the most direct route to get there unless she modified the directive.

That gave her time to think. Pickus was blessedly silent, other than the clatter of his keyboard. So what would the coming days require of her? She'd come to help Ternus, but beyond bringing this ship she wasn't sure what she could offer the war effort. She knew little of Nebiat's plans or ultimate motivations. And that would make answering this Governor's questions all the more difficult.

He'd want to know why she was here, instead of New Texas, and explaining that auguries and premonitions were why she'd chose not to assist probably wasn't going to go over very well.

They circled the planet in high orbit, the sky around the planet lit with a lethal array of glittering stars, each a missile or drone platform like those she'd seen at previous battles. There were so many of them. Hundreds. More, perhaps. This world was a fortress, one even the Krox would be hard pressed to assault. One that couldn't be easily bound or subverted through magical means.

They rapidly closed with the most impressive of the stations, this one affixed to a long metal tube extending up from the surface. "What is that...thing?"

"That's a space elevator," Pickus explained. "They use it to move men and material into orbit via lift. Different stations can dock with it, though I think Alamo Station's been parked there for decades since most shipping takes place off world now."

The *Spellship* maneuvered expertly around dozens of satellites, stations, and departing craft as they made their approach. Voria straightened her jacket, and took a moment to re-tie her hair into a tight bun. It would have to do. "Ikadra, teleport Pickus and I to the aft officers' cargo bay, please."

"Ooh, field trip!" Ikadra's sapphire pulsed happily. Voria smiled. It was a welcome change.

There was a moment of vertigo, then she was standing in the cargo bay. She moved to the airlock membrane and waved a hand before it. The energy field winked out and exposed the docking tube that the station had extended. She walked briskly up the tube, noting the turrets installed every three meters.

Again she felt the prickling across her skin, a faint whiff of magical power as something in the tube scanned her. It pleased her to know that Ternus took magical security so seriously, and the fact that a world famed for their ignorance in all things arcane had *much* better security than Shaya, the undisputed magical master in the sector.

A door slid into the wall as they reached the end of the docking tube, and she spotted a quartet of Marines just beyond. They wore the standard olive uniforms, and each stood with relaxed readiness, their rifles cradled in both hands, ready to snap to their shoulders.

"Ma'am," a blonde soldier called, "you're expected at the forum. If you'll follow me please. They're waiting."

"They?" She asked as she fell into step with the Marine. Pickus dropped a step behind her, assuming the role of an aide. That seemed to come readily to him, and she suspected he didn't enjoy the kind of attention being an officer warranted.

"The subcommittee, ma'am." The Marine set a brisk pace. He reminded her of a younger, more stern version of Davidson.

That sounded like the most Ternus thing she'd ever heard. A subcommittee? Really? She shook her head, but managed to contain the sigh. Goddess save her from bureaucrats.

The Marine led her down a long, circular corridor that snaked around the outer edge of the station. They passed more Marines at several check points, and she noted that every intersection had a pair of turrets. This place would be an absolute nightmare to assault, even for a Krox binder.

"Through here, ma'am." The blonde Marine gave a polite nod at a pair of double doors flanked by more Marines. The doors slid open at her approach.

"Thank you for the escort," she began, glancing at the bars on his uniform, "Lieutenant."

He nodded again and she walked through the now open doors. The room she entered wasn't at all what she expected. Every taste of bureaucracy on Shaya had left her wanting to shoot herself in the face. She could already tell this was different.

Seven men and women sat around a rectangular table, and all bore the weariness that accumulated from too little sleep over a prolonged period. A young man at the far side of the table rose, and Voria noted that each of the others eyed him deferentially before doing the same.

"Colonel Voria," he called in a strong Ternus Drawl, "welcome to Alamo Station, and to Ternus. My name is Pierce Austin, duly elected governor of the Ternus Colony. I ain't going to bother introducing the rest of these people, unless you feel the need."

"I appreciate the expediency, Governor." She walked to the table. "May I?" She nodded down at a seat.

"Of course."

Voria set Ikadra in the air, and he used his own magic to keep himself aloft. She sat, and folded her arms on the table before her.

"As I understand it, you're no longer a part of the confederacy. That right?" Austin—she couldn't think of a boy that young as governor—undid the top button of his collar.

"That's correct." She shook her head sadly, toying with the edge of her sleeve. "Would that it were otherwise, but Tender Eros believes an attack is imminent. He refused to send aid to Ternus, our sworn allies. I had no choice but to break ranks and come with the forces I could muster."

Fleet Admiral Kerr gave a tired smile. "We're grateful for that, Major. The *Hunter* arrived at New Texas this morning and, as I understand it, made quite the stir by inserting a company of tech mages into Fort Crockett. You've no idea what that's done for our morale. My people see the Krox as unstoppable machines, and fear that our only recourse is to give up this space and flee for a new world. Some have already done exactly that."

"Kerr," Austin interjected, "if we're quite finished fluffing the Colonel's ego, perhaps we could get back on task? Colonel, we're grateful for your help, but the question I want answered is why are you here? Why didn't you accompany Davidson to New Texas? You've seen our defenses. Our world is hardly at risk, but New Texas is about to fall."

In that moment Voria understood why Kerr worried about her reaction to the man. Thankfully, her ego wasn't so fragile that she couldn't handle being challenged. This part, at least, she'd been prepared for. She glanced over her shoulder at Pickus. "Can you transmit the sector map I was working on?"

"Yes, ma'am." Pickus didn't even look up from his comm, but a moment later, a hologram sprang up over the table. It showed the sector with an overlay of Krox attack waves.

"I've had a great deal of time to ponder the Krox strategy. As you can see every recent battle is charted here, complete with the estimated cost to the Krox forces." She rose and moved to stand near the hologram. "Notice that while the Krox have hit Marid, Danton, Starn, and Vakera, they've left Colony 3 completely untouched. This despite the fact that it is quite clearly in their invasion path."

"It doesn't wash." Austin rose, too, and leaned in to inspect the hologram. "Colony 3 represents most of the sector's food supply. If the Krox wiped out that world we'd have shortages all over the sector in a matter of months. In a year. at least a half dozen new colonies would starve."

"Precisely my thought, which is why I came here. I believe that New Texas, while a legitimate target in its own right, is not Nebiat's true goal." She turned her attention to Austin. "Make no mistake, Governor. The Krox have only just begun. They will hit you hard, and they'll do it where you least expect it. Soon. When they do, I want to be in a position to respond with all the force I can muster."

34

BREADCRUMBS TO A GOD

Kazon looked instinctively over his shoulder, but anyone with the magical clout to slip past the wards on his quarters could no doubt cloak themselves from his sight. There was nothing in the shadows there by the bookshelf. That was his imagination.

He waved a hand and a soft, white glow emanated from the ceiling, dispelling the shadows. But it also exposed the walls of his quarters, which were made from the same oily metal as the rest of the ship. When he'd first been given the ship he'd thought it futuristic somehow. Powerful.

Now it had become a coffin, somehow claustrophobic despite being spacious.

He knew he was close to answers, but the closer he got, the more he realized that Skare couldn't allow him to live, if Kazon somehow discovered the secret to this metal.

And then there was the mystery surrounding Inura. Kazon could find no mention of the god's death, but also no mention of his direct involvement at any time in the last two millennia. For that entire time, the Consortium had grown and prospered, but Kazon couldn't help but wonder. Was their founder still alive and guiding the organization? And how could he learn more? Every lead he'd chased so far had gone cold.

Still, it was enough that he felt it prudent to express his concerns to those allies who might be able to do something about it. He sat in the chair behind the desk and tapped a missive on the scry-screen. Kazon couldn't cast one himself, but the screen drew the magic from an assistant who possessed *fire* magic.

"What is it, brother?" Voria's prim face filled the screen, and, as usual, she had a harried look to her. She stood on the bridge of her new ship, which gleamed behind her.

"I know you are at war, sister," he began, attempting to collect his thoughts. "I will keep this brief. Mother has been compromised. Her behavior has become…erratic."

"Erratic? What do you mean erratic?" Voria asked with that faintly bored tone he'd come to expect. She glanced to the side, then lowered her voice. "She's always erratic."

Kazon shook his head. "Not in the usual ways. She's focused. Driven. And she is working hand in glove with Skare, but they won't tell the board what they're working on."

Voria eyed him critically for a long moment before she finally spoke. "I know you wouldn't bother me with trivialities, but I'm not hearing anything worthy of special note."

It occurred to him he was going about this all wrong. Voria was an agent of long-dead gods, their instrument in all this. He should have led with this.

"I have begun this badly. Allow me to begin again. Take a look at this, sister." Kazon held up the bracelet Aran had sent him. "This is Aran's spellarmor. Look at the runes around the outside. I know you inspected this briefly before sending it on to me. You concluded this was, in fact, the work of a goddess, yes?"

"Yes, Virkonna's handiwork, quite clearly," Voria allowed. "Where are you going with this?"

"Well, you'd expect Mother to be just a tad bit more interested in a magical binding that could prove that her greatest rival's new alloy was unsafe. Even the spell itself should have fascinated her." He set the bracelet down and leaned in to the screen. "She showed no interest. None. Then she had a meeting with Skare, and ever since, she's refused to see me. All of her resources have been placed at Skare's disposal."

"What?" Voria blinked several times. "She'd never allow him control of so much as a single mage, much less her entire armada."

"Finally." Kazon leaned back, and breathed out through his nostrils. It calmed him, the idea that he might have a real ally. "You begin to see why I'm concerned. This metal isn't safe. But it is very, very lucrative and somehow Skare has won Jolene over."

Voria tapped her lip absently with a finger. Her eyes took on a faraway look, and Kazon had the impression she was using some sort of ability. Her eyes snapped back into focus, then landed on him. "You were right to contact me. We very nearly approached the Inurans to cleanse the *Spellship*, instead of bringing it to Shaya. I don't know what Skare is planning, but I do know that his magical defenses, those preventing me from seeing his possibilities, were erected by a god. He's working with someone. Krox, or Nefarius, or a player we haven't met."

"So you agree that I'm right to be alarmed?" Kazon asked. He needed to hear it.

"Yes." She gave a tight nod. "And you need to get out of

there, Kazon. You're likely to be their next target, the very instant they realize you mean to oppose them. Something they can detect easily via scrying."

He shook his head slowly as he considered the implications. "I can't leave. Not yet. There's a lot I can do with just a few more days, things that might salvage a little if it turns out I am right about Mother. I've been slowly moving resources, but I need more time. Besides, I'm close to puzzling out Inura's whereabouts. I think so, anyway."

"Inura?" There was a single moment of incredible excitement, then Voria straightened and took on what he was beginning to call older-sister face. "Kazon, not even locating a god is worth losing you. If you stay and fight, or even stay and gather, you run the risk of being captured. If they turned Jolene, they can turn you. We've seen what Nebiat can do. I don't know what Skare's involved in, but binding is nothing to toy with. Get out, brother."

"As soon as I safely can." He touched the screen. "Be safe, sister."

The screen went dark. He needed to move quickly, before Skare finished consolidating power.

LEVEL 28

A wave of dust washed through the bright corridor as the tunnel collapsed behind them. Aran waited for that dust to settle, then removed his helmet. The seal hissed open and his eyes adjusted to the bright halogens above. The corridor reeked of smoke, and less pleasant things.

He turned to Tharn, who still wore her silvery armor. "I know you aren't military, but do you have any idea how they might react to our presence? Or what the layout of this facility might be?"

Before the archeologist could answer, heavy, booted footsteps sounded on the metal walkway. They were moving double time, and he counted a half dozen sets. Marines, most likely. Aran turned to the company. "Lower your weapons and get your helmets off."

One by one, the squad did exactly that. Tharn was the last to remove hers, and a wry grin creased her age-spotted face. "I like being the one doing the observing. Keeping my helmet on lets me do that. But, I suppose if you kids can do it I can too."

Crewes popped his faceplate and loomed over the reporter. "Oh, we're kids, are we?" He grabbed one of her drones and crumpled it between his armored hands. Then he seized the other one and peered into the lens. "How many of these things you got? 'Cause every time you address the LT as kid, I'm gonna crush another one."

A squad of soldiers in olive uniforms sprinted into view. They minimized their profile against the walls, and moved with the kind of impressive skill he'd come to expect from Ternus Marines. He recognized their rifles as the same ones Davidson and his men used. They were fully automatic, though he had no idea how many rounds each magazine held.

"Identify yourself," a harsh feminine voice barked.

"We're Aran's Outriders, contracted by Admiral Nimitz," Aran called out. He took a cautious step closer to the Marines. "Looks like you guys had some Krox tunneling into the facility, so we decided to show them out before introducing ourselves."

"Excuse me," Tharn's voice rang out. She walked boldly up the corridor, and the drone Crewes was holding strained to follow her. He raised an eyebrow, and Aran nodded. Crewes released the drone, and it zipped after the reporter. "Captain? Or Sergeant or whatever, surely you recognize me. I can vouch for these people. Turn on Channel 1 and you'll see exactly why you want to take these people to your commander immediately."

The Marine she was speaking too, an impressively muscled woman in her mid-twenties, reached into her pocket and withdrew one of the portable comms Pickus used. She tapped the screen, and a moment later a holographic image sprang up over the device.

"Holy crap," Bord called. He hurried over to the

Marines, who snapped their rifles to their shoulders. Bord stopped and raised his hands. "Hey there, fellas, no need to get testy. I just want to see the footage. That's me and my girl looking all heroic-like."

The Marines lowered their weapons, so Aran approached as well. The woman leading the squad wore lieutenant's bars, making her his rank equivalent. Well his confederate rank anyway. He could probably call himself a captain, or whatever else he wanted to now.

"This is you guys?" the woman looked up at Aran's face, her hard eyes bathed in the glow of the hologram.

"Yeah." He nodded, then jerked a thumb over his shoulder at Kheross. "That's the dragon."

Her face went white. "You brought a...dragon into Fort Crockett?"

"Yeah, but he's our dragon," Aran pointed out. "Trust me when I say we're going to need him if you want anyone in this facility to survive the next few days."

"We've done all right so far." The woman's jaw tightened. Aran's gaze flicked to the name stenciled on her uniform. Hernandez. "This is the first breach we've had."

"Did you not joost see that missive thing?" Kez stabbed an armored finger at the hologram. "We wiped out hundreds of corpses, and the Wyrms they'd have sent up that tunnel. If they'd gotten in what was your plan? Shoot them with little pieces of metal? What do you think that's going to do?"

Aran raised a hand and the fiery drifter subsided. "Would you be willing to take us to your leadership? I can share our intel, and they can decide if or how they'd like to use my company. Sound good?"

Hernandez nodded. "Fine by me."

"Sir," a stocky man hissed at Hernandez. The muscles in

his arms were taut, as if he were still ready to fight. "We sure we want to allow these people in wearing their armor? Shouldn't we ask them to remove it?"

She shook her head slightly. "If they wanted to use that armor, they could do it right now. There isn't anything between them and command that would stop them." She turned back to Aran. "Follow me. And please don't mention the dragon until I deposit you with high command."

Hernandez moved up the corridor, and Aran followed. The rest of the company fell into his wake, and Hernandez's squad fell in behind them. The tension thickened as they walked, and Aran wished he could think of something to say that might break it.

It took several minutes and many corridors to reach a thirty-meter-wide blast door. Four turrets lined the roof over it, and while Aran couldn't identify the caliber they fired, he was willing to bet he wouldn't enjoy being hit by them.

Hernandez stepped forward and spoke to a camera set between the turrets. "Sir, we've discovered the source of the incursion. Request permission to bring 'Aran's Outriders' down to level 28."

The camera whirred, and the door began to rise. It exposed a lift with a latticed metal floor. He peeked between the cracks as he stepped on, and saw a shaft descending into the darkness. It extended at least a kilometer, if he was judging the perspective correctly.

"Who are you bringing us to meet?" Aran asked Hernandez.

She eyed him with an unreadable expression for several moments before speaking. "We're bringing you to meet the joint chiefs and the governor herself."

"We met a governor back on Marid," Bord piped up. "So she's the leader o' the whole planet then?"

"Kind of." Hernandez's tone made no move to disguise her impatience. She slapped a button inside the door, and the lift began to descend. It picked up speed as it fell, and numbers began to flash by on the wall.

"How do you get oxygen down here?" Aran asked. "We're inside a mountain, right?"

Hernandez gave a put upon sigh. "I'm not a tech. There are airshafts, but I don't know how they work. They're too small to be used tactically."

Aran very much doubted that. They might be too small for a person, but a Krox could employ any number of magical options to exploit a very confined space. He made a mental note to speak to the governor about it, assuming he was given a chance to speak.

Numbers continued to whir by until they hit the 20s, then the lift slowed. It stopped next to a faint, stenciled 28 on a blast door that mirrored the one they'd entered through above. The door slid up to expose a heavily fortified position. Sandbags were piled around a trio of turrets, with Marines using the sandbags for cover. The turrets appeared to be fixed emplacements, but he'd guess the Marines were added after the fact.

A hard-eyed man in an olive uniform stepped out from an emplacement. He had an assault rifle trained on Aran, but his finger wasn't on the trigger. "Remove your armor, and lay your weapons against the rear wall."

"Do it," Aran ordered. He sketched a sigil with his thumb and slid out the back of his spellarmor. Aran reached into his void pocket and withdrew his sword, then turned to the man who'd spoken. "Is it all right if I bring this? If we get jumped by Krox I don't like the idea of being unarmed."

"No weapons," the man snapped. His eyes narrowed, and he very deliberately slid his finger over the trigger.

"Fair enough." Aran put Narlifex back in the void pocket, then walked slowly to the edge of the lift.

The rest of the squad exited their armor, all except for Tharn, who apparently considered herself exempt. Once they'd finished, they moved off the lift and onto level 28. The Marines behind the barricades didn't at all share Hernandez's relaxed stance, and covered Aran as they moved up a narrow corridor.

The entire ceiling was lined with heavily armored turrets, each of which swiveled in their direction. He paused for a moment when he sensed a whiff of...*fire* magic? "Are we being scryed?" He turned to Hernandez.

"I guess." She shrugged. "There are magical scanners, but I don't know how they work. You do see the tag on the shoulder, right? You get that I'm a Marine, not a scientist?" Her words were sharp, but there was no real heat to them. A couple of her squad members laughed.

"LT ain't no scientist, either," Crewes pointed out. He moved to stand next to Hernandez, who sized him up like a slab of beef. Crewes seemed oblivious to her attention. "He's a war mage and a leader. He thinks about problems before they happen. Seems like there might be a lesson you could maybe learn here."

"Yeah?" Hernandez looked up at him with grin. "Maybe you'll have to tutor me. I'm a slow learner."

Bord opened his mouth to say something, but Kezia elbowed him in the ribs and he fell silent with a grunt.

The corridor dumped them into a wide conference room dominated by an oval table. About thirty people were seated around it, most wearing the business suits he'd come to associate with their merchant class. There were also a few Inuran outfits, probably those who held some sort of allegiance to the Consortium. Only three men wore olive uniforms, and Aran recognized the one he'd guess was in charge.

"Admiral Nimitz." Aran inclined his head at the grizzled man. He had spoken to him since resigning on Shaya. "Voria sends her regards."

"'Course she does." He rolled his eyes, then spat suddenly to the side of the table. "I notice she ain't here though, is she?"

Aran suppressed a sigh. This was going to be fun.

36

GENOCIDE

The first day was the hardest for Nara. The *Talon* had a pair of cells tucked under the crew quarters, but they'd never had to imprison anybody and so she'd never even seen the cells until being locked in one. She'd briefly considered lying about the *Talon*'s location, but not giving that particular bit of information was a route to a speedy execution.

Nebiat hadn't even bothered to inspect the vessel herself, instead placing Frit in charge and going back to her own ship. She had dispatched Kaho to serve as an advisor, but from the little Nara had overheard he had even less love for Nebiat than she did, so perhaps Nebiat had assigned him as a way of eliminating multiple problems at once.

Hours passed in silence and gave Nara the one thing she least wanted. More time to think. Her only solace was her new-old suit. She spent hours practicing its uses, and relearning everything it could do. The suit was impressive, and allowed her to go invisible at will while using almost no magical energy. That alone made the suit invaluable, but there were a number of other toys that proved equally impressive.

Most of those were through the visor, and included pierce invisibility, but also technological toys like the ability to see heat signatures through walls. The combination made the suit devastatingly effective, and she could already envision uses for it in the field.

Her reverie was finally broken when she heard three sets of footsteps approach down the wide curving ramp that led into the brig. The first figure to appear was Frit, still carrying Nara's staff. Her fiery hair had been bound into a simple ponytail, and the chrome ring Frit had used to bind it glowed orange from the heat.

Behind Frit came Kaho, and then a few paces behind both was Fritara, her hand wrapped around the hilt of her spellblade. Frit and Kaho were chatting together in low tones, and something Kaho said made Frit laugh and… blush? That was new. Fritara eyed both with intense dislike, and she stalked into the brig after them while she glared her hatred.

Frit looked up at Nara, and her eyes softened. It comforted Nara more than she'd ever be able to express. "I'm sorry we left you down here for so long."

Frit approached the bars, and Kaho moved to stand next to her. Fritara approached, but stood a little distance away. Nara badly wanted to know why she was here, but of course couldn't ask in front of her.

"What are you going to do with me?" Nara asked.

"May I?" Kaho turned to Frit to ask permission, and Frit nodded. "My mother departed, and while we have been given a task to fulfill, the manner we choose is up to us. That means we can utilize the tools available to us, and you are one of the most potent. This vessel is another."

"Thank you for that," Frit interjected. "I know you didn't have to tell us about the *Talon*."

Nara took a deep breath. Her patience was non-existent, and she couldn't allow it to make her say something stupid. "You'd have found out anyway. So, are you letting me out of this cell?"

"Conditionally." Frit withdrew a red-gold necklace forged from *spirit* and *earth* sigils. "After discussing it with the crew, we've decided that we can only let you out if you're properly bound. You'll need to wear this. No one will make you do anything, and we won't give you unrealistic orders, but we want the ability to control you if we have to."

"Speak for yourself," Fritara snapped. She moved to stand next to the bars. "I will make you do whatever I need done, whenever I need it done. And Rita might too. It's time you had a little taste of what it's like to be a slave."

"Fritara." Frit's tone was dangerous. "I said it above, but let me repeat this for your benefit. If you harm Nara, then you and I are going to exchange more than harsh words. She is my sister, too, and she's cooperating. And Nebiat placed me in charge, not you."

"Why she placed a traitor in charge I'll never know." Fritara frowned darkly. "You think the only woman to ever take pity on or help us is some sort of demon. Why can't you accept that she wants to help us?"

Kaho began a sharp, hissing laugh. "Ah, child, I do not mean to be patronizing, but you know far less of my mother than you think. She is quite capable of playing the magnanimous goddess, but I assure you that she will snuff you out like a candle when it is convenient. I've seen many of my siblings die, bartered away like scales in a Kem'Hedj match. It will be no different with you."

Fritara glared angrily from Kaho to Frit, and her mouth

worked silently. Then she spun on her heel and stalked back up the ramp.

"That one is going to be trouble," Kaho rumbled softly. "If you were wise you'd put an end to her now."

"I'm not going to kill a sister, even as one as annoying as Fritara." Frit sketched a sigil in front of the cell door, and the glowing bars winked out of existence. "In time she'll see reason, and if not, I'll deal with it. Here." She handed Nara her staff, which Nara accepted gratefully.

"Give me the collar?" Nara extended a hand, and Frit passed her the necklace. Nara clipped it around her neck, and the instant it snapped shut she felt a tingling across her entire body. It was like being stuffed into a shirt that was a size too small, except she felt it over her entire body. She blinked up at Frit. "My gods, this is awful. I'm so sorry you had to deal with this for so long, Frit."

"It can be...worse." Frit bit her lip, and for a moment she was the scared student Nara had met back on Shaya. "If you need to talk, let me know. Once you've proved yourself I'll make a case for removing the collar."

"Okay." Nara nodded. "So what now?"

Frit squared her shoulders, and seemed to be seeking strength. "Now we go to Colony 3, and we murder an entire world."

37

TRAITOR

Voria had the bridge to herself for the first time in weeks. Pickus had busied himself coordinating the drifters and their complement of tech mages. They weren't anything resembling a fighting force, but they could become that given time and attention.

She raised a hand and willed the bridge to shift back to its natural state. The *Wyrm Hunter* vanished, replaced by a large room with sigil-covered walls. The whole place still filled her with awe, as it had quite clearly been constructed by someone whose understanding of both magic and technology far outstripped her own.

"Are you going to do something cool?" Ikadra piped up in the corner, where she'd set him upon entering the room.

"I hope so." She turned in a slow circle. "You might be able to help with that. I'm told I can use a temporal matrix to enhance my godsight, and I want to inspect the possibilities around this world and other key targets."

"That's why gods have such an advantage. They cheat." His tone was all proud parent, a tone he adopted whenever she'd done something clever. "Simply using your ability in this room will tap into the latent power of the matrix. When it was designed, the thought was that the user should be able to keep their mind free to focus on the possibilities. I don't know, though. It means the matrix sees you all the time." His voice dropped to a conspiratorial whisper. "Like when you touch yourself."

Voria snorted, but managed not to laugh.

"Yes, well then." She cleared her throat, then closed her eyes.

A rainbow of light danced at the edges of her vision, endless reflections of possible futures. She saw people on this world growing prosperous. She saw them die from a mysterious plague. She saw them live, and thrive, and conquer the entire sector. She saw their world detonate, destroyed by the foul magic of Krox. It spun on and on in countless directions, and she struggled to hold on to any single possibility.

Navigating the flow was harder than it had been on her own. There were more possibilities, and they stretched further. To utilize this, she'd need to learn to follow a specific possibility to its logical conclusion. Unfortunately, there was no manual on doing so, and Ikadra had been remarkably little help beyond 'fluffing her ego' as the Ternus governor had said.

Voria started with places, rather than people. She quested through the sea of realities around New Texas, and saw a hundred ways the battle might end. Then she shifted to Ternus, but there was nothing to suggest a Krox attack. No possibility where Nebiat breached their defenses.

Finally she looked at Colony 3, and her blood ran cold. A Fissure opened, and some sort of probe emerged. So did a cloaked vessel, but the dozens of scans run by the Ternus defenders didn't detect it. She quickly realized why.

A glittering ship appeared in orbit, its golden hull unmistakable. She was looking at the *Talon*, undoubtedly piloted by Nara. After a few moments a spray of missiles shot from the cargo bay, and spread out to descend to different points across the planet.

Each missile detonated, and a wave of grey-green, magical death swept across the world. All living things died, right down to the bacteria in the soil. In one instant, Nara murdered an entire world.

Voria forced her breathing to calm. She could feel her heart racing, and the anger clouding her vision. It was vital she remain detached. There was one other route she needed to investigate, particularly in light of the information about Nara destroying Colony 3.

She thought of Nebiat, and began navigating through a sea of possibilities that stretched in many directions. Almost instantly something bright exploded in her head, and she lost vision in her right eye for several moments. When it returned, it brought a spike of pain with it. She disconnected, and cradled her head in both hands.

"What happened?" Ikadra oozed concern.

"I—well, I'm not certain, honestly." She blinked away the worst of the pain, and focused on Ikadra. It took several more moments than it should have. "I ran into something I couldn't see. It was...blocked somehow."

"Oh shit." Ikadra's sapphire pulsed very rapidly. "Did your head get all explode-y, and if so, what were you thinking about when it happened?"

"Yes, quite." She rubbed her temples, then looked up. "I was trying to think of Nebiat when it happened."

"I'd test it a few more times, but if you keep running into blocks, that suggests someone with some serious mojo doesn't want you to know what's going on with her."

"Hmm." She channeled a bit of *life* and the pain subsided. "I'll forgo immediate testing, but I strongly suspect that's what I encountered. Someone is hiding the Krox plan, perhaps Teodros himself."

"Well, that sucks." Ikadra pulsed forlornly. "I was hoping we'd get somewhere."

"I was fighting and winning battles long before I could perceive the omniverse." Voria rolled her shoulders, and picked up the staff. "All it means is that we must proceed with what I did forage. Colony 3 is going to be attacked, and I think we have time to do something about it."

She didn't mention that she'd seen Nara.

Voria strode over to the little folding desk Pickus had set up. Something he called a 'sticky note' was attached to the screen. It read, 'push and say your name'. She depressed the button on the little black comm unit the note was affixed to, and the screen lit up.

"Majo—no, Colonel Voria, to speak with Ternus—"

The machine cut her off. "Thank you, *Majo—no, Colonel Voria*. The meeting organizer will join the quantum call shortly. Would you like to use the ambient audio or an external device?"

"I'm an external device!" Ikadra piped up, sapphire flashing excitedly. "Use me for audio, and I'll relay the feed to Majo here."

"Ambient audio is fine." Voria overrode Ikadra with a threatening look.

A moment later she was saved from further awkwardness when the screen resolved into Fleet Admiral Kerr's face. "Ah, Fleet Admiral. I wasn't certain I could get this device to function."

"Glad to see one of the most powerful mages in the sector figured out a basic comm." He didn't bother to hide his amusement. "So what did you want to speak with me about? Or is this something best discussed in person?"

"I think this device is fine." She considered her words carefully, in case she was wrong. "I've performed an augury, and I know where the Krox are likely to strike next. You were right about Colony 3." The risk of someone eavesdropping was outweighed by the gravity of the situation. "Worse, I identified one of our vessels there. We had a defector recently, a true mage of some strength."

Kerr removed his cap, and seemed to age years in seconds. "Are you talking about Private Nara? The same woman who saved Marid?" He scratched under his beard. "Doesn't wash. If she were a spy, she'd never have completed that ritual in the first place."

"Yes, a question I've been turning over as well," Voria admitted. "I don't understand, unless she was recently bound and we were unaware of it. So far as I know there was no opportunity for that to occur, and even if there were, the girl has strong mental defenses. Quite frankly, Fleet Admiral, I don't know why she did what she did. But the fact remains that Colony 3 is under imminent threat, and if you do not arrive quickly and in force you will lose that world."

Kerr's face fell. "We've gotten word that New Texas isn't faring well. They can't survive without reinforcements. Are you telling me that we need to abandon them?"

"Not at all." Voria's mouth firmed into a determined line. "I will take the *Spellship* to New Texas, and I will break that siege, so long as you can reinforce Colony 3 as quickly as possible. Remember that Nara can cloak the *Talon*."

Kerr nodded gratefully. "My thanks, Colonel. I'll speak to the governor and get things in motion. We're not totally defenseless against invisibility, and should be able to catch them when they come through the Fissure. Godspeed."

As the scry-screen went black Voria was left with a lingering doubt. Who had obscured the timeline around Nebiat? Clearly they wanted her at New Texas, and had ensured she'd be there. It smelled like a trap, but she had no idea where that trap lay. Who was manipulating events so deftly?

Soon she'd know, one way or the other. And she had a feeling she wouldn't very much like the results.

38

BAD NEWS

Aran let his gaze roam the assembled Ternus leadership. There was a good deal of fear, but not the wild-eyed kind that led to panic. These people knew they were in deep, but still thought maybe they could swim with the current. He needed to know if that was false bravado, or if they actually had a chance.

"Admiral," Aran began, interrupting Nimitz's string of insults aimed at Voria and the confederacy in general, "the Krox aren't going to react kindly to my company punching through their lines. They'll be on us, and soon. Respectfully, we need to get this place situated. Now."

Nimitz's jaw clicked shut and a vein throbbed in his temple. Aran got the sense the man wasn't used to being interrupted, by anyone. "Son, if we weren't at war—"

A tall, dark, mahogany-skinned woman rose at the far end of the table. Her dark hair was pulled into a smooth ponytail, and she wore one of the elaborate suits, complete with the rope around the neck. Why you'd voluntarily pre-tie a noose around your own neck remained a mystery to Aran.

He noticed that every last person at the table deferred to the woman. Even Tharn adopted a respectful stance, the first he'd seen from the grizzled reporter.

"May I have the floor, Admiral?" the woman asked in a clipped drawl. It was similar to Davidson's, but more refined.

"'Course, Governor Bhatia." Nimitz tipped an imaginary hat in her direction. His expression hardened again when it fell on Aran.

The governor licked her lips, and the instant she spoke he understood why these people showed her such deference. "We are in an unprecedented crisis. If the Krox seize this room, they not only co-opt our leadership, but they also gain control of enough weaponry to end all life on this world. Our own forces are insufficient to stop them. Since conventional arms have failed us, our only option is the arcane. We may not understand magic, Admiral Nimitz, but in this we do not need to. This man kills binders. Our people saw that on Marid. They saw it on Shaya. They saw it on Virkonna. Now, he fights on our world. The decision is yours, of course, but I would highly recommend deferring to this young man's wisdom." She raised an expectant eyebrow at Nimitz.

Nimitz gave the world's most put upon sigh, then frowned at Aran. "You're a damned fine soldier, I get that. Davidson wouldn't shut up about that. But I ain't seen any real proof that you can lead, and that scares the piss right outta me. Save our asses, son, and I'll be gods-damned grateful."

"Excellent." The governor seized control of the conversation once more. She stepped from the table and glided gracefully toward a holomap dominating one corner of the room. The governor extended a long finger to spin the map, then she faced Aran. "As you can see, we're on the 28th level of this facility. The Krox will need to penetrate each successive level of security, but if they do so, eventually they will reach us here. There is nowhere else to run. No secret tunnel out of the mountain. The battle will come down to this room, and both sides know it."

Aran walked to the hologram and extended an experimental hand. He moved the image, and was pleased to see it responded just like a spell might have. He zoomed it outwards to show the entire facility. "These narrow lines, what are they?" A trio of white lines paralleled most of the areas of each level.

"Ventilation shafts," Nimitz called. He rose from the table and approached the hologram. "That's our air, son. We've got two levels of filters. The first are more conventional. The second are from the Inurans. Consortium claims they'll clean any magical toxin, and the salesman was real convincing. You think they'll work, or should we consider that a point of failure?"

"They'll work," Aran allowed. The Consortium did fine work, as his armor attested. "But that doesn't mean they can't still be exploited. *Air* magic will allow someone to become gaseous. A binder could send minions through there, and they could burst out wherever you've got a vent."

"LT's right," Crewes boomed. He approached the hologram. "I saw some on the way in. Wights. Nasty critters. Incorporeal, so you can't hurt 'em with normal weapons. You've got to use magic, though fire can put the hurt on 'em too. You got any flamethrowers? Please tell me you got flamethrowers."

"Admiral?" Bhatia turned to Nimitz, who stood with his arms folded.

"Only a handful." He gave a frustrated sigh. "Son, I'm going to level with you. We got caught with our pants down.

When the Krox hit the system, we had no idea how quickly they'd make atmo, or that they even knew this facility existed. We had three hours notice, which was just enough time to call in a battalion of Marines. We've got plenty of ordnance, and years of food, but not enough men to hold the line."

Aran considered that. He studied the hologram again, taking in the entire facility. "The good news about wights is that they can't inflict mischief, as they can only affect living tissue. The first thing I'd suggest doing is pulling back all living squads, and relying on automated defenses on all levels above this one." He turned back to the admiral. "I realize that may sound extreme and that we're effectively ceding 27 levels, but if we're short on troops we can't protect that much ground."

The Admiral gave a sharp nod. "Sound logic, son."

"Can we expect any relief from Ternus?" Aran asked.

"Possibly," the governor ventured. "Ternus is not so immune to politics as we appear, and there's bad blood between New Texas and the capital."

"Bullshit," the admiral snapped. "That's not enough to keep them from riding to our rescue. That ain't the real worry. They'll send relief, unless they believe there's an assault coming on Ternus, or on Colony 3."

"Colony 3?" Aran asked.

"It's the breadbasket of Ternus, of the sector really," Bhatia explained. "Eighty percent of our food comes from Colony 3, and that percentage is higher on the capital. If it were assaulted, Ternus would have no choice but to respond, so I believe they will wait to commit their forces until they ascertain the extent of the invasion."

"Do you have a way to communicate with ships in orbit?" Aran stroked his beard as he studied the map. "If we can't get immediate support, maybe Davidson can keep the pressure on their fleet."

Nimitz turned to one of the techs hovering around the edge of the room. "Get Davidson on the line."

"Yes, sir." The olive-uniformed tech snapped a tight salute, then punched away at a datapad. A second hologram sprang up, this one directly over the table. It showed the *Wyrm Hunter*'s command bridge, with Davidson staring out from the command matrix.

"Captain Davidson," Nimitz rumbled. He leaned closer to the image. "Can you give us your current fleet disposition? What are those scaly bastards up to?"

"Sir, it looks like they're concentrating all ground forces around Fort Crockett. Their orbital defenses have taken up position around it, and appear ready to respond if we make a play." Davidson's face fell. "I've also got some bad news, sir."

"Don't keep me in suspense, son."

Davidson looked uncomfortable. "Sir, we've got intel that Colony 3 is going to be hit. The capital just issued an eyes only priority one that we're responding with full force. The primary kill target is the *Talon*, sir."

Aran's grip tightened around Narlifex's hilt. Nara was working with the Krox?

"Has Ree heard?" Aran asked, though in his heart he knew she already had. That was why she wasn't on the bridge with Davidson.

"I'm sorry, man." Davidson shook his head. "She took every last spellfighter and headed for Colony 3. We're down to the *Wyrm Hunter* and a few surviving platforms up here. We can keep their air in line, but there's no way we can reach you on the ground. You're on your own."

Aran nodded. He looked around the assembled faces,

and saw realization dawning on many. They were starting to understand how unlikely it was that any of them would survive. This was the moment when each would be tested. He couldn't change that, but he could offer a little help. Seeing a leader would give these people hope.

He shrugged as if Davidson had just related an incoming storm instead of their almost certain deaths. "It is what it is. If those bastards want this room, it's going to cost them—I can promise you that. Send word if Voria contacts us. We've got a lot of work down here to do in the meantime." He turned to the admiral. "Permission to set up some defenses, sir?"

"Granted, son. Save our gods-damned bacon."

39

THE PRICE

The door hissed shut behind Skare, sealing him inside Jolene's office. A week ago he'd have considered this hostile territory. Now, it was the abode of his closest ally.

"Skare." Jolene inclined her head, then rose from behind the desk. She approached until she stood within easy reach, and offered a tentative smile. "I'm ready."

"No, you aren't. I cannot stress this enough, Jolene." Skare rested his hand on the matron's shoulder, and was pleased she accepted the gesture. His old rival would have recoiled, or possibly attacked. "Talifax isn't like anyone, or anything, you have ever met. He could snuff one or both of us like candles."

Jolene laughed derisively, then raised her hands to take in her office. "We are in the most heavily warded room in the sector. I don't care who this Talifax thinks he is. He—"

Skare froze. The temperature had dropped several degrees, and the tiny hairs on his arms were standing up in a terrifyingly familiar way. Talifax had arrived. Skare knew how heady the blood was, and hoped that Jolene possessed the good sense not to challenge a demigod.

"Please, do not let me interrupt," rumbled a voice from the shadows. A patch of darkness obscured Talifax. Interesting. It appeared he was unwilling to reveal himself fully to Jolene. "You were saying that you did not care who I believe myself to be."

Jolene's jaw worked, and for the first time Skare experienced a small swell of pity for an opponent. He remembered the terror when he'd discovered that Talifax could completely ignore wards. It was impossible to forget the bloom of horror, the knowledge that all your power and magic meant nothing. That they were wayward children who'd finally met an adult.

"I apologize, mighty Talifax," Jolene managed in a near whisper. Her face had gone nearly bloodless, and her eyes were fixed on the darkness in the corner. "Please excuse my arrogance."

"Skare tells me that you have been converted to our cause." Talifax spoke as if Jolene hadn't. "I have come to ascertain the truth of this. If I find that he is incorrect, your existence will end." Skare hated that emotionless voice, so calm and measured. He had no doubt Talifax could and would do exactly as promised.

"Of course, Master. I—what do you wish to know?" She returned to her seat and folded her hands in her lap, probably aiming for meek. Even now, she couldn't disguise her eagerness, though to be fair Skare hadn't been able to either when he'd been in the same situation.

Jolene's body shot suddenly into the air, and her arms and legs bent backward as her body went rigid. Skare detected a wave of magic emanating from the darkness. The spell contained all eight aspects, though *spirit* was the strongest in this case. A binding of some form? Did he bear a similar one?

Her body slumped back into the chair. She shivered violently, and her pupils were nearly wide enough to swallow the entire eye. Skare edged a bit further away from her.

The darkness vanished, revealing Talifax's dark grey armor, and too-thick limbs.

"There is no deception in you." Talifax took a step closer, looming over both of them. "You will sacrifice anything to achieve your goals. That is good. I can offer you power and immortality."

"What will this cost me?" Jolene whispered. She stared up at Talifax adoringly.

"Your son is a threat. He represents a possibility I have not foreseen." Talifax frowned. "Capture him, and bring him to me so that I might unravel his mind and find out who is tugging his thread. Almost, I believe it must be Neith."

"Of course, Master." Jolene bowed low. "I will have him subdued and brought before you immediately."

40

WIGHTS

Aran knelt to inspect the drone. It was nothing more than two barrels bolted onto a squat frame. One barrel fired conventional rounds, and the other, fatter nozzle fired a thick sheet of flame. They had two dozen of the boxy little contraptions, which was enough to cover about 70% of the vents in the command bunker itself.

That left the vents in the corridor outside exposed, and several near the doors leading inside. They'd arrayed the Marines around those weaker points, each armed with a backpack attached to a portable flamethrower. Each heavy Marine was protected by a squad armed with more conventional rifles, though Aran noted each had one of the heavy pistols belted to their thigh as well. Those would probably be of more use when it came to close quarters. And it would.

"Crewes, I need you, Bord, and Kezia to reinforce the Marines holding the room itself." Aran nodded toward the blast doors at the end of the corridor. "Kheross and I will help the Marines at the base of the elevator shaft. If we have to fall back we're going to need you guys in a hurry. Nothing gets through that door."

Crewes gave a broad smile. "I got a real special surprise for anything that comes through that door. Spoilers, it ain't a fucking surprise. It's *fire*. Lots and lots of *fire*."

"I almost feel bad for those wights." Aran clapped his friend on the shoulder, then strode back up the corridor to inspect the defenses near the lift itself. There were some positives, at least. The Krox could only come at them down the shaft itself, which let them set up an easy kill zone. The barrel of every rifle and every turret already pointed directly at the door. Anything vulnerable to conventional ordnance was going to die quickly.

"Kheross?" Aran called to the Wyrm. He stood inside the lift itself, staring up into the shaft.

"Can you feel their approach?" The dark-haired man rumbled.

Aran stepped onto the lift and followed Kheross's gaze. The shaft disappeared up into the unrelieved darkness. He couldn't see anything, but Kheross was right. Something... sang in the distance. A potent, many-layered power he was familiar with.

"That's *void* magic. A lot of it." He cocked his head. "I've felt something similar before, at the Skull of Xal. Demons."

"You sound surprised." Kheross eyed him with mild interest.

"The Krox use *spirit* magic. *Earth* sometimes. We don't often see *void*." Aran's hand fell instinctively to Narlifex as he assessed the strength of the approaching magic. Narlifex thrummed in greeting.

"A wise mage harnesses all eight aspects as quickly as they are able," Kheross offered. He returned to staring up at the darkness. "Evolve past your enemies, and they will move to counter who you were, not who you are. You said that, or a future version of you, anyway."

It chilled Aran that there was this whole other version of him, one that had apparently lived centuries and helped to define an entire culture. Right now, though, he was more concerned about the approaching enemy. "I don't know a lot about demons, beyond that they don't go down easily. Any advice we can offer our allies?"

"Stay out of the way and pray for the best?" Kheross gave a half smirk. "You and I both know these tiny men will be as saplings against the ferocity of the storm about to crash over us. They may distract a stray attack, but I expect little else."

Aran glanced at the hard-eyed Marines behind the barricades. "I think they might surprise you. Magic is powerful, but there's a reason that the Krox haven't been able to conquer Ternus yet."

"Let's pray you are right." Kheross tensed. "Our enemy is nearly upon us."

Aran could feel the *void* magic growing closer. He darted back off the lift and spun to face the Marines, "Don't be shy about explosive rounds. Overwhelming force."

Marines moved smoothly into position, and the action of multiple rifles sounded in quick succession as the soldiers prepared themselves. Aran rolled into position behind a pile of sandbags, and waited.

Inhuman screams split the silence, their otherworldly wails echoing from the very walls around them. The scream passed down the corridor, the terrible sound moving steadily toward the command bunker itself. Aran tensed, but resisted the urge to sprint into the bunker and help. He needed to trust his people. Crewes would deal with the wights there. He was needed here, to hold the line.

"Brace yourselves," Aran roared. He reached into his

void pocket and withdrew his rifle.

One of the vents on the wall to his right burst open, and a pallid, grey fog boiled out. It strongly resembled the breath weapons they'd seen the Krox use, but the breath coalesced into a rough human outline, a ghostly woman of exquisite beauty.

Her eyes were utterly devoid of color, holes in reality that led into the depths themselves. A chill passed over Aran, and he grew numb as he met that gaze. He was dimly aware of the magic the wight used, some sort of paralysis designed to slow him long enough for it to make a kill.

The wight lunged suddenly, its ghostly form melting into an ancient hag with cracked, weathered skin. She slashed at him with wicked claws, and he leapt backwards at the last instant.

The wight seemed surprised, and he capitalized on that. Aran snapped his spellrifle to his shoulder, and filled the weapon with *fire*. A glowing, orange ball the size of his head streaked into the creature's face, and the parts of the creature that came in contact dissolved into dense, black smoke.

Aran smiled grimly and fired a level one fire bolt at the creature's chest. A ghostly shriek echoed down the corridor as the creature broke apart, then dissolved entirely.

"Guess *fire* does work," he called to Kheross as he pivoted to find another target.

Wights burst from many vents at once, a dozen or more attacking Marines up and down the corridor. Pandemonium broke out. Automatic weapons fire echoed up and down the corridor, drowning out all other sound, and filling it with the acrid odor of gunpowder and sweat. The bullets did nothing but ricochet off the walls—that, and fill the corridor with smoke that made the wights even more difficult to see.

A Marine with a flamethrower stepped up to a wight,

and aimed the barrel at its ghostly back. A sheet of orange-white flame engulfed the spectral creature, which fell back with an enraged cry. It flew back into the vent, disappearing from sight. The Marine stuck the nozzle into the vent, and unleashed another torrent of flame. The wight's death cry echoed through the walls.

Aran sighted down his scope at the next nearest wight. He gently stroked the trigger, and his chest tightened as more *fire* magic was pulled into the weapon. The level two fire bolt caught the wight where the chest would have been on a human. It shrieked, and then its energy dissipated. Much cleaner than the first kill.

"Crewes," Aran barked into the comm, "level two seems to be enough to one-shot these things."

"On it, LT," Crewes panted back. A moment later Crewes's laughter echoed from the other room. "Oh, yeah! Get some, you skinny bitches."

Danger. We. Kill. Now. Narlifex's voice pulsed in his mind. It was thick with battle rage, but tinged with caution too, a new emotion.

Aran spun to face the elevator shaft just as shadowy forms began landing around Kheross. They stood head and shoulders taller than Kheross, with thick arms, curved horns, and smoldering, purple eyes. The dark-skinned brutes looked a great deal like the tech demons he'd faced back at the Skull of Xal, though these wore battered armor that looked like it might have been stripped from tanks.

Kheross's axes materialized in his hands, and he began to dance. Demons swung at him with clawed hands, but he flowed around each strike, then delivered wicked counter attacks. The blows wounded the demons, but their armor and their own thick hides prevented any single strike from killing them.

Aran dumped his rifle back into his void pocket, then guided his spellarmor into a quick dash toward the corridor. He needed to trust Crewes to deal with the rest of the wights. If these demons made it past the lift the Marines wouldn't stand a chance.

"Hernandez," he roared over his shoulder. "If those things get past us, fall back to the bunker."

The dark-haired Marine gave a thumbs up, and then went back to firing from her position behind a pile of sandbags. She used a pistol, and at first Aran wondered why. Then he saw one of the tech demon's knees explode. The creature staggered, and Kheross decapitated it with a sudden strike.

Okay, he stood corrected. Maybe the Marines did stand a chance.

He drew Narlifex, and flew toward the demons. Several pivoted at his approach, their hungry eyes settling on him. Aran blurred forward, and dropped low at the last second. He braced Narlifex against his arm. "Burn them, bud."

Narlifex flared to blue-white brilliance, a hotter shade than he usually used. Aran accelerated and his momentum lent Narlifex incredible force. The blade quivered eagerly, then sheered through the closest demon's legs.

The suddenly legless demon toppled to the ground with a deafening roar. Three more leapt over its body. Aran rolled past the first, and slashed at its side. Narlifex cut through the demon's thick carapace, but the wound was superficial.

The second demon raised a rusted claymore, and brought the massive sword down on Aran. He was about to dodge, but the legless demon seized his ankle in a death grip, pinning him in place.

Aran snapped his spellshield into existence, and interposed it just in time to intercept the falling blade. The force of the blow knocked him to the floor of the lift, but his spell-armor protected him from the worst of it.

He filled his body with flame, enhancing his strength and speed. Aran whipped Narlifex around, and brought him down in a slash that hummed through the air. The blade sliced cleanly through the demon's wrist, and the claymore clattered to the deck. He reversed the stroke, and sliced off the arm pinning him in place.

Aran flipped to his feet and seized Narlifex with both hands. He had room to swing now, and he used it to full effect. He leapt into the air, dodging a slash from another demon.

Aran brought Narlifex's flaming blade plunging down at the handless demon. It brought its arm up to deflect the blow, but Narlifex crashed down on him like the judgement of the gods. It cut through the arm, through the demon's snarling face, and deep into its chest. Smoke billowed from the wound as Narlifex cauterized the demon's terrible flesh, but the demon was no longer in a position to feel anything.

"Outrider!" Kheross bellowed. The word was panicked.

Aran turned to see Kheross pinned to the deck under the weight of a half dozen demons. They swarmed him, biting and clawing at his scarlet armor. Had he not been in human form he probably could have dealt with them, but the lift was too small to accommodate a dragon's massive size. That left him vulnerable and the demons were taking full advantage.

Aran risked a quick glance up the corridor, and his heart sank. Nearly a quarter of the Marines were down and dying, and only a few resisted the remaining wights. Hernandez barked orders and was guiding the survivors toward the bunker.

41

HOLD THE LINE

Aran took a single moment to assess the organized retreat. Hernandez and her Marines were falling back in good order, and they were laying down withering suppressive fire that actually gave the demons pause. "Good gods, those Marines are tough."

Confident that the governor was protected, Aran sprinted toward the knot of demonic bodies obscuring Kheross from view. He infused his entire body with *air*, as he had when he'd killed Tobek. But this time Aran had spellarmor.

He grinned as the blue-white magic crackled around his armor. The glow intensified until Aran, his spellarmor, and Narlifex all became lightning. He grounded himself into the closest demonic bodies over Kheross, flowing between them in lethal arcs of pure *air*. Aran entered a demon's nostril, cooking its brain before flowing out its other nostril and toward the next target.

They screamed and beat at their faces, trying to cover orifices as Aran wove a deadly path through their ranks. He could feel the energy burning away, and knew he wouldn't be able to sustain it much longer. Aran released *air*, and hopped backward as he reached for his dwindling reserves of *fire*.

A jet of white flame rushed over the demons, blackening their armor and completing the work he'd already begun. All but one collapsed to the floor of the lift, and Kheross was already dealing with the final assailant. The Wyrm flipped to his feet, and his fist rocketed out, shattering the demon's spine just below the neck. Kheross threw it to the ground, then stomped on its skull with an armored boot.

"Eww." Aran winced as demon brain splattered his armor.

Something beyond conscious thought drew his attention, and he glanced up, into the darkness. In the distance, many floors above, Aran caught sight of a pair of violet eyes. They stared down at him, unblinking.

"Why isn't he attacking?" Aran muttered. He shifted into a defensive stance, but the figure above made no move to approach or to flee.

Kheross flicked ichor from his boot, and moved to stand next to Aran. He stared up into the darkness. "He isn't attacking because he wants you to chase him. He seeks to provoke you."

Aran nodded thoughtfully. "Makes sense. Bait me into following, so he can ambush me."

A rustling, like autumn leaves in Shaya's upper gardens, grew around them until it resolved into a voice, "If you followed me there would be no ambush, only an execution."

Aran couldn't help but laugh at that. "Man, I never get tired of the clichéd villain crap. You're a Krox, aren't you? I'd recognize that arrogance anywhere." He assumed the spell would allow the binder to hear them, or that he had some other way of listening. Clearly he must.

"I am no mere Krox. I am Arkelion, son of Drakkon," the voice whispered back. "I give you one day to regain your magic. One day to rest. Then I will return, and when I am finished no stone will be piled atop another. I will lay waste to this place, to you, and to any who remain."

"'Kay. We'll be here." Aran buckled Narlifex around his spellarmor, and by the time he glanced back up, the eyes were gone.

Kheross chuckled, shaking his head. "That was cruel. My kind pride themselves on our posturing, you know. Cutting him off like that will enrage him."

"That was the point. Our only hope is him overextending himself so we have a shot at taking him down." Aran turned wearily, and guided his spellarmor back up the hallway. A half dozen medics had already darted out and were pulling survivors to safety. Far too many men and women lay unmoving, most clustered around their machine gun emplacements. "Looks like Crewes and the others took care of the wights, at least."

He drifted up the hallway, and back into the command bunker itself. Crewes stood protectively inside the doorway, but stepped aside for Aran. "Those skinny pieces of shit burn like everything else. How'd it go on your end, LT?"

A shimmering, white ward blocked the rear half of the room, and Aran could see silhouettes behind it. Bord's work, almost certainly. He removed his helmet and brushed his hair out of his eyes. "I'm not sure. We dealt with the demons, but I get the sense this whole thing was just a test."

"You are not wrong about that." Kheross glanced nervously back through the doorway. "Some Wyrms, like me, are brash. We are an apex predator after all, and that lends itself to aggressive tactics. Yet others are more cautious. More practical. I believe we are dealing with the latter."

"That surprises me." Aran rested a hand on Narlifex's hilt, and the blade hummed. "Drakkon style is all about offense. This Arkelion guy said he's the son of Drakkon."

"That's the mountain-sized lizard on Marid, right, LT?" Crewes rested the barrel of his spellcannon on his shoulder, and followed Aran as he picked a path toward the ward. The walls he passed had all been scorched, and while there were fewer bodies in here they'd still clearly been hit hard. So many dead.

"Yeah, that's the one," he finally muttered.

"I am not familiar with Drakkon," Kheross ventured. "He sounds impressively powerful. Who is he?"

Aran paused, and turned to look back at Kheross. "I find it odd you haven't heard of him. Drakkon is the guardian of Marid, a goddess killed by Krox during the godswar."

Kheross merely shrugged. "Neither name is familiar."

Aran filed that fact away for later. If Kheross didn't know either, there was a high chance that both Marid and Drakkon were nothing but a memory in his timeline. It could be important, but not right now.

"Bord," Aran called as he approached the ward. "We're secure."

The shimmering, white ward winked out of existence, and revealed a placid governor and her aides. Only Nimitz wore his stress openly, which manifested as a vague aura of annoyance.

"And that's a wrap," Tharn's warm voice sounded from behind him, and Aran tensed, but didn't turn to face her. He'd forgotten that all this was being recorded, and if he turned, cameras would be waiting.

Aran again forgot all about the cameras when

Hernandez strode up to Crewes, and the sergeant fell back to chat with her. Something eased in his chest. Aran didn't know most of the Marines who'd died, but he'd spoken with this one, and knowing she lived helped somehow. The battle had cost them, but they'd held the line.

"Archeologist Tharn," the governor's imposing voice echoed through the room. "A word, please? Lieutenant Aran, would you join us as well?" She led them over to the far corner of the room, which was as isolated as they could get given the circumstances.

Aran risked a glance at Nimitz, and was unsurprised to see the admiral frowning in his direction. He wasn't sure why the governor had excluded him, but it seemed a tactical error.

"Our options," Governor Bhatia began, "are rather limited. We have no choice but to stay here, and try to live as long as possible. But that does not mean we are powerless. Tharn, presumably you recorded that last battle?"

"I was about to upload it." She nodded at the governor, showing none of the deference everyone else did. Tharn folded her arms. "What do you have in mind?"

"Before you do, I'd like you to interview some of the Marines for additional commentary. Pick people local to New Texas. Tell their stories." Bhatia's gaze shifted to Hernandez, who was giving the few surviving Marines orders. "Capture this. Show the world that we are still fighting, and show them we're making the Krox pay for every step they've taken. Show them we can resist, so that when our light here is extinguished, the rest of the sector will keep fighting."

42

COLONY 3

Frit turned a slow circle in the opulent room. A comfortable bed floated near one wall, a bed that she was able to sleep on without turning it to ash. The bed's internal magic seemed to prevent damage, and that meant that for the first time in her life Frit understood what it was like to sleep comfortably.

A full-length mirror sat against one wall, next to a large scry-screen. There was also a golden dresser with four drawers, but Frit hadn't touched it. It was full of the previous captain's belongings, and while Frit hadn't known Aran well, she knew enough to know that he was a good person. Still, she reminded herself, it wasn't as if she'd stolen the ship. Nara had done that.

"Frit?" Kaho's voice rumbled from the doorway. "We've reached Colony 3, and can open a Fissure on your order."

"Thank you, Kaho." She gave him a tentative smile, which he returned. That smile might have terrified her, once, as it exposed a mouthful of fangs. But the more she got to know him, the more she liked Kaho. He was honest and wise, and thoughtful. And one of the few people to see through Nebiat's bullshit.

Frit sucked in a deep breath, which instantly turned to smoke, and then exhaled her stress. Command was tough, but she'd seen some of the best commanders in the sector and what they all had in common was not letting the people under them see the stress.

She squared her shoulders and strode onto the bridge with the same brisk walk she'd seen Voria use. Nara stood in the central matrix, while the other two were manned by Rita and Fritara respectively. She moved to stand before the scry-screen, which of course showed nothing but unrelieved blackness.

"Kaho, relieve Rita, please. Be prepared to open a Fissure." Frit clasped her hands behind her back, but that didn't feel right. She tried letting them hang at her sides but that didn't feel right either. Where should she put her damned hands?

"Shouldn't Nara open the Fissure?" Fritara interjected, the soul of innocence in front of Rita.

"Nara, please cloak the ship." She turned to Rita, who'd exited her matrix. "Rita, would you mind running down to the cargo bay and jettisoning the drone we took from the facility?"

Rita nodded, and seemed relieved as she left the bridge. Frit wished she could leave. Instead, she turned back to the scry-screen and waited. Ordering other people about was much more stressful than simply doing things yourself. That was going to take some getting used to.

Nara began touching *air* and *dream* sigils, while Kaho focused on *void*. Each completed their respective spell at nearly the same instant, and the *Talon* shimmered out of existence at the same instant the Fissure cracked across the sky.

A tiny, silver drone was punted out of the cargo bay, and tumbled end over end through the Fissure. "Let's hope they buy this."

Fritara's lip turned up in a sneer. "They cannot possibly be foolish enough to believe a probe is capable of opening its own Fissure."

"Respectfully," Nara said in a low, submissive tone. "The Ternus military knows next to nothing about magic. If they believe this came from the one facility where they were experimenting with magic, they're far more likely to accept our ruse."

Nara guided the *Talon* through the Fissure, which snapped shut in their wake. It afforded Frit her first view of another world, and it couldn't have been more different than Shaya. Shaya was small, comparatively. Just a slice of a single moon, with a few hundred million inhabitants.

She had no idea how many hundreds of millions of people called Colony 3 home, but they must be nearly uncountable. Cities dotted the surface, each surrounded by a sea of green and gold farmland that made this world so very valuable. And, if they succeeded, all of it would be ashes soon.

Dozens of orbital defense platforms clustered not only around the planet's umbral shadow, but also the rest of the planet. How could anyone ever breach this place? These people were just so...massive.

"Hold on," Nara called. There was a moment of vertigo as the ship blinked, then another, and another. Five more came in quick succession, which was more than she could have managed. By the time they stopped, they'd made it nearly ten kilometers from their entry point.

Nara leaned against the stabilizing ring, but Frit couldn't see any other obvious strain. "Okay, I'm taking us away at maximum speed."

A wave of magical energy, *fire* in this case, washed through the area they'd just vacated. Frit smiled. "Nicely done, Nara. Looks like we avoided their initial scans.

Several dozen fighters zipped up to the probe, encircling it like hungry sharks. Frit froze. Three of those fighters were golden, and smaller than their Ternus counterparts. "Those are Shayan spellfighters. They have war mages."

"You don't think." Nara gave her a horrified glance.

"I do think. There's only one woman crazy enough to be out here." Frit sighed. "That has to be Ree."

"You know them?" Fritara asked suspiciously.

"You do too," Frit snapped, just to cover the other woman's grating tone. "It's the leader of the war mages we faced when we departed Shaya, and I'm willing to bet she's here to finish what she started."

That complicated things. Frit already had massive reservations about this plan, but adding Ree into the mix underscored how dangerous this all was. If she wasn't careful, they'd all end up dead. If she was, then billions of people ended up dead.

It felt like there was no right answer, no proper path forward. None of this felt right. "Circle to the third moon, and hide behind its shadow."

Fritara gawked at her as if she'd suddenly sprouted frost. "We're not going to finish the mission?"

"Not yet we aren't." Frit rounded on Fritara and stalked up to the edge of the matrix. "Ree is canny. She's powerful. And we don't know what other resources she brought. We get one shot at this, and if we mess up we're all dead. So yeah, I'm going to wait. I'm going to let Ree wonder. Are we really here? Maybe the probe was a coincidence. Then, in ten or so hours when she's exhausted, I'm going to strafe the planet. Do you have a problem with that?"

Frit made it a challenge. Maybe this wasn't the right way. Maybe she should back down, and be reasonable. But that didn't feel right. She was a battle mage. She was trained to kill, to overcome. Fritara was going to challenge her, and she needed to show her she was ready for that challenge.

After several long moments Fritara relaxed. "It's a good plan. I just didn't understand what you were doing is all."

"Good. Then I'm going to get some rest. I suggest you all do the same." She stalked off the bridge, and then entered her quarters. This time she waved her hand and the door slid shut behind her.

She had a lot to think about. Very soon she'd need to make some very difficult, very permanent choices.

43

DEATH APPROACHES

Nara was alone on the bridge, and had been for the better part of six hours. Frit and Kaho had spent most of their time together in the mess, while Rita had remained in what used to be Kezia's quarters. Fritara poked her head in every hour to glare at Nara, but beyond that had left her in peace.

Despite her earlier threats, Fritara hadn't used the collar, and other than the claustrophobic feel of the thing it hadn't really limited her much. Apparently it could lock magical ability entirely, but as they needed her to fly the ship, they'd left her that.

"Death comes," Talifax rumbled, popping into existence right next to her.

Nara bumped into the stabilizing ring, and her hand shot down to the spellpistol they'd allowed her to keep, probably because she couldn't even think about harming anyone carrying a control rod without being overcome with blinding pain. Not that she'd tested that.

She relaxed when she realized who the intruder was. A quick glance around confirmed they were still alone. She had no idea if anyone else could see him, but the last thing she needed was the crew thinking she was insane.

"What do you want?" she whispered fiercely. "Now is not a good time."

"When the moment comes I will disable the collar," Talifax explained. He folded his thick arms, and stared impassively at her. "Frit must live. Remember that."

Then he was gone. He'd simply vanished, with no apparent spell use.

"Who are you talking to?" Fritara's voice had an extra layer of suspicion slathered on.

"Myself," Nara snapped, then immediately chastised herself. She took a breath, and offered Fritara a week smile. "I'm sorry. I was just muttering to myself. Ree scares me, is all. If you'd met her, you'd be scared too."

"I did meet her." Fritara narrowed her gaze, and the flames all over her body surged hotter. She wrapped a hand around the hilt of a slender spellblade, and delivered a milk-curdling scowl. "I will meet her again, and this time no more of my sisters will die. This time she will, and so will her smug friends."

She hadn't seen Fritara fight, but the way the war mage carried herself would have put Aran on guard immediately. She knew how to use that sword, and while a true mage could cast some amazing spells...well, Nara doubted she could stop her if Fritara decided to cut her down.

Footsteps sounded from the mess, and Fritara's ire shifted to Frit and Kaho as they strode onto the bridge. Both wore smiles, and under other circumstances Nara would have been thrilled for Frit, even if her boyfriend was a Krox.

"Have we cowered long enough?" Fritara crossed the bridge to stand before Frit, and Nara didn't miss that her hand rested on the hilt of her spellblade. "Let's finish this, for good or ill."

Frit slowly folded her arms. She kept her composure, for the most part, but Nara knew her well enough to see she was struggling. She licked her smoldering lips before speaking. "You are not going to like what I have to say." She cupped both hands to her mouth and called, "Rita, we need you to hear this."

Fritara stared daggers at anyone willing to meet her gaze, which Nara wasn't. No sense drawing attention to herself. A cautious Rita appeared, blinking owlishly. Well as owlishly as a girl made of fire could manage.

Death approaches. Talifax's words echoed in her mind.

Frit unfolded her arms, and rested her hands at her sides. "I've decided not to do as Nebiat has asked us. What we'd be doing isn't just murder. It's killing on a scale this sector has never seen, or at least maybe not since the godswar. Killing this planet ends all other resistance in this sector, and—"

Fritara's blade was in her hand, and she advanced toward Frit with murder in her eyes. "I knew you were a traitor. Nebiat has asked nothing of us, except this one thing. This thing that will ensure we win the war. And you don't want to get your hands dirty? Fine. Get out of my way, Frit. I'll do it myself." Dark, purplish, void flames burst up around the blade.

In that moment, Nara understood Talifax's warning. Time seemed to slow as she considered the situation with the gift Neith had granted. Talifax wanted her on that station, because it placed her in Frit's path. He wanted Frit to have an ally when in a situation where she'd be killed, because if she were killed then Colony 3 would be wiped out.

If Colony 3 were wiped out, then Ternus lost the war. Shaya probably lost it as well, or would at least be hampered by the loss. It would cripple the entire sector for a generation while entire economies shifted to provide the necessary food. On the surface she didn't understand why preventing that benefited Talifax, but it could be as simple as bleeding his enemy. By stifling Nebiat's plan, if she succeeded here, she kept Ternus in the fight, which kept the Krox forces occupied and allowed Talifax to operate freely.

Nara eased her spellpistol from its holster. No one noticed, least of all Fritara. The war mage had advanced on Frit, who'd had no choice but to back into a corner. Kaho couldn't help, as he appeared to have precisely zero combat training. He was a true mage through and through.

Rita looked as if she wanted to say something, but lacked the courage.

That meant if Nara did not intervene in this moment, that Krox would win here. A tiny, frigid voice in her wanted her to let things play out. To let Krox win, because it would harm Talifax. She ruthlessly crushed that voice.

"I can't let you live. I'm sorry, sister." Fritara launched a roundhouse that Frit was too slow to dodge. The blow knocked Frit into the wall, and she went sprawling at the mouth of the ramp leading to the mess.

Frit began sketching a sigil, but Fritara flung a counterspell with incredible speed. Frit's spell shattered, and Fritara raised her blade for a killing stroke.

Nara's spellpistol snapped up, and she relaxed her grip, cradling it in both hands. She sighted at the back of Fritara's head, then crafted a killing spell. She began with a core of *earth* refined down into a super dense sliver. Around that she added a thick layer of *void* to burn away flesh, and magic alike. Finally she added *air*, to shatter the *earth* once it reached its target.

The pistol kicked slightly, and the spell shot from the barrel. A purplish-brown orb streaked into the back of Fritara's head. The void splashed against her defenses, and the sliver of earth pierced the back of her skull. Once inside, it detonated. Fritara's eyes flared briefly, and then her lifeless corpse slumped to the deck.

Nara holstered her pistol, then raised her hands and faced Rita and Kaho. "I'm sorry. I was just saving my friend."

Kaho had his hand raised, ready to sketch. He watched Frit, apparently waiting for instructions.

Rita's spellblade was half out of its scabbard, but she abruptly sheathed it. She shook her head sadly. "That needed to be done, but I'm glad I wasn't the one who had to do it." Fiery tears streaked her ebon cheeks.

"Thank you," Frit whispered as she climbed to her feet. She was also crying. "I didn't want it to come to this, but...if you hadn't stopped her, I'd be dead."

"Frit, look!" Kaho pointed at the scry-screen, which still showed Colony 3. Nine points of light were streaking toward the moon where they were hiding.

"It can't be coincidence." Nara's heart sank. "You know who it is. Ree's found us."

44

LAST MINUTE

"Pickus, establish contact with the local authorities." Voria deftly sketched the final sigil, and a Fissure split the black. She willed the *Spellship* through, bracing herself for what lay on the other side.

Much to her surprise, there was no immediate Krox assault. In fact, there was no sign of any vessels, enemy or otherwise. The entire umbral shadow was empty, save for some glittering stations and satellites in near orbit of the planet below.

"I'm connecting to the planetary defense network," Pickus explained as his fingers flew across the keyboard. He glanced up at the scry-screen. "There we go. Take a look for yourself. I've got up to the minute casualty reports, top news stories, and everything else you could want."

"I see." But Voria didn't see. What kind of nation would publicly broadcast all news of its war? What was to prevent enemies from listening to those transmissions? Then it hit her. A smart commander would seed the news with false information. An enemy could never know what was true, and what was planted. "The data is helpful, but can you get me a person to converse with?"

"I'm trying." The clacking of the keyboard continued. "Okay, one sec."

The scry-screen flickered just as Voria caught sight of the top news story. It read 'War Mage Single-Handedly Saves Command Bunker', and it contained a picture of Aran's face. Before she could investigate, another familiar face filled the screen.

Where Kerr had been the best case, this was the worst. "Hello, Admiral Nimitz."

He folded his arms and gave her a once over, clearly unimpressed. "Let's get the preamble out of the way, shall we? We're screwed, and as usual, you've arrived at the last minute. Unless you can magic away hundreds of thousands of corpses dotting cities all over the globe, and somehow deal with the binders, then as usual it's too little, too late."

Voria hesitated. This ship was impressive, but could it muster a feat like that? She had no idea if they could do anything to help.

Ikadra's sapphire pulsed a deep, slow, angry beat. "I don't know who pissed in your cereal, but you should treat the woman saving your planet with a little respect. We'll take care of the binder problem, and when we do you'd better be ready with an apology."

Nimitz ignored Ikadra, and locked eyes with Voria. "I've got a battle to plan. I'm not expecting much out of you, Voria. Sure would be nice if I was wrong for once." Nimitz reached toward the screen, and the feed terminated.

Voria turned slowly to Ikadra. "Please tell me that this ship actually *can* clear up an endless army of corpses, and somehow deal with the binders that summoned them."

"Uh." Ikadra pulsed nervously. "I mean, theoretically..."

"So you have no plan to remove these corpses, but you just promised that we'd do so?" Voria snorted, more in amusement than exasperation. When one was surrounded with impossibilities every day, either one learned to laugh, or lay down under the weight of it.

"I'm pretty sure we can do it. This ship is the ultimate spell amplifier," Ikadra offered. "You can empower almost any spell, and with enough magic, it will engulf the planet. The ship will pull from all crew, so you've basically got access to all of their collective magic."

"So what would happen if I amplified a void bolt?" Voria waved a hand and the scry-screen shifted to a closer view of the planet, the area over Fort Crockett, specifically.

"Uh, you'd punch a big hole through their planet?" Ikadra offered.

Voria tapped her lip and considered that. After a moment she smiled. "So if I were to tailor, say, a counter-spell that targeted *spirit* magic, it would engulf the entire planet?"

"Sure." Ikadra flashed enthusiastically. "It wouldn't stop the binders or anything, though."

"But I could cut off the bulk of their armies." She smiled wickedly. "That would buy Aran and his company time, which we could use to craft a more permanent solution to the binders." She glanced at Ikadra. "So what's involved in this amplification?"

"Well, it does take a while. And it needs to be powered, which, like I said, will require the help of everyone on board."

Voria blinked. "That seems so obvious. We tap into all the tech mages aboard, and use their magic to fuel the amplification spell. That's what makes this vessel so powerful."

"Yup," Ikadra pulsed, "and it means that if we get more mages, we become totally badass."

"Pickus, inform all mages that their services are needed." If she could organize this ritual, then in a few hours the planet would be free of corpses, and any other creatures the binders had enslaved.

45

TEODROS

Eros knew doom had come to Shaya the very moment the Fissure cracked the darkness behind their moon. He glanced up at the sky through the *Arcanaca*'s transparent ceiling, and dread mired his feet to the deck. Tremendous black claws seized the edge of the Fissure, and a scaly monstrosity emerged.

At first, Eros assumed it to be a Void Wyrm, massive in size, yet otherwise unremarkable. Then he saw the milky, white eyes, and the gaping wound in the chest. A binder had animated this monstrosity, and while that would make it slower than its living counterpart, it would also make it immune to all but catastrophic damage.

His hand shot up and he sketched a missive to Erika. The spell whizzed away, and an instant later an illusory version of her appeared next to him.

"Tender?" She blinked. She appeared to be in the middle of oiling her sword.

"Scramble every fighter we have, and contact Ducius. Tell him to get the fleet mobilized over Shaya." Eros kept eye contact the entire time, and she picked up on the gravity of his tone.

"At once." She slid her blade back into its scabbard. "Shall I meet you on the *Arcanaca* when it's done?"

He nodded. "As soon as you can manage."

Eros killed the missive and turned his attention back to the Fissure in the sky above. It hadn't stopped growing. Cracks now veined across the night sky, their edges crumbling only when they reached the direct starlight outside the planet's umbral shadow.

The beast had emerged entirely now, but made no move to approach. Instead, it drifted further from the world, and another Wyrm began to emerge. And another. All titanic monstrosities, with centuries' thick scales. All had the same rheumy eyes, and most had identifiable wounds. Their sheer size would make animation costly. Who possessed enough magic to bind so many?

Smaller Wyrms began to emerge, each moving to join the larger flight. Eros counted twenty-nine by the time the flow stopped. He turned toward Shaya's upper branches, tensing when he saw his own navy lifting off. They had twenty-seven ships of the line, the oldest, strongest vessels Shaya had ever created. Reinforcing that were seventeen spellfighters, though their pilots did not number among the finest he'd seen.

Below his armada, chaos had erupted on the tree itself. Mages reported to battle stations, while civilians made for shelters built into the tree itself. They would offer scant protection if their fleet were overcome, as Eros knew in his heart that it would be. He'd dreamed this moment countless times, fragments of it, at least.

He knew what came next. He knew what came out of that Fissure, though somehow the name had been kept from him. Only now did he realize the awful truth, that the being clawing its way through the Fissure had obscured his identity until it no longer mattered if Eros learned it.

"Teodros," he whispered in awe.

The titanic Wyrm extended a pair of city-sized wings, then fixed its hellish gaze on Eros. Not on his world, or even on his ship. It saw through all that, and it looked him directly in the eye. He saw no sigils, but a missive arrived, whispering in his ear. "If you flee, you will live. She will not."

Eros sketched a missive of his own, flinging it into orbit. "I do not run from Wyrms. I slay them."

He extended a hand and withdrew his eldest staff from his void pocket. The dark haft hummed in his grip, a silent welcome. "It is time to fulfill the task for which you were created, my friend."

The staff pulsed understanding. It knew that it would not survive this, but it also knew why the sacrifice was necessary. For some to live, others would die today. He would die today.

Eros raised the staff toward the sky, and held it aloft as he pulled deeply from the well of magical power in his chest. The golden energy surged down his arm, flowing into the staff in a frenetic staccato of pulses. The staff began to glow, slightly, then with increasing brilliance.

That brilliance grew to a level that would blind any who looked at it, until Eros and his ship appeared to be a star in the sky over Shaya. But the light did not blind him. He was of the light, and the light was of him. Eros held that light as the approaching dragon flight neared the edge of the prismatic barrier protecting Shaya from the lifeless moon that lay beyond.

He waited until the smaller, faster Wyrms passed

through. Then Eros finally released the torrent of life, amplified through the diamond at the staff's tip. A beam of golden light streaked into the shield, and a ripple of golden energy passed along the entire surface, painting it gold.

Spellfighters screamed by overhead, and Eros smiled grimly as they converged on the Wyrms he'd allowed through the field. Those few had been cut off, and stood no chance on their own.

He watched the next wave of Wyrms fly unerringly toward the field, but when they reached it the golden energy flared and each Wyrm was incinerated. Puffs of ash drifted away into the void—first one, then two, then a dozen. Nearly all the smaller Wyrms were destroyed, save those the spellfighters were quickly dispatching.

A gust of wind breezed through the room, delivering another missive. "Well played, Tender. A costly spell, though."

Eros winced as a sharp crack echoed across the deck. He looked up to see the staff's diamond split, then shatter. The golden energy in the staff flickered, and then died. His connection to the staff died with it, and inexplicable sadness welled up in him. It was a tool. A construct. Yet in many ways, he'd been a friend, and now that friend was dead.

The shield flickered, then returned to its previous translucency. The rest of the Wyrms advanced, winging their way through the shield and toward the spellfighters. Eros raised a hand and sketched a *void* sigil, then an *earth*, then three more intricately-woven *void*. When the spell completed, he raised his hand, and then swept down suddenly.

The first Wyrm to reach the fighters—one of the original six massive ones—dropped from the sky like a rock, slamming into acres of farmland near the edge of the bubble. A titanic cloud of dust burst into the air, temporarily obscuring the dragon. When it cleared, the abomination was already clawing its way back to its feet, though thankfully minus a wing.

The spellfighters had used the reprieve to retreat safely behind the fleet, which had just began its first salvo of spells. A cascade of golden bolts lanced out from every vessel and they converged on the front rank of dragons. The brilliance washed over them, burning away wings, faces, legs, until a grisly rain of desiccated corpses began over those fields.

Then Teodros entered Shaya's bubble. He sketched so swiftly Eros could barely track the spell being constructed. He had enough time to marvel briefly, then Teodros released his spell. A ball of earth appeared in the sky above the Shayan fleet, but that ball quickly flattened into a disk that spun out wider and wider, like a pie crust being made.

The disk had no apparent ill effect, save that it cast a deep shadow over the fleet. Shadow. "Goddess, no."

A Fissure split the sky over the fleet, veining out in the darkness provided by the disk—out of reach of the sun, and cast in the momentary gap when the Shayan mages were recovering and thus unable to use their *life* magic to summon the kind of light to destroy a Fissure.

The very instant the cracks were wide enough, a sea of fleshy, grey tentacles slithered through every gap. They came in all sizes, but large and small they wove unerringly toward the closest vessels. The rope tendrils wrapped around each vessel they could reach, then yanked the unfortunate ships back into the lightless depths.

Eros sketched a counterspell, and flung it at the disk. The disk shattered, and the rays of light fell upon the twisted tentacles and the Fissure itself. Both tentacles and the Fissure began to dissolve, but not before carrying a half dozen ships back into the darkness to be devoured by whatever the tentacles were attached to.

Another missive whispered through the room. "You should pay more attention to your surroundings, Tender."

Eros spun around, scanning the sky for whatever threat Teodros had in store for him. He spotted movement below and realized that several beetle-like creatures had burrowed from the earth near the dims. They were laying waste to the town, which was thankfully less sparsely populated now that most of the little pikeys had departed with Voria.

Then the beetles reached the tree, and began to burrow. The magically dense wood proved little barrier, and the black carapaces disappeared inside the holy tree. There could be only one destination, as Teodros no doubt intended him to know.

It left him in an impossible position. If he stayed here to battle Teodros, those beetles would reach the pool and drink it dry. If he left to respond to them, then Teodros would quickly finish his fleet, and come for the pool anyway.

Not far below him, a Wyrm grappled the *Eternal Branch*, savaging the hull with the claws on all four limbs. The ship responded with a burst of golden light, drawing a shriek from the animated Wyrm. When the energy passed, the binding had been severed, and the now limp corpse plummeted from the sky. The ship righted itself, and began coming around for a pass at another Wyrm.

"Blast it. What do you want from me?" He looked down at Shaya. "What is the right answer?"

In the end there was only one choice. If he faced Teodros inside the tree, then the Wyrm would have no choice but to face him in human form. That would make it a contest of sorcery, rather than a physical confrontation. It meant that most of his fleet would be destroyed and his mages slain. But if it saved the mother, that was all that mattered.

He began sketching the teleport spell, forcing himself to watch the Wyrms annihilate his fleet as he fled.

46

LAST STAND

Aran peered through the command bunker door toward the lift at the end of the corridor. Halogen lights flickered, making shadows dance. Everything was quiet, as it had been for the past twenty-four hours. Arkelion had made no move to probe their defenses.

"Captain?" Hernandez asked from behind him.

He shifted to face the Marine, but kept his spellrifle aimed at the doorway. "Hey, Hernandez, what's up?"

"I brought you one of our sidearms." Hernandez extended a pistol, grip first.

Aran propped his spellrifle against the wall, and blinked when a wave of empathic indignation washed over him. It seemed to be focused on the pistol. Did his spellrifle not want him to have it? Was it jealous? It wasn't as advanced as Narlifex, but maybe it was time he started treating it the same way. He'd never had a pet that he could remember. Looked like now he had two.

"Thanks." Aran accepted the weapon and took a moment to inspect it. The heavy pistol had a simple trigger with a guard, and his armor just barely allowed him to get a finger inside of it. A magazine had already been inserted in the clip, and contained six purple rounds that he could see through a slit on the grip. "What do I need to know about it?"

"The rounds will detonate on impact, so don't fire at anything closer than two meters." She raised a hand to stifle a yawn. "Other than that it should work just like your spellpistols. Hopefully you won't need it."

"I'll take all the help I can get." Aran opened his void pocket and slipped the pistol inside, then picked up his spellrifle. It pulsed relief, but still seemed irritated about the pistol.

"Hey, Cap." Crewes came trotting over. "Chronometer's got two minutes until the twenty-four hour mark. You wanted to be informed."

"Thanks, Crewes." Aran nodded gratefully. "Hernandez, if you and your Marines can hold this doorway, that frees my people up to push the hallway without needing to hold back on big spells."

"Do you really think we dealt with all the wights?" Hernandez asked. She glanced nervously at the nearest air duct. "If they get in here and we don't have you to protect us..."

"I'm sure," Aran replied confidently. "Existing creatures, like most of the megafauna on this world, can be bound instantly and then sent into combat. A creature like a wight requires a ritual to create, and that requires time. Kheross can probably explain the process."

The white-haired Wyrm lounged against a nearby wall, doing his best imitation of feline boredom. "You are correct. The army we destroyed represents countless magical hours. It will take months to raise a similar army."

"Any thoughts on what we might face today then?" Aran

leaned around the corner to peer at the lift again, but it was still empty and he felt nothing approaching.

Kheross uncrossed his arms and moved to stand next to Aran. He peered down the corridor as well, and his eyes took on the far away look of memory. "A binder of that strength has two choices. They can send endless waves of cheap fodder, or they can gather their remaining minions and push with everything they have. Given the age of our assailant, I suspect he will choose the latter. He's going to come at us with every creature he still has bound—his reserves and a personal bodyguard if he has them."

"At least it ain't gonna be more wights." Crewes sounded genuinely relieved. "Those witches make my skin crawl. I hate that depths-damned laugh."

"Excuse me." Tharn floated over in her silvered spellarmor. "Would you mind giving that speech one more time, Kheross? I'd like to get a better angle on your face."

"What?" Kheross blinked at her, and then his face twisted into a feral version of itself. "Do you lack any understanding of our present circumstances? We face annihilation, woman. And you want to take pictures? Go away, or I will ease my boredom cracking your bones."

"Quiet, both of you," Aran snapped. He raised his rifle to his shoulder and sighted through the scope. "I feel something approaching. Get into positions, people. Tharn, you can record whatever you want, but stay out of the way and don't leave this room—only your drones, got it?"

"I make no promises." Tharn's tone was hesitant, but Aran didn't have time to investigate.

"Corporal Kezia." Aran swiveled the rifle across the bottom of the lift, but didn't see anything yet. A great deal of *void* magic was approaching.

Kezia trotted up in her heavy armor, each step booming on the metal floor. Aran sized her up approvingly. "If Tharn leaves this room your primarily responsibility is shoving her right back inside."

"Yes, sir," Kezia said cheerfully. "I'll see that she keeps a proper distance."

"Incoming," Aran barked as a figure dropped into sight near the center of the lift.

He studied it in the scope for just a moment, noting that it was a three-meter-tall demon not unlike those in the last wave. This one, however, wore a spellblade. Horns curved from her forehead, but if not for that and the ebony skin she'd have passed for your average Shayan. She was certainly less bestial than any demon he'd yet seen.

Three more demons landed next to the first, also wearing spellblades, and also female. All four moved with the kind of coordination that Aran recognized. He recognized it, because he shared that same coordination with his own squad.

"All right, everyone." Aran lowered his rifle a hair so he could study the four figures without looking through the scope. "The one in the center with the falchion is the primary target. Crewes, I want you to engage spell amplification once we close the gap. Burn it all, or until they go down. We'll use mine on whatever the next wave is. I want to save Bord and Kezia's until we face Arkelion himself, if possible."

"And me?" Kheross demanded. He swung his axes in slow, lazy twirls.

"Look for an opening, and do as much damage as you can." Aran frowned as he studied the four demons, who'd yet to leave the lift. "They're waiting for us. Let's not disappoint them. Crewes, you're on point."

"Oh, good, I'll go introduce us." Crewes fired the thruster on his armor and rocketed into the corridor on a plume of flame. All four demons watched him with interest, but none made a move to approach as he closed the gap. Aran fell in behind him, keeping his rifle cradled in his arms as he approached.

Kheross trotted past them both, giving a nod as he moved to engage.

Bord and Kez came last, with Bord waiting near the door while Kezia stood protectively between them. They all knew their roles, and executed without needing to be told.

Crewes stopped about twenty meters from the lift, and called out cheerfully to the demons, "Hey, there. You ladies look lost. You sure you want to be in this neighborhood after dark? 'Cause people have a tendency to get hurt. Here, let me show you a little trick I've been practicing."

The lead demon gave a delighted laugh. She stopped laughing when Crewes raised his cannon and fired a continuous stream of superheated flame. It poured from the barrel like water from a hose, and Aran quickly realized that Crewes had somehow found a way to unify the two elements. Whatever he was firing burned like flame, but moved like water.

It flowed around all four demons, and coated every bit of exposed skin. Cries of rage came from the lift, and the lead demon charged Crewes. The sergeant snapped down his hands and his wrist spikes extended. He dropped his spellcannon at his feet. "Looks like you want to tussle. Come get some, skank."

The demon raised her falchion, a large, curved blade not unlike Narlifex. She brought it down on Crewes in a brutal slash, but Crewes was ready. The Sergeant knocked the blow to the side with his right hand, then jabbed the claws on his left wrist into her midsection. All three blades snapped against her armored skin, and the broken weapons clattered to the ground.

She delivered a roundhouse that sent Crewes skidding across the floor in a shower of sparks. Aran snapped his rifle up and sighted down the scope. He aimed for her chest, and thumbed the selector to level three. "Crewes, can we get that amplification?"

"On it, sir." Crewes's armor flared gold, and a wave of energy shot out from his armor. An answering resonance came from the rest of the squad's spellarmor, and a tendril of golden energy attached to each of them.

The effect was instant. Aran could move faster, think more quickly. He was stronger, and his magic was also stronger. He smiled as he fired an empowered level three void bolt at the demon's chest. The energy knocked her back a half step, but Aran blinked in disbelief when his strongest spell had no visible effect.

A fifth figure dropped suddenly from above, and slammed into the ground behind the four demons. It gave Aran his first real look at Arkelion, an ordinary looking man with long, blue hair flowing loosely around his shoulders. A bit like Kheross, but even more emo. The hair shimmered and glistened like water, and Aran realized it reminded him a great deal of Frit.

His features were handsome, but not supernaturally so. He was well-muscled, but again not supernaturally so. He looked rather ordinary, with the exception of the hair. Arkelion's face split into a cruel smile. "I see you've learned that my daughters are quite impervious to magic, and I've warded them against flame since your squad seems so fond of its use."

Aran switched to his internal microphone, which meant

Kheross theoretically couldn't hear. "Switch to non-fire-based attacks. Let's see what kind of mileage we can get with water."

The lead demon charged Crewes, who was struggling back to his feet. Kezia rushed forward and leapt into the air over him. She raised her right hand to fling a ball of water at the demon's feet. The spell hardened instantly, and the demon tripped. Kezia wrapped both hands around her hammer, and brought it down on the demon with immense force.

The blow knocked the demon prone, and her sword went skittering away.

"You will," the demon panted as she rose, "pay for that." She began struggling to her feet, but clearly the blow had done something. That gave Aran hope.

He snapped open his spellshield, and shifted Narlifex to his free hand. If magic wasn't going to work, this needed to be settled the old-fashioned way. "Kheross, Crewes, let's form a line."

Aran moved to stand in the center of the corridor, while Kheross hurried to his right. Crewes trotted up on his left, and seemed no worse for wear other than his missing wrist blades.

Kezia and the first demon were still scrapping in the corner. The others charged, each leaping toward one of them. The demon Aran squared off against topped three meters, and had the range to match. Her spear was larger than Aran's sword, and afforded her even greater reach. Combined with her natural magic resistance that deprived Aran of almost every available strategy.

Almost.

Aran leapt at her, and as expected she brought her blade

around in a defensive strike that should have forced him to leap back. Instead, Aran shifted his entire body to *air*, and the enemy's spear whistled harmlessly through the space he'd occupied.

He rematerialized and yanked the pistol Hernandez had given him from its holster, then aimed it at her face from a half-meter away, which probably wasn't a great idea given what Hernandez had said about close range.

Aran stroked the trigger, and the pistol kicked in his grip. A purple round shot into the demon's face, and detonated on impact. The resulting explosion sent Aran tumbling away, though he was able to roll with it, and came back to his feet a dozen meters away. Several angry yellow warnings sprang up on the spellarmor's HUD, but nothing critical.

The demon wasn't so lucky. The round had caught her in the temple, and while her chest still rose and fell, she was very much unconscious and out of the fight. For now at least.

Aran turned back to the rest of the combat. Kheross was being forced back by a demon with a pair of short swords. She was larger, faster, and impervious to all of Kheross's responses.

Crewes was faring better, and clung to his target's back with an arm around her throat. She rammed him into the wall, but he refused to budge.

Behind him, Kezia was still squaring off against her opponent, and getting the worst of it. Their line was about to buckle, and there wasn't a damned thing he could do about it, except keep Arkelion occupied. Aran knew that, in all likelihood, he was about to die.

He dragged Narlifex's tip along the floor, drawing a line

of sparks as he approached the ancient Wyrm. "I hear you fancy yourself a blade master. I seem to be short a dance partner. Shall we?"

Arkelion's smile grew more predatory. "Let's."

47

COUNTERSPELL

Voria settled into a full lotus position, the kind of thing she rarely liked doing. In this instance, the pose was fitting, and it meant that she wouldn't have to focus on standing while attempting the single most complex spell she'd ever witnessed, much less cast.

She'd set the walls of the matrix to be their natural state, a sea of ever-changing sigils. Their energies bathed her in brilliant power, and she drank eagerly of that strength. It originated from all over the ship, from anywhere that a tech mage happened to be. The ship siphoned the energies they were willing to part with, and fed them to Voria.

She breathed. Deep and slow, the rhythm running counterpoint to her own heartbeat. When she was ready, she sketched the first sigil. She began with *life*, then added *spirit*, then *life* again. She added *water*, and finally she sketched an *earth* sigil to harden the spell. So simple for such a massive endeavor.

It took moments, no more than a simple void bolt might have. Yet the energies flowing through her dwarfed the power a mortal could wield. It dwarfed the strength of the ritual used to cleanse Kheross and Rhea. For the first time, she suspected she was experiencing what a god felt. The feeling of unlimited power was heady, and dangerous.

Voria focused. She envisioned the planet below, seeing it through the eyes of the *First Spellship*. A human saw in one spectrum. The ship saw in all of them, hundreds of layered senses, and countless possibilities. She could feel the abominations below, clogging the cities dotting the surface on every continent.

She could feel the life force of the millions of surviving humans. She could even sense their dread and their resignation. Under that, for some at least, lay hope. New hope, inspired recently. That was growing, though not quickly enough. Perhaps she could speed it along.

Voria completed her spell, and a blue-grey counterspell streaked from the *Spellship*'s hull. It slammed into the surface of the world in an inaudible explosion of light. That light flowed over the planet's surface like mist, covering every centimeter.

Everywhere it passed, the abominations flared as they were touched, then simply ceased to exist. Corpses toppled to the ground all over the planet, while bound creatures found themselves suddenly freed, able to turn on their former masters. The counterspell completed its work, and the blue energies faded.

"You okay, ma'am?" Pickus asked quietly from the corner. "Looks like it took something out of you."

"A great deal." She rose shakily to her feet, and vertigo nearly stole her balance. Ikadra was suddenly in her grip, and she sagged against the staff. "Thank you."

"I want to make a joke about sweeping you off your feet, but I got nothing." Ikadra's voice had returned to full enthusiasm. "That. Was. Awesome. I bet those binders are so pissed right now."

"Ma'am," Pickus called, "I'm putting the admiral on screen."

"Of course," she slurred. She shook her head to clear it, but that was a mistake. It loosed a wave of fatigue that saturated every muscle. She badly wanted to sleep, and realized in horror that like it or not, she wouldn't have much choice soon. The spell had simply taken too much out of her.

She blinked a few times to force her eyes open, then focused on the scry-screen. It held an impossibility. Nimitz was smiling. "I take back at least half the bad things I've ever said about you, ma'am." He removed his hat. "I don't know what you did, but my people are taking back over a dozen cities as we speak."

"C-can you handle the remaining binders?" She raised her free hand to stifle a jaw-cracking yawn.

The smile faded, replaced by grim resignation. Nimitz replaced the hat, and straightened it before answering. "Your boy, Aran, is a sight to see." Something bright exploded in the distance, and a trace of smoke drifted across the monitor. Nimitz cleared his throat, and pointedly ignored whatever was happening around him. "If this is the last time we talk, you've got my apologies. I've got to get my rifle now. If we go down here, avenge us, Colonel."

The screen died. Voria wrapped both hands around Ikadra and pulled herself to her feet. Sleep would have to wait. She was about to order the *Spellship* into low orbit when a fiery-red border appeared around the scry-screen to indicate an incoming missive.

Voria waved impatiently and the screen lit. A haggard Eros stared back at her, then staggered as the *Arcanaca* lurched behind him. Smoke and flame belched into the room, but Eros sketched a ward with incredible speed. The white runes swirled around him, protecting him from the blast.

He turned back to the screen. "We are ruined, Voria. Teodros has come. Our fighters burn like candles. We are naked before the fury of a demigod, and I do not possess the strength to stop him."

Erika suddenly entered the picture, and moved to wrap an arm under Eros. "I've got you. Hang in there, Tender." She turned to face Voria. "We'll get to the Chamber of the First, and try to slow Teodros down. It's all we can do."

The implications slid a blade into her heart, cleaving it permanently in two. "I cannot reach you in time to make a difference. I'm so sorry, Eros. I was so very wrong."

Only in that moment did she realize the terrible extent of the manipulation. She'd been maneuvered like a Kem'Hedj scale, every piece set in such a way to cause her next, very predictable move. Teodros had been behind it all, and had ensured she'd be far from her homeworld when he came to claim the body of their goddess.

"We are past apologies, Voria. I forgive you, for what it's worth. I have no interest in grudges, only in saving our goddess." He lurched closer to the screen, soot smeared across one cheek. "Avenge me, Voria. The fight won't end here. He can drink the pool, but not even he can uproot the tree and get to Shaya."

"Don't give up," Erika snapped. She glared hard at Eros. "We can still prevail. Get us down there."

"Goddess be with you, Voria." Eros threw her a tight Confederate salute, and then the screen went dark.

"What have I done?" She sank to her knees. Sleep no longer beckoned, her grief keeping exhaustion at bay. Under it all lay anger. Rage. She'd been used, but she was still in this fight. She rose shakily to her feet, leaning heavily on Ikadra. "Pickus, I'm going to open a Fissure. Pilot us through, and then set a course for Shaya."

"Yes, ma'am." His tone was somber.

Voria raised a trembling hand and began to sketch. The three sigils took an eternity, but when she completed them, the familiar hellish glow of a Fissure split the sky. She prayed that Aran would be able to protect these people, and she prayed she reached her own in time to make a difference.

Then Voria toppled forward, asleep before she reached the deck.

48

SHARDS

Aran raised Narlifex into a guard position with both hands, and shifted his body so the spellshield on his left wrist faced Arkelion. He knew he had no chance of taking a full Wyrm as old as Arkelion, but he was certainly going to go down swinging.

Arkelion drew a gladius, the sword a little over a meter long, with a thick blade that could either be used to chop or to stab. He swirled it once in one hand. "Whenever you are ready."

Aran reached deep into his magical reserves. He increased his speed and his strength with *fire*. He made himself more agile with *air*. Finally, he triggered the spell amplification on his armor.

Then Aran charged. He rained a flurry of blows upon Arkelion, every one a test. Arkelion casually batted each aside, and each time he moved the gladius only enough to deflect the blow. The fact that Aran was using a two-handed weapon with enhanced strength didn't matter at all, and Aran was unable to force him even a single step backward.

Arkelion gave Aran a contemptuous look. "Teodros

claims that you are some sort of champion of the gods, and that several have imbued you with their might. Thus far, I am not impressed."

Then Arkelion rushed Aran, his blade seemingly in a hundred places at once. Aran wildly parried, and dodged what he could. Warning lights still bloomed all over the paper doll on his HUD as the blade master scored hit after hit.

Aran flipped backwards, dodging a kick, then ducked under a slash. He rolled back to his feet and brought Narlifex around in a low slash that Arkelion hopped over. He reversed the stroke and brought it up toward Arkelion's side, but the dragon seized Narlifex at the last moment. He held the blade firmly in his hand, ignoring the trickle of dark blood where the sword had pierced his hand.

Aran strained against him, struggling to yank his blade away. Arkelion didn't budge. His hand began to shake, and the muscles on his arm bunched. "Allow me to demonstrate the differences in our relative strengths, mortal." His fist tightened suddenly, and the last quarter of Narlifex's blade shattered into shards.

The blade screamed in Aran's head—pain, rage, and horror. Aran echoed those emotions, but it was the rage he held onto. He reached instinctively for *air*, and gathered the shards before the landed on the floor of the lift. Each rose, and they swirled around the now jagged end of Narlifex.

Aran launched an attack at Arkelion, which the master easily parried. Only, he didn't parry the dozen shards rotating around the sword's jagged tip. They zipped past his defenses and sliced into his face and neck. Arkelion hopped back with a roar, and Aran retreated into a guard position.

"How you holding up, bud?" Aran whispered to his blade.

Narlifex strong. We kill. Then heal.

Aran wasn't sure exactly what was involved in the healing part, but he caught the gist and figured he could deal with it later. For now, he had a fight to win.

Arkelion had fallen back several meters, and now circled Aran with a calculating gaze. The wounds on his face healed as Aran watched. He risked a quick glance at the rest of the combat, and all over Aran saw his people being pushed back by the demons. No one had gone down on either side, except for the demon Aran had dropped. That meant a stalemate, at least until the tech mages started running out of spells.

"I notice you've gotten awfully quiet," Aran taunted. He kept his distance, until he saw an opening anyway.

"Do not bait me, child." Arkelion leapt into the air, and came down on Aran with a fist to the jaw. Aran's armor cracked, but held, as he was thrown to the ground several meters away.

Arkelion advanced, and Aran hurriedly climbed to his feet. He raised Narlifex, and used the wounded weapon to desperately deflect most of the blows Arkelion leveled at him. Then a blow slipped through, and the paper doll showed red over Aran's chest. The next hit there and he was done. Aran hopped backwards and looked to the company for help, but no one was in a position to provide it.

No hope. Narlifex thrummed in his hand. *We die well.*

Aran raised the blade over his shoulder and shifted into a guard position. "Come on, Wyrm. Let's end this."

Suddenly a wave of pale, grey energy washed through the lift. The spell reeked of *spirit* as it enveloped everyone, swirling over them all, and passing through their bodies, and then disappearing inside the walls. Aran wasn't sure what the spell was, or who had cast it, but the effect was immediate.

All around him combat ceased. As one, the three surviving demons—no, four, Aran realized as the last one climbed to her feet—turned in his direction. They rushed Arkelion as one, each voicing a shriek of wordless rage. The demons came at the ancient Wyrm from all sides with a savage flurry of blows.

Arkelion's blade was everywhere, but a few hits slipped through. The desperate concentration on his face showed the effort it was costing him.

"You know," Crewes panted as he rose to his feet, "those demon chicks are strong as hell, but they seem to be a little temperamental. What in the depths just happened, sir?"

"I don't know how, but that was a counterspell," Aran explained in wonder. "The biggest I've heard of, much less seen. Someone incredibly powerful just saved our bacon."

"Oh, come on." Crewes barked an amused laugh. "We both know who it was. She ain't never let us down before, and the major ain't about to start now."

Arkelion leapt into the air and shot out of sight into the darkness. Three of the demons followed, but the fourth turned to Aran. It was the one he'd shot. He was certain of it, though whatever damage he'd inflicted appeared to have already healed.

"Thank you, Outrider. For our freedom. It is centuries in coming." Then she leapt into the air and disappeared, leaving them alone.

Somehow, they'd survived. Aran held Narlifex up for inspection, and watched with fascination as the shards arranged themselves back into place of their own accord. The cracks were still there, but the weapon appeared otherwise whole. "Did you just repair yourself?"

No. The shards broke away again, and then returned to form the blade. *Shards useful. Narlifex will keep. Nasty surprise for foes.*

"Man, I love having a living spellblade." Laughter bubbled out of Aran, mostly the relief at still being alive. He turned to Kheross, who'd just limped over. "You think Arkelion will escape?"

"Almost certainly." Kheross wore a truly evil smirk. "But he will not enjoy it, and I suspect those lovely ladies will never stop hunting him. Was that one of your tricks? How did you break the binding? I didn't even see you cast anything."

"Wasn't me," Aran admitted. "If I had to guess? Crewes is right. Voria arrived in the *Spellship*. It's the only thing that makes sense, because a true mage had to have cast that spell."

A drone whirred into Aran's field of view, and unsurprisingly, Tharn wasn't far behind it. She appeared to be mid-broadcast. "—has done it again. The latest demonic assault has been repelled, and as you can see, Captain Aran did it without losing a single member of his company." She turned to face him. "Captain Aran, how does it feel to have survived another harrowing battle?"

Aran sheathed Narlifex and removed his helmet. The air was blessedly cool against his skin. "You broadcast the entire fight to the audience, right?"

"That's correct, Captain. They saw it all as it unfolded, as they saw the battle before this one." The drone whirred closer and a light came on over the camera.

Aran winced at the sudden bright light. He forced himself to look directly into the camera. "Then you've seen what we've been through. You know what we're up against. The Krox threw everything they had at us. They came as hard as they will ever come, and you know what? We're still standing."

"Compelling words, Captain." Tharn smoothly seized control of the conversation once more. "And what will you do now?"

"Now?" He looked back into the camera. "Now, I'm going to find out where the Krox will be next, and I'm going to get there first. And when they arrive, they'll get exactly the same welcome we gave them here."

49

THEM OR US

Frit's mind reeled as she stared down at her sister's body, but she knew she couldn't afford to wallow in shock. She needed control. She focused on facts, as she always did. Fritara was dead. Rita supported Nara's actions, so the dissension had been quelled. The next threat was Ree and the approaching fighters.

"How did they find us?" Rita asked as she stared up at the approaching fighters on the scry-screen. Their golden forms were still little more than twinkling stars, but that would change quickly.

"Flame readers," Nara supplied as she ducked into one of the matrices. "Probably other Ifrit, like you. They're using slaves to hunt runaways. Frit, how do you want to handle this? I'd recommend we flee. We don't have to fight this battle. We can just leave. I can open a Fissure right now."

Frit took a deep breath. Then she shook her head slowly. "I am so tired of running. Besides, it's not a fight we can run from. Ree will follow us wherever we go. She'll hunt us and the sisters who went with Nebiat. If we don't end her here, then eventually she'll end all of us. This is survival."

"It's more than that, isn't it?" Nara asked quietly. Frit detected no accusation in the question.

"Okay, vengeance then. I'll admit it." Frit took in Kaho and Rita as she sought the words. "Ree killed my friends, in front of me. All she had to do was let us leave and they'd still be alive. If that had been the end of it, then maybe I could let this go. But it isn't. She's flown across half the sector specifically to hunt us. Nara, you care about Aran, don't you? I bet a dozen spellfighters would be pretty helpful on New Texas right now. But she isn't there. She's here, because killing us is her obsession."

"Our course seems clear," Kaho rumbled. His scaly tail flicked behind him, reminding her of a cat. "Who do you want in the last matrix, Captain Frit?"

"Don't call me that." Frit drummed her fingers on her thigh as she considered. "Nara, myself, and Kaho to start. Rita, stand second. You can relieve one of us if we run dry."

"And our plan?" Nara asked. Frit noted she didn't use the title, which was good, since hearing it made her feel like a thief.

"Um." She gave Nara a helpless look. "I can fly, and I can fight, but plans aren't my thing. You're the brainiac, remember? How do we survive this?"

Nara closed her eyes for a moment, and began whispering to herself. If Frit didn't know better she'd say that Nara was speaking to an imaginary person on her right. Alarming, but not surprising given all the recent trauma.

"First we ensure that we aren't hunted for the rest of our lives." Nara tapped a *fire* sigil to initiate a missive. "I'm setting up an open missive, so Ternus should have no trouble intercepting this. Just play along."

Nara took a moment to adjust her hair, while Frit hurried over to the only unoccupied matrix.

"Kaho," Nara hissed. "Get off screen. Rita take his place."

"Ah, excellent point. I doubt they'd react well to the sight of me." The hatchling ducked nimbly from the rings and move to a corner on the same wall as the scry-screen.

The screen ignited and Ree's angry visage appeared. Her eyes flashed in triumph. "Pirate Girl. Confirmation at last that you're working with the runaways. I knew you were in this together. How far back does your collusion go? Have you been doing Nebiat's bidding the entire time?"

"Ree, please. Just listen." Nara raised a hand, and there was a slight quaver to her voice. She looked scared and small. And disarmingly beautiful. "Nebiat was in control of some of the Ifrit. We stopped that, and took back the ship. We have the magibombs created by Ternus at their secret facility. These things wipe out worlds, Ree. Nebiat was going to use them on Colony 3 to wipe out not only this world, but the food supply for the entire sector. We stopped that, and are more than happy to turn over the bombs. Please, Ree. Work with us."

Ree gave a sharp, bitter laugh. "I'm not falling for it, Pirate Girl. You're not dealing with some wide-eyed mongrel you can trick into thinking you need protecting. This time you won't get away. There will be no quarter. No mercy. We will exterminate you. I want the whole sector to see what happens to those who betray Shaya."

Frit gasped and raised her hands to her mouth. The words were bad, but the vicious tone was worse. Ree hated them all so blindly that it had eroded everything else...and Nara had just arranged for her entire rant to be broadcast to Ternus.

"If you attack us we will defend ourselves," Nara cautioned. "Don't do this, Ree. Turn your ships around, and let Ternus take possession of their bombs. We all walk away safely, and you can go back to your war with the Krox. You know, defending those people you swore to protect?"

"Run, Pirate Girl." Ree's eyes had narrowed to near slits. "I will find you. Or stay, and meet your end now."

The missive was terminated from the other end.

"And the government of this system saw the broadcast?" Kaho asked. He blinked large, slitted eyes. "How will they respond?"

"They'll stay out of it," Nara said. She turned to Frit. "I've bought you the space we need to fight. If you want to take down that many fighters, we need to get them to chase us. We're faster. All we need to do is kite them."

"Kite them?" Frit asked in confusion.

Nara blinked, and an uncomfortable expression bloomed. "It's a returning memory, something from Ternus. It means keep them at extreme range so we can hit them, while they can't hit back. Anyway, never mind. Make for the Ternus lines around the umbral shadow like we're trying to flee the system. We're faster. We can reach it around the same time Ree does."

"Around the same time worries me." Frit tapped a *fire* sigil and seized control of the *Talon*. She poured as much magic as the ship would drink, and immediately battled vertigo as it flowed from her into the ship. She shook her head to clear it. "Kaho, do you have anything to add or suggest? We'll take any help."

Kaho finally rose from the corner where he'd sat with his wings wrapped around him. "I am not a tactician, as Nara can attest. She got the drop on me, and my brother. An encounter he did not survive. I'd trust whatever tactics she suggests." He gave her a deferential nod, which pleased Frit. She sincerely hoped those two could learn to get along, though setting aside their past would be difficult.

Frit studied the approaching fighters, and compared them to their destination. It was going to be close, and both parties were still several minutes away. "Nara, do you have time to explain the rest of your plan? There is a rest of the plan, right?"

"It's simple, assuming we can pull it off." Nara brushed a dark curl from her forehead. "When we get close I'll use a displacement spell. We'll be cloaked, and they'll see an image of us. We fly close to a Ternus station, and let Ree fire on the illusion. Their shots pass through the ship and hit the Ternus facility."

Frit eyed Nara sidelong, and wondered how well she really knew her friend. "That's horrifying."

"Devious, but effective," Kaho pointed out.

"It's them or us." Nara shrugged. "And it's a damned sight better than us fighting them all and dying."

"Do it." Frit said. She touched another *fire* sigil and adjusted the scry-screen to show the rapidly approaching Ternus lines. They'd be flying between two of their massive stations, and every one of their hundreds of guns was now pointing in the *Talon*'s direction.

Frit was confident in her piloting abilities, but what Nara proposed added a new layer of difficulty. She needed to fly them safely, while positioning the illusion so as to get Ree or her companions to fire on the station. There had to be a way to do that without killing a bunch of innocent technicians.

"They're almost within spell range," Kaho cautioned from his matrix. He tapped *earth*, then *spirit*. Flows of pale-grey and deep-brown energy flowed from him into the deck, and an unfamiliar spell rippled through the entire ship. "I've reinforced the hull with an earth ward, and have prepared a spirit ward against their spells."

Frit tuned out their voices, and became the *Talon*. The

vessel was more refined than the spellfighter she'd trained in. It was far more intelligent, and capable of supplementing her piloting if she let it. Frit surrendered herself to its control, allowing it to actually fly while she thought about where she wanted to go.

"Spells away!" Kaho roared, though she could already see them, both on the scry-screen and through her connection to the *Talon*.

A volley of life bolts rained down on their position, but the *Talon* easily spun out of the way. "Nara, are you ready with that displacement?"

"On it," she called back. Nara's hands flew across sigils on all three rings, and a river of *dream* and *air* magic flowed from her into the deck. When it ceased, something cool rippled out from Nara, and enveloped the entire ship. "We're cloaked. No more offensive spells, or we'll reveal ourselves."

Frit didn't reply, instead giving herself to flying. She willed the cruiser closer to the nearest station, and threaded it through a pair of gauss cannons mounted along the deck. Their illusionary double followed in their wake, about three hundred meters behind them. It duplicated their movements perfectly, replicating each a few seconds after the *Talon*.

The cluster of golden fighters unleashed a second volley of light bolts, and they'd have converged on the *Talon*, had it not been an illusion. Instead, those bolts slammed the hull around the pair of cannons they'd flown past.

Those cannons detonated spectacularly, and sprayed shrapnel hundreds of meters into space.

"Okay, Nara. You're on." Frit poured more speed into the ship, and hugged the hull of the station as she zipped past it. The illusion was gone now, and their position was clear to the enraged Shayan forces. This was the most dangerous part of the plan.

"Here goes." Nara tapped a *fire* sigil and the scry-screen connected to the Ternus HQ. A grizzled-looking man in a scarlet cloak of all things filled the screen. "Ternus defense forces, this is the Confederate ship, the *Talon*. We surrender. Repeat, we surrender."

The man's fleshy face drained of all color. "I see. I will inform high command. Please stand by." He sprinted away from the screen, stumbling in his haste to make it up the stairway behind him. His muffled voice came over the missive. "Captain Rogers, Captain Rogers. I've got the mage lady on the line, sir. She wants to speak to someone in charge."

Frit tuned out the scry-screen for the moment and focused on flying. She wove around more turrets, then put on a burst of speed and headed for the next closest station. That opened a gap between her and the fighters, but it wasn't enough. They fired another volley, and this time she was too slow.

She winced as a pair of light bolts hit the aft side of the ship, but felt nothing on impact. "Did they hit us?"

"Oh they hit." Kaho gave her a toothy grin. "My wards deflected them. I can reapply the ward several more times before I need to rest." He raised a scaly finger and tapped another pair of *spirit* sigils as he erected another ward.

Frit gave a joyous whoop, and turned back to piloting. They'd reached the next station, and she interposed another set of cannons between her and the approaching spellfighters. This time, those cannons were active. They loosed a volley as the fighters approached, one the fighters seemed completely unprepared for.

The lead fighter was unmistakably Ree's. How she knew,

Frit couldn't say. Perhaps it was part of being a flame reader. But she knew it was her nemesis, a woman she could have been friends with in a different reality.

A tear slid down her cheek as white streaks lanced into Ree's fighter. Once, twice, a third time. The fighter came apart in a slowly expanding ball of flame, and Frit covered her mouth with both hands. There was no way Ree had survived that.

She expected glee, or satisfaction, or even more anger. She did not expect the inexplicable tide of regret.

"The other fighters are breaking off," Kaho called.

Frit watched mutely as the surviving fighters limped away from the stations. They were now effectively trapped in the system, unable to reach the umbral shadow.

"Nara." Frit spun to face her friend. "Can you cloak us and get us out of here?"

"If you want me to, but Frit, I think we should stay." Nara gave her a pleading look. "I know it's scary, but we said we'd surrender. Let's show them your people can be trusted."

Frit considered that. Nara was right. They could flee, but if they did, Ternus would always see them as enemies. If she stayed, maybe she could convince them that the Ifrit were not to be feared. Depths, she might even make a friend for her people.

Still, the cost had been high. She stared at the glittering debris field that was all that remained of Ree. She felt nothing. No satisfaction. No vindication. Not even the brief regret. Only weariness.

50

LAST LAUGH

Eros's teleport resolved with a pop and he appeared next to the Pool of Shaya, in the Chamber of the First. Its golden glow bathed the room, the only light source needed. He could feel the magic singing to him, a seemingly infinite amount. It was that power that no doubt drew Teodros, but there was nothing to say they couldn't use that very power against him.

He scanned the rest of the chamber, and was relieved to see Erika standing with her back to him. She faced the chamber's only entrance, a wide arched hallway that gave her plenty of room to use the naked spellblade in her hand. It was the first time he'd ever seen her wear the spellarmor of the Tender's guard, but if ever there was a fight that required it, this was it.

"It's good to see you wearing the gold once more. Keep me safe while I prepare our defenses," Eros called as he knelt next to the pool. "Deal with the summoned minions, and I will see that we are warded by the time Teodros arrives."

He knew this was merely the preamble to their battle.

Teodros would send minions, which Eros's 'minion' would dispatch. Eros would erect defenses, which Teodros would study. Only when he was satisfied that he understood what he faced would the ancient Wyrm approach, and therein lay Eros's only really hope of altering the future of their world.

He couldn't overpower a Wyrm, and he couldn't overcome him with magic. Not directly, anyway. The Wyrm was simply too old and too prepared. A demigod in his own right, one with millennia of experience. Yet that did not make him infallible, and that gave Eros a chance to make his death matter. To be remembered not as an ignoble coward, but rather as the man who sacrificed everything for his goddess.

Eros scooped up a handful of golden *life* magic, then drank deeply. He took a second, then a third scoop. It was more power than anyone had ever been allowed to take, and it crashed over him in a wave. His godsight, an ability he ignored as often as possible, leapt into clarity. Possibilities snaked in all directions, and nearly every one of them was equally horrifying.

Yet one tiny thread remained that would allow him to influence the far-reaching consequences of Teodros's victory here.

He turned to face Erika, suffused with an immensity of magic he'd not dared dream of, not even when he'd first been elevated to Tender and understood the truly massive power the position imparted. Today, he was as close to a god as he would ever come. In that instant there were no more than a dozen beings in the sector who could have met him in equal combat.

Unfortunately, as Erika cut down the last abhorrent beetle, one of those beings stepped from the tunnel the beetles had bored. Eros spent a millisecond examining his foe. So far as he knew this was the first time anyone had seen the human form that Teodros chose to wear.

His hairless body was slate-grey, not so different from the shade of his scales. A suit of ebony spellarmor covered his body, but that armor bore little resemblance to the suits the Inurans produced. It was a series of interlocking plates, and resembled that worn by knights in their earliest myths. Teodros cradled a spellspear in his right hand, and like the armor it too bore a style from a previous epoch.

"You could have run," Teodros rumbled. He stepped into the room and gave Erika a contemptuous look, then turned back to Eros. "It would have bought you a handful of years, perhaps as much as a decade. That possibility was nearly as great as this one."

Eros raised a hand and sketched a *life* sigil. Teodros made no move to counter it, so Eros added another, and then a third. A golden ward sprang up around him, shielding the pool. Eros cleared his throat. "If you believe there was any possibility where I would have run from this confrontation, then your godsight is deeply flawed, monster."

"Oho, a little fire." Teodros smiled, and thumped his spear heartily against the wooden floor as if clapping. "So tell me, little Tender. Do you wish to converse before I kill you and drain your little pool? Have you questions you wish answered, because I would be happy to gloat?"

Would delaying Teodros have any value? Who could come to save them? No one. Voria was half a sector away, locked in a pointless battle with Teodros's underlings. And, so far as he knew, no living god existed to come to their aid. He was well and truly alone, and would be dead soon no matter what he did.

"I'll indulge you." Eros glanced at Erika, and she

nodded. "So, what is your grand plan for the sector, Teodros? Resurrect your dark father, and then grovel before him in the hopes that he doesn't consume your mind? There is a reason you were one of his few progeny to survive Krox's wrath. He'll be hungry when he wakes, and I've no doubt you'll make a tasty morsel."

Teodros gave a hearty laugh as he began to slowly twirl his spear. The casual skill was meant to intimidate, and Eros noticed Erika tense when she saw the motion. "Do you think me a fool, little Tender? Krox will never rise, not as he was. I have labored for centuries to engineer the rise of a god, but not the one you believe." He smiled then, revealing dark fangs. "I will rise in Krox's place."

Eros began sketching again, this time a protection spell. He gathered sigils of *life*, and *water*, and *spirit*, until he'd completed a sixth level spell. It was the most complicated he knew, and constructing it was laborious. It would have been a perfect time for Teodros to strike, but he merely stood, twirling his staff. Waiting.

The spell completed and a rain of golden energy cascaded down over Erika. Each drop that struck her armor disappeared within, and as that energy was consumed, Erika began to glow. She grew larger, half again as tall as she had been, and much, much faster. The spell imparted a certain amount of magical protection against *void* or *spirit*, the two most likely to be used in attack spells against her.

"A potent defense," Teodros mused. He raised his spear in a salute to Erika, and then he blurred toward her.

Eros was not idle. He sketched as quickly as he ever had, aided largely by the Shaya's grace effect he'd gained when drinking the blood from the pool. He completed another of the most complex spells he was able to cast, this one also designed to enhance the user. A dozen images sprang from

Erika, each a perfect mirror. However, unlike the lesser version of the spell these images were not harmless. They had a magical form, and could harm those vulnerable to such things.

Erika swept her blade up, and a dozen blades answered in near perfect unison. Her own blade clanged off Teodros's spear, and sent her sliding back a step. Several of the illusions connected, and wherever their blows hit, little wisps of magic floated from Teodros, over to Erika. Stolen essence.

"Ingenious. I've never seen the like." Teodros spun his spear, and the tip lanced out for thirty meters or more around him, far further than it should have been able to extend. Something he was doing bent space, and allowed the weapon to strike any target he could see, apparently.

The spear cut down image after image, and all Erika could do was desperately parry and fall before the storm of blows unleashed by Teodros. The flow ceased, but only then did Eros realize why. Teodros had paused to fling a disintegrate at Erika. In the same instant, he loosed his spear, aimed at a spot above and behind her.

Erika somehow twisted out of the path of the disintegrate, which avoided instant death. It placed her in the path of the spear, which caught her in the chest and carried her across the room. She slammed into the wall with bone-cracking force, and if not for the protection spell Eros had cast, he was certain she would not have survived.

As it was, she hung limply from the spear, clawing ineffectually at the haft of the weapon with the hand that still worked. The other arm hung limply at her side, a stream of blood flowing down the index finger of her gauntlet from the wound in her chest.

Teodros blurred across the room and wrapped both hands around the spear. Eros sketched a disintegrate with his right hand, but began a second, more subtle spell with his left. The casual ease with which Teodros had dealt with one of the finest war mages Shaya had ever seen confirmed his worst fears. It was time to think about what came after, and he could still do something about that.

The Wyrm lunged out of the way of Eros's hastily cast disintegrate, but his hands never left the spear. Pulses of bright, white light began flowing out of Erika, up the spear, and into Teodros. Each pulse seemed to sap a bit more of Erika's will, and to his horror Eros realized she was beginning to age. Lines creased a once beautiful face. Rich, scarlet hair faded to pale orange, and then white.

Eros hurried his casting, but rather than fling another disintegrate he focused on the myriad possibilities connected to this one. He followed Teodros back to his home, a system in the Erkadi Rift. He watched him perform a terrible ritual to awaken the mind of Krox, and he saw Teodros enslave that mind to do his own bidding.

He thought furiously. How could he disrupt that spell? He smiled, and began tailoring the binding. How fitting that he use the magic of his enemies to bring them down in the hour of their triumph. Teodros would think he had won, but he would learn very quickly just how mistaken he was.

"You are already a god," Eros murmured, infusing the words with awe. As a man who lived by his ego, he understood the effect that could have on the arrogant. And Teodros did not disappoint.

The demigod released the spear, and left Erika's limp form impaled against the wall. He walked to the edge of Eros's ward. "Not yet. Soon, I will be. Soon I will control the mind of Krox. I will *be* Krox."

Erika groaned, and began pulling the spear from her wound. Teodros's expression shifted to irritation, and he turned to face her. In that instant Eros struck. He flung the spell, and the binding sank into the back of Teodros's skull and settled there, its touch so light that even a Wyrm of Teodros's age and skill could not feel it.

Such a binding was, by nature, weak. The compulsion would only last a few seconds. But when the time came those few seconds would be enough to alter history for the entire sector. He could die knowing he'd saved what he could.

Teodros sketched a disintegrate, faster than Eros could track. In the same instant, he extended a hand, and a tendril of air ripped the spear from the wall and into his grasp. Erika landed awkwardly, and as she began to rise, Teodros flung his disintegrate. This time, Erika couldn't dodge.

She had a single instant of awareness. She knew her fate. Eros read it in her eyes. Erika closed her eyes, just before the bolt took her in the chest. There was an explosion of particles, and then she simply ceased to exist.

Eros fell to his knees.

"Lower the ward and I will make your death painless," Teodros offered. He paced outside the ward like a hunting cat. "Or stay inside, and watch me drink your pool dry."

He crossed to the golden pool and knelt beside it. "Are you certain you would not like to face me, and die with dignity? Or are you so eager to witness this place's desecration?"

"Do what you will." Eros nodded at the pool. "I cannot stop you."

Teodros bent to the pool, and began lifting handfuls of golden power to his lips. He drank deeply, and in that moment Eros struck again. This time he created a simple teleportation spell, centered on the bottom of the pool. He removed hundreds of liters, and deposited them in a secure location. Teodros wouldn't have it, not all of it at least.

The Wyrm continued to drink, and seemed unaware of the missing portion. When he had finished, Teodros finally rose to face Eros. His eyes were lit with golden light, and he blazed with power, far more so than he already had. "I see all, little Tender. I see your deceptions and your hopes and your fears. I see every moment. Every possibility. My victory is at hand."

Teodros flung a counterspell at Eros's ward and the ward shattered into mana shards. Eros reached into his robes and flung a dagger at the Wyrm. Teodros knocked it contemptuously aside, and then appeared next to him. He wrapped a hand around Eros's throat, then the other seized both of his hands. Teodros crushed them, shattering every bone in each delicate hand.

Eros screamed into the hand over his mouth, the agony drawing tears he hadn't realized he'd been holding. Teodros bent close, and whispered into his ear. "Now I drain your magic, as I did hers. And then, I resurrect a god."

Eros gritted his teeth and thought fondly of death. His greatest regret was that he wouldn't be alive to see Teodros's face when the Wyrm learned what Eros had done.

51

EMBERS OF LIFE

Voria braced herself as she guided the *Spellship* back into normal space over the moon where she'd been born. At first glance, that world appeared just as peaceful as it always had, but only at first glance. Plumes of dense, oily smoke rose from many points on the plains outside the roots of the tree.

Scattered among them were the grisly remains of dragons. They came in all shapes and sizes, though most were catastrophically large. Where had the Krox come by so many? How had they mustered an army of such size, and if they'd had it, why not use it in previous battles?

And then she felt the lingering energies around the bodies. They had a definite spirit residue. "Those creatures were bound. Corpses, most likely."

"Undead dragons?" Pickus adjusted his glasses as he stared at the field on the scry-screen. "No disrespect or nothing, but I'm kind of glad I wasn't here to deal with them. I don't even want to meet the regular variety."

Voria was too distracted to chastise him. "My goddess, Teodros must have collected bodies from the battlefields where we faced the Krox. Vakera. Starn. Marid. Every battle gave him more corpses to work with, ones that our navy couldn't ignore."

She could already see the pitiful remains of that navy. The wounded *Arcanaca* was their center piece, smoke billowing from numerous holes on the stern. She was surrounded by a half dozen battered ships of the line. All that remained of the once proud Shayan fleet. The fleet that had terrified an entire sector into signing the Confederate Accords.

Yet at the same time, the fact that the fleet still existed meant that the Shayans must have won. Didn't it? There was only one way to be certain. She faced Pickus. "If anyone contacts the ship via missive, tell them I've gone to the Pool of Shaya to meet with the Tender."

Pickus snapped an absent salute, so she tightened her grip around Ikadra and then sketched a teleport spell. Time and space warped around them, and when the vertigo faded she was standing in the room where Kheross and Rhea had been cleansed.

"Wow, this place has been trashed." Ikadra gave a low whistle. His voice became more somber. "Oh, crap."

Voria scanned the room until she found the cause of his distress. The room was much more dimly lit than it had been the last time. The fierce glow from the pool was all but gone, embers in place of a bonfire. A body lay next to the pool.

She focused on the body next to the pool, which was still moving. Voria hurried over, and it took a moment to recognize Eros. His jet-black hair had faded to a brittle white, and his once handsome face was lined and spotted with age.

"V-voria." He raised a trembling hand, and she took it in hers. "Teodros. Came." He paused, fighting to catch his breath. His chest rose and fell rapidly, and a thin sheen of sweat covered his brow. "Drained the pool. Drained me. Killed Erika."

"We've lost, then?" She sat back on her haunches, but didn't release his hand.

"No!" The word was fierce and his eyes flashed as he delivered it. Then his trembling lips slid into a smile. "Teodros believes it so. He returns to the Erkadi Rift, where he will awaken the Mind of Krox." Eros was interrupted by a fit of coughing, and it took long moments for his breathing to stabilize. "I implanted...a compulsion. At the very moment of his triumph he will learn that I am—," more coughing, "—not to be trifled with."

"We need to get you to the Caretakers." She released Ikadra and slid her hands under Eros. It terrified her how easily she was able to lift him.

"Won't matter." He wheezed a bitter laugh. "Teodros drank my magic. Did the same t-to Erika." He inhaled a long, slow breath through his nostrils before he seemed to find his strength. "You have much work to do. You must rally the Caretakers. I left...a reservoir of *life* magic. In the room with the Mirror of Shaya. It's enough to...stabilize the tree. For a time, at least."

Voria's eyes widened as she looked up at the tree around her. She hadn't realized it, but the tree was connected to the magic of this place. Without the magic, the tree would wither and die. And so would the people who lived here.

"We can still get you help." She was about to ask Ikadra to teleport them, when Eros seized her sleeve with a weak grip.

"No." His eyes blazed, the only part of him she still recognized in that aging face. "I forbid it. I have no wish to live without my magic."

She gave him an irritated glance. "If you think you get to abdicate your responsibilities as Tender that easily, then you are a fool. Our people still need you, magic or no."

"Stubborn—," more coughing, "—wench."

"There's the man we know and love." She nodded to Ikadra. "Take us up to the third branch. Directly to the palace."

"Sure." Ikadra's tone was muted, but dark energies rolled from the staff, and a moment later they appeared in the center of the Caretaker's massive hall.

Ducius and several others she didn't recognize sat wearily around a table showing a map of Shaya and the immediate orbit. At the sight of her, Ducius shot to his feet. "Of course you return after the attack. I shouldn't be surprised."

"Ducius!" Eros croaked. "I—tire of your rancor."

Voria brought Eros to the table where they'd gathered, and gently laid him across the surface. Ducius's face shifted to horror when he took in Eros's visage. The other Caretakers had similar reactions. Unsurprisingly, from a race that could—theoretically at least—live forever. Age was the worst possible end for them.

"Yes, see your possible fate if you do not listen." Eros paused for breath, his angry gaze roaming the Caretakers. "I tell you now the secret passed from Tender to Tender." Strength seemed to return then, enough for him to speak at the very least. "Shaya is no tree. The tree was planted over her grave, to mark it. Shaya looked much as you or I, and began life as a mortal before she was elevated."

Gasps echoed through the room, but no one interrupted. Other than the swish of robes as nervous Caretakers shifted, there was only silence.

"Shaya can be resurrected. We very nearly had all the

pieces. The pool was one of those pieces, but only one." He closed his eyes, but did not stop speaking. "You must find a way to restore her. Krox rises, and will be upon us soon. Only the might of another god can oppose him."

"How are we supposed to revive her?" Voria asked numbly. "Wasn't the pool the magic we needed to do exactly that?"

"And what of the tree, and our people?" Asked a stern-faced young woman Voria had never met. "If the tree dies, they die too. This world will be abandoned."

"That," Voria said, "we can most definitely correct. The tree thrives on *life* magic, and we possess more *life* mages than any world in the sector."

"S-she is right," Eros whispered, "The reserves I set aside will be enough to keep the tree alive for several years, but you will still need to find a way to restore Shaya." He fixed his gaze on Ducius. "It falls upon you to lead them, old enemy of mine. If Shaya cannot be restored, you must take them far from here. Yanthara, perhaps, where I secreted Rhea."

To Voria's horror she noted a single teardrop slide down Ducius's face. "Of course, you old bastard. I will take care of them, I promise."

Eros reached up a trembling hand and rested it on Ducius's sleeve. "I name you Tender, as the goddess will no longer be able to confirm one." His voice had faded to be nearly inaudible. "Please, Ducius. Learn to work with Voria. Do not make my mistake. We need her. She is the key…"

The light left Eros's eyes, and his chest stopped its frantic rising and falling. Voria ignored the tears, and reverently closed Eros's eyes. Somewhere in the room a man began to sob.

Voria looked up to find Ducius watching her. He licked

his lips. "He was no friend to me, but he loved our people. I love our people. Whatever I believe about you, I know that you love our people too. Will you help me?"

Voria nodded. "We'll find a way, Ducius. I cannot believe the gods have led us this far without a plan. Somehow, we will bring back Shaya, and she will help us oppose Krox."

She didn't really believe her own words. Bringing Shaya back had seemed impossible when they'd had the pool. Now? There was no being in the sector that she was aware of with the strength to bring a goddess back from the dead. Without that, they were doomed.

52

AFTERMATH

Aran leaned back in his chair, and stared up at the holoscreen over the conference room table. It had been tuned to some sort of news channel, which, of course, was filled with news about the war. It shocked him how brutally honest the reports were, including casualty reports. But, apparently, this was a populace that could handle it.

Crewes shifted uncomfortably in the chair next to Aran. "Man, I keep feelin' like something is going bust through that wall."

"I think the Ternus folk call that PTSD," Bord supplied. "One of their medics told me about it. They've been all over me trying to figure out how I can heal. Drives them a little batty, I think, my immense power does." He steepled his hands behind his head. "Why, if I wasn't spoken for, I'm sure I could have my pick of the lovelies on this planet."

"But you are spoken for," Kezia pointed out with an eyeroll. "And why I did the speaking, I'm still not sure."

"It was my wily charm." Bord shot her a wink, and both Aran and Crewes laughed.

"Children." Kheross rested his booted feet on the table at the far side of the room, as far as he could get from them. He shook his head. "Can you not maintain focus for even a day after the crisis has abated? It is unlikely, but still possible that Arkelion resides on this planet and seeks vengeance."

Tharn's drones circled, whirring as they recorded it all. The woman herself sat silently sipping coffee. Every once in a while she'd make an observation on her datapad, but she said nothing.

The door opened and two Marines stepped inside. Nimitz entered a moment later, followed by Governor Bhatia. Both seated themselves, while the Marines flanked the door at attention.

"I apologize for the accommodations," Nimitz grumbled. He removed his hat and tossed it on the table near Kheross's feet, then sat in the chair next to the Wyrm. "We're not exactly equipped to handle guests."

"We mostly just want a place to sleep." Aran rubbed at the back of his neck. "Were coming up on thirty-two hours without sleep."

"I understand." Bhatia gave a sympathetic nod. "This will not take long, I promise. But it could not wait. Before I deliver my news, let me start by confirming what we all believed. Colonel Voria arrived and used the *Spellship* to destroy every corpse on the planet with a single spell. I don't know much about magic, but frankly I find a spell of that magnitude terrifying."

"You and me both," Aran admitted. "We didn't really know what that ship was capable of when we rescued it."

"And that brings me to the second piece of news." Bhatia gave a heavy sigh and rested her elbows on the table. She fixed him with a sober look. "We have your friend Nara in custody. She surrendered the *Talon* at Colony 3 after staging a coup against the Krox loyalists on the vessel. As a result, she saved that world. However, that doesn't change the fact that she fought against the Confederacy in a time of war. The law seems pretty clear."

"Respectfully, Governor, was there a question in there?" Aran took a deep breath. The exhaustion was getting the better of him.

"Can she be trusted, Captain? Should I release her into your custody? Should she rot in a cell? And what about the Krox she was caught with, a true mage named Kaho I'm told? As if the whole issue weren't sticky enough, she was caught with two Ifrit whose only crime seems to be trying to escape from the Shayan forces in system hunting them."

"Shayan forces? Are you talking about Ree?" Aran straightened, and his heart began to thunder.

"I'm sorry if she was a friend, Captain, but she was killed in action, by Nara." The governor's mouth firmed into a line. "Nara was defending herself, and we have the entire thing recorded. She did nothing wrong, and had already offered to surrender. The Shayan commander attacked anyway, and in the process did catastrophic damage to one of our own stations."

"Ree's dead." Aran shook his head slowly as he struggled to process the idea. He didn't even know how to feel. He hadn't ever really liked her, but he'd never doubted she was fighting for the same thing. She was a strong ally, at the very least. And in time he believed they could have become friends. And even if they never did it was still his fault she'd come. His responsibility.

"Wow." Crewes gave a low whistle. "So you got Nara and her cronies on ice. Nice. What are you going to do with our ship?"

"I lobbied hard for that." Nimitz broke in. "High command has seen reason. They'll turn over the vessel, with a stipulation."

"Stipulation?" Aran asked wearily.

"This one isn't so onerous, I hope," the governor said. "We'd like you to allow Tharn aboard as crew. Ternus has deemed you vital to the war effort. You've single handedly turned around morale, and they want to tap into more of that. If you're going to continue fighting the Krox, then we'll fund your contract, and give you whatever bonus you want. That's our only condition."

"You're right," Aran allowed. "It isn't that bad. All right. You give us our ship back, and we'll let you record the payback we're going to deliver to the Krox. What about Nara?"

"Truthfully?" the governor asked. "I don't know. I suspect she will be remanded to Colonel Voria's custody, alongside the other prisoners. My government would love to make this someone else's problem, and seeing how she trained the girl they'll probably find that the most fitting."

53

TIME WILL PROVE ONE OF US RIGHT

Nara had assumed she'd be terrified, but being remanded into Ternus custody was instead a genuine relief. She'd made a choice, and now for good or ill she'd taken herself out of the war. Talifax couldn't use her if she was languishing in a cell on some space station, and there was no way Ternus would let her go given the company she kept. They'd loved finding a Krox on board.

She waited patiently as a technician injected something into her arm. In moments, she was sick to her stomach and her hands began to tremble. She looked around the little cell, with a reasonably comfortable bed and a simple desk. There. The bed.

She staggered over, and slumped onto the lumpy mattress. "What did you give me?"

"A magical suppressant," the tech explained without looking at her. It was covered head to foot in a white plastic exterior. Though, now that she thought about it, she had no way of knowing there was a living person inside. This could be one of the robots she'd heard about. "It will prevent you from casting spells while under its effects. I apologize for the side effects."

"Of course, I understand." And she did. Ternus wasn't taking any chances, and she didn't blame them. "Are you allowed to answer questions?"

The white figure moved fluidly, but Nara was increasingly certainly it was artificial. "I have not been expressly forbidden from doing so, and I can see no reason not to tell you what I know. The surviving Shayan spellfighters were allowed to depart the system without further hostilities. Your companions have been put into custody in this system. None have been harmed, so far as I know. I will be conducting medical exams of each."

"Thank you." Nara relaxed back against the bed and wished the nausea would go away. And it did. Instantly. She blinked a few times. She felt much better.

The doctor gave her a nod, and then departed the room.

"I already know you're here," she said, more than a little sourly. "Have you come to gloat?"

"To converse." Talifax materialized in the chair next to the desk. Somehow, it contained his bulk without breaking. "You have done well, and completed the tasks in the manner of my choosing. I am pleased."

Nara closed her eyes and took a deep breath. "I am not pleased. I used my friend, Talifax. I don't like manipulating her. Frit deserves better."

"Your wishes are irrelevant. Your species is irrelevant, ultimately. Nothing more than a galactic footnote." Talifax rose and approached the bed. "Was anything you asked her to do wrong, or not in her own best interests? You convinced her not to eradicate hundreds of millions, while starving billions more. Certainly that is worthy of your persuasion, yes?"

Nara sat up and scooted down the bed, away from Talifax. The nausea was getting worse. "Yes, and that's what infuriates me the most. Everything you want me to do seems like the best thing at the time. I'm not sorry I convinced Frit to stay. I think it was the right play for her people."

"Yes." Talifax's voice was amused. "She and her sisters will be much better off, and Krox will be denied a powerful asset. What's more, their chief enemy is still very much in fighting shape. One of the wonderful things about humanity is the speed with which you reproduce. In a single generation, Ternus will recover, and so Krox will have no choice but to deal with them before that happens."

Nara nodded. "You weaken both sides while prolonging the war. How noble."

"Come, now, that descriptor applies to neither of us, 'Pirate Girl'." Talifax gave an amused shake of his head. "You will do what it takes to survive, and to protect who and what you love. Where your companions balk, you will do what needs to be done, even if it is distasteful."

"Yes." Nara hated admitting that, but it was the truth. Especially after recovering many of her memories. She glared fiercely up at Talifax. "But I am not your plaything. I will not do as you wish, unless it coincides with my own goals."

Talifax boomed a metallic laugh. "Passion born of ignorance. You do not yet grasp my plans. Your reward is great, Nara. Great enough that I believe you will betray anything and everything to achieve it."

She rolled her eyes at that, but Talifax merely sat there. "Okay, let's hear your offer."

"I intend to elevate you to godhood," Talifax explained as if relating the weather. "Your divine incarnation will be born to oppose Krox, and you will triumph over him."

Nara began to laugh. She couldn't help it. It rolled out of her in waves, the kind where she couldn't stop giggling, until she struggled for breath. "Oh, that's rich."

"You do not believe I can achieve this?" For the first time his voice was brittle and cold.

"Oh, no, it isn't that." She folded her arms and stared defiantly up at him. "It's the idea that I'd put myself in a position to serve you. That's the part that's ludicrous. What's the point of becoming a goddess if I'm on a leash, and at your beck and call?"

"Perhaps you are not as cognitively gifted as I was led to believe." Now he sounded disappointed. "Consider the alternative."

That gave her pause, a moment's worth at least. If he really were offering to make her a goddess, and the reason was to oppose Krox, what chance would the sector have if she turned it down? Krox would win. Talifax knew that, just as he knew she'd reach the same conclusion.

"I will never serve you. I'll let the sector burn first." She pulled her knees to her chest, and rested her forehead atop them so she didn't have to stare at Talifax.

"Time will prove one of us right." The amusement was back. "Rest, vessel. The days ahead will be long and bloody, but they will end in your ascension."

54

RHYMES WITH SHINURA

Kazon snapped his helmet into place and took a deep breath as the HUD flared to life. The Mark XII spellarmor had just been completed, and he'd secured seventeen sets. Sixteen of those were stowed in the cargo hold, alongside the other gear and munitions he'd squirreled away. Combined with what he'd gradually siphoned, it might be enough to keep Voria's unit—and Aran's—fighting until the end of the war.

He doubted he could reach New Texas in time to make a difference, but it couldn't hurt to try. He still owed Aran, and even if he didn't, he was smart enough to see how important Aran, and his sister, were. They had some sort of divine purpose, and he was in a position to help them achieve it, if he could safely escape the Inuran fleet.

The door to his quarters shimmered out of existence as Kazon exited. He made his way toward the bridge, struggling to calm himself as he walked. His heart rate remained elevated, and he didn't have any idea how to control it. This whole endeavor terrified him, and it probably should terrify him.

Only his mother could eclipse Skare's ruthlessness. Having both focused on him meant his odds of survival were slim. His only hope was sneaking away before they made their move, but now that he was leaving he was about to find out what contingency plans they'd put into place.

And they had—of that he was certain.

Kazon ducked onto the bridge and moved to the closest spell matrix. He'd considered bringing a real pilot, but he possessed *void* magic, and he'd been practicing. He should be able to open a Fissure and bring the ship to meet Aran on New Texas. If the ship was corrupted, he could abandon it, after turning over its contents.

A soft chiming echoed over the bridge and the scry-screen flared to life of its own accord. Kazon jumped, then relaxed a moment later when he realized what was happening. His vessel had been designed to mostly run itself, and this was simply normal operating procedure.

The screen showed three dozen spellfighters zipping out from the Inuran fleet. All were headed in his direction.

"That didn't take long." Kazon tapped the *void* sigil on the silver ring, then the gold, and finally the bronze. The ship's drive rumbled to life. "Good luck catching me."

He guided the ship away from the dock and began to accelerate away. The *Hermes* was, quite literally, the fastest thing the Inurans had ever built. His mother had given it to him, assuming it would impress him. How ironic that her gift was going to be the thing that saved him.

The dock fell away behind him, and he began gaining distance from the fleet. A large, scarlet number began counting down in the lower right corner of the scry-screen to indicate their approach to the planet's umbral shadow.

Six, five, four, three—the vessel came to a sudden and complete halt, and the spelldrive powered down. He wasn't even drifting. The vessel stopped moving entirely, a mere thousand kilometers from the umbral shadow.

Kazon inspected the matrix, but found nothing amiss. Everything seemed to be working.

"I should have seen this coming," he muttered. Kazon shook his head. "The ship came from my mother, but ultimately it must have been Skare who built it."

The scry-screen flashed red to indicate an incoming missive. Kazon tapped the *fire* sigil to accept, and the screen filled with his mother's face. Skare lurked behind her, a ghastly smile making Kazon's hands twitch. He'd give nearly anything to wrap them around that skinny bastard's throat.

"By now, you're aware of your predicament," Jolene began. Her tone was empathetic, and while she was an excellent actress, he was fairly certain her concern wasn't feigned. "Our fighters will arrive in moments. Surrender, Kazon."

In that moment, he realized that while the concern wasn't fake, its motive wasn't at all what he'd thought. She didn't fear for his safety. She was concerned he might get away. He considered a clever retort, but couldn't spare the time. Kazon stabbed the *fire* sigil and the scry-screen went dark.

What were his options?

He ducked out of the matrix, but had no clear idea where to go. If the vessel wouldn't move he could take an escape pod, but those had also been built by Skare. He could try flying out of the ship using the Mark XII armor. Unfortunately, its anti-detection countermeasures required magic he didn't possess, so Jolene would simply scry his location and track him.

He'd never make it to the umbral depths, not with three squadrons of spellfighters chasing him. The dilemma was maddening, but he wasn't willing to merely surrender. Maybe they'd catch him, but right now his only option was leaving the ship and using the spellarmor to flee.

Kazon started toward the airlock, but pulled up short when a man appeared next to him. He was tall and regal, and had long, white hair. Yet he seemed no older than Kazon, perhaps a few years younger even. Until you reached his eyes. Warm, golden light flowed from the holes where the pupils should be.

A pair of draconic wings extended behind him, flaring outwards as he gave Kazon a friendly smile.

Kazon extended a hand to grab his hammer from a void pocket, but the stranger crooked a single finger and Kazon froze. Or more precisely, the spellarmor did.

"Constructs such as your armor offer an immense degree of power, but they also open up weaknesses." He moved to stand in front of Kazon, affording a good look at the man. If it was a man.

A tail flicked back and forth behind him, and the light glittered off green scales all along it.

"What are you?" Kazon asked. He figured it couldn't hurt, and right now it seemed the only move left.

"The short version?" He brushed long, platinum hair from a face so handsome it bordered on feminine. "I am your god, Kazon. You may call me Inura, the Wyrm Father of *Life*."

"Oh." Kazon quietly emptied his bladder, which wasn't as cowardly as it sounded. The suit was designed for that, after all. "So, uh, why are you here, Inura?" Kazon figured it would be rude to ask a god directly for help, especially when that had to be the reason he'd shown up at this precise instant.

"My enemies have finally revealed themselves. Even

now, in this very moment, Krox rises. Worse, Talifax has openly seized control of the organization I founded so long ago. You represent the last of the faction still following the ideals I initially created." Sharp, golden light emanated from Inura's eyes, and his beautiful face curved into an ugly snarl. "The time has come to fight back. The godswar has come again, and our enemies will soon learn that I have not been idle. Together, we are going to elevate your sister to godhood. She will lead us to victory against Krox, and then against Nefarius.

"But first," he continued, sketching a brilliant bouquet of golden sigils, "I will give Skare and your mother something to ponder."

The spell disappeared and Kazon tracked it through his connection to the ship. A single, pulsing ball of golden energy streaked toward the thirty-six spellfighters. It had nearly reached them when it exploded into countless light missiles. The missiles swarmed toward the fighters, and one after another they peppered the hulls with superheated death.

Fighter after fighter exploded, until every vessel pursuing him ceased to exist. Any doubts Kazon might have had that he was dealing with a god vanished instantly.

Finally, they had a fighting chance.

55

KROX RISES

Nebiat inhaled deeply as she stepped onto the bridge of her little cruiser. The ancient vessel had served her well, and had already begun to serve as an interim home for the displaced Ifrit she'd convinced to flee from Shaya.

Each of the three spell matrices was occupied by a true mage, and one of those mages was already in the act of opening a Fissure. The sky split, and they began maneuvering back into normal space.

The void on the other side of the Fissure was tinged purple, as everything in the Erkadi Rift was. Scientists from previous millennia would have called the effect a warm dust nebula, but mages knew the truth. They were seeing the magical leakage from the corpse of a god. The essence of Krox, slowly drifting in all directions like blood in water. It wreathed the unnamed system where her world lay, and where her father ruled.

"Miss Nebiat?" An Ifrit called tentatively. Nebiat couldn't remember the girl's name for the life of her. "I think you should see this."

The Ifrit tapped a *fire* sigil and the scry-screen shifted to show the system's red star, or rather what most people believed to be a star. The Mind of Krox slumbered before them, pulsing slowly with immense power. But there was something new as well.

Twelve rods had been erected in geomantically charged positions around the star, and lines of blazing, white power connected them. *Life* magic, enough to make a god weep. The lines all flowed towards a fixed position at the nadir of the star.

A sea of glowing, interlocking wards, many layers deep, had been erected around a ritual summoning circle that dwarfed the one she'd created on Marid. In the center of that circle hovered a minuscule, bipedal figure, his slate-grey skin bathed an angry orange from the light of their god.

Her father, the mighty Teodros.

Nebiat turned smoothly to face her younger cousins, each Ifrit staring timidly at her, like cats ready to bolt for a deep closet until the stranger goes away. She gave them all a warm, encouraging smile. "I am going to speak to my father, and let him know we've arrived. When I return I will take you to my world, and we can show you your new homes. Each of you will have a villa, and servants to care for your every need."

They smiled at that, and most seemed to accept the promise.

Nebiat sketched furiously, trying not to let the Ifrit see her nervousness as she completed the teleportation spell. She popped into existence a dozen meters from her father, the wonderful light of Krox bathing her, but not as it should.

She glanced up and realized the wards her father had created sat between her and Krox, and were completely shunting those energies. Even now, he added another layer, which drew the others together.

"Ah, daughter." Teodros's words appeared in her mind, a simple telepathy spell. "You arrived later than expected. Did you run into any trouble?" He added another *life* sigil, and a *water*, then flung another layer of wards atop those he'd already created.

"Father," she thought back, "I don't understand what your goal is. We lost at Colony 3. We lost at New Texas. Our offensive failed. Ternus stands. Everything you've asked of me, all of it was supposed to culminate in our victory here. Yet it hasn't. And still you take no direct hand. Why, father? Your presence would have turned the tide at New Texas, or ensured no battle was even necessary at Colony 3."

Nebiat hated the pleading in her tone, but she couldn't disguise it. She'd spent centuries dutifully enacting the will of Krox, and now it seemed all of it had been a ruse. A ruse she still didn't understand.

"Your failure at Colony 3 is an unexpected complication." Teodros looked up then, and his slitted eyes fixed on her. "I intended Ternus and the sector to be crippled for a generation or more. Thankfully, it wasn't the sum of my plan. Once my ascension is complete I can intervene directly."

His ascension? Not Krox's? She studied the wards he'd erected, and the roads gathered around the Mind of Krox. Her father didn't possess the kind of magic necessary to do this, or hadn't last she'd been aware. So where had he acquired it? Her eyes widened.

"You assaulted Shaya directly." Nebiat drifted closer, peering at her father's unreadable face through the wards. "How did you manage it without a fleet?"

Teodros beamed an arrogant smile in her direction.

"Every time one of my progeny has fallen I've had the corpse brought here, where I animated it. I have been slowly building an army for over a century, dozens of potent Wyrms who feel no pain, and do not flinch from death." A sinister smile crept onto his face. "That army is ashes now, but so is most of the Shayan fleet. And I came away with their precious Pool of Shaya. I finally have enough power to accomplish my plan."

That made no sense. The *life* magic wasn't being used to resurrect. It was being used to ward. And what need did Teodros have of wards against the Mind of Krox, the being that had given him birth? Nebiat simply couldn't understand the logic. Unless her father was doing something Krox would want to stop. Then the wards made complete sense.

"Father, what are you planning?" She suspected, but she wanted to hear it from him.

He raised his arms expansively, bathed in the energies of his wards. "I will bind the Mind of Krox, and I will drink his power. In his place will rise a new god, dark and terrible. Teodros, the unassailable."

His eyes shone, and Nebiat's stomach roiled in fear, and anger, and sadness. Her father would break the sector, and she had no idea what image he would reforge it into. She had no idea what Krox's motivations were, but she had trouble imagining them as being worse. Her father was mad, and she had no desire to live in the version of the universe he crafted.

But what could she do? She couldn't harm him, or stop what was about to happen. She could only observe, and hope he treated his one surviving child with a shred of mercy. A vain hope, in all likelihood.

"What will become of me?" she asked forlornly.

"Daughter." His mental voice contained...was that

compassion? Teodros waved a hand and a hole appeared in his wards. He extended that hand and caressed her cheek. "I am so proud of you. Of all my progeny, you were the only one to have never disappointed me. You need not fear. I will not bind you or harm you. I will gift you with power, once I have ascended. You will aid me in creating a paradise, one I alone control."

Teodros turned back to the star. "That won't be long now. I am pouring all the power we acquired in the war, every Catalyst I have visited, all the artifacts I have drained. Everything is being fed into the Mind of Krox. Soon now, he will begin to re-awaken. In that moment, I will supplant his consciousness. I will become Krox."

A puff of magical energy burst out from the back of Teodros's head, and she raised a curious eyebrow. Nebiat was a master of binding. In fact, she doubted any other binder in the sector could rival her. She knew every available binding, and every tangential spell that might aid in the process.

She instantly recognized the compulsion spell someone had laid over her father. A sixth level, both powerful and insidious, if short lived.

Teodros blinked suddenly, then bent back to his wards. He added more sigils, but Nebiat realized that there was something off about them. They were fragile and malformed, poorly drawn, as if by a novice mage. The sigils were such a tiny imperfection in the vast sea of magic, but they were a weakness. A weakness her father was far too canny to have introduced.

The energies from the rods intensified, and each now fired a beam into the smoldering, red star. The star bubbled and shifted, the surface roiling like a cauldron brought to a boil.

A tendril of liquid magic lashed out from the Mind of Krox, and latched onto Teodros's wards. Then another, and another. They probed the wards desperately seeking a way in. At first, the wards held. They had been erected by a demigod at the height of his power, after all.

Teodros had thought of everything. Except for the petty retribution of a very clever Shayan, one who knew that even a simple imperfection might be enough for a god to exploit.

The wards cracked, shattering into a brief puff of mana shards. Teodros's shocked face gaped up at the star, and then the tendrils dove for him. The first encircled Teodros's waist. Then another lashed his leg, and another his arm. Horror dawned on her father's face as he realized his predicament.

The tendrils dragged him closer to the star, and several more roped out around him. Teodros shifted then, assuming the form of one of the most powerful Wyrms in the sector. But he had never had to face the full might of an elder god.

Krox's tendrils pulsed with power, draining Teodros's magic. Pulse after pulse flowed back into the star, and Teodros's struggle weakened after each one.

She shivered as Krox pulled her father into his brilliant depths. The Wyrm disappeared as if he'd never been, while the final magical energies began pouring into the star. She was out of time.

Nebiat hastily examined the incomplete spell her father had been working on, the one that fueled all twelve rods.

"You were going to kill a god, but how?" The spell was a ninth level—she was certain of it. Thankfully, it had very nearly been completed. Only one section was unfinished, an area rich with *spirit* and *earth* wards. Binding. "What's the last step?"

Below her the star began to rumble. The god was waking.

She frantically scanned the sigils and tried to understand exactly what her father had been attempting. There was no time. If she was going to complete the spell it had to be now, even if she didn't understand what it would do.

Nebiat added *spirit* and earth *sigils* to each unfinished chain, quickly completing the last three and then sealing the spell. The ritual completed, and beams of energy from the closest neighboring rods shot into Nebiat.

She shrieked in agony, thrashing as an ocean of magical power crashed over her. She could only watch in horror as her body unraveled, every molecule separated as she disintegrated into nothingness.

No, not nothing. Her essence—her soul—remained. The energies gathered around it, then suddenly shot into the mind of Krox. She pierced the star like a spear hurled by the Creator, sinking all the way to Krox's core.

Krox's immense rage assaulted her from all sides as magics beyond her comprehension fought to dismantle her mind. Her father's wards shunted them away, the layers of wards slowly peeling away as they made it deeper toward the center.

Finally, she reached the very core of the god, the center of his mind. The wards were nearly gone, but she no longer needed them. The energies her father had channeled had all been collected around her, and they swirled outwards —*spirit*, and *earth*, and *water*, and *life*. She didn't understand everything they did, but they seemed to be scouring away parts of the god, rewriting it to fit some new plan.

Suddenly she was no longer alone. Something lurked near her, a vast unknowable presence, watching.

What have you done? It rumbled in her mind, the words

terrifying, and alien. *I live, but I cannot act. You have enslaved me.*

All of Krox's power lay before her, and she realized that power existed to serve her. She could will Krox to do whatever she wished. Effectively, she *was* Krox. If she'd still possessed a mouth, she'd have smiled.

Nebiat had become a god, and very soon her enemies would finally feel her wrath.

Want to know when the next **Magitech Chronicles** book goes live?

Sign up to the mailing list!

Check out MagitechChronicles.com for book releases, lore, artwork, and more!

Made in the USA
Monee, IL
26 January 2020